Soldiers and Lovers

LESLIE THOMAS

Soldiers and Lovers

WILLIAM HEINEMANN: LONDON

Published by William Heinemann, 2007

2 4 6 8 10 9 7 5 3

Copyright © Leslie Thomas 2007

Leslie Thomas has asserted his right under the Copyright, Designs and Patents Act 1988
to be identified as the author of this work

First published in Great Britain by
William Heinemann
Random House, 20 Vauxhall Bridge Road
London SW1V 2SA

www.rbooks.co.uk

Addresses for companies within The Random House Group Limited can be found at:
www.randomhouse.co.uk/offices.htm

The Random House Group Limited Reg. No. 954009

A CIP catalogue record for this book
is available from the British Library

ISBN 9780434016136

The Random House Group Limited makes every effort to ensure that the
papers used in its books are made from trees that have been legally sourced from
well-managed and credibly certified forests. Our paper procurement policy can be found at:
www.randomhouse.co.uk/paper.htm

Typeset in Baskerville Mt by Palimpsest Book Production Limited,
Grangemouth, Stirlingshire
Printed and bound in Great Britain by
CPI Mackays, Chatham ME5 8TD

For Mark and Caroline

'We'll Meet Again'

Wartime song

1939–45

Prologue

On the flank of the hill local people had now placed a wooden bench. Although it was at the bus stop it faced away from the road so that whoever sat there could take in the scene as well as wait for the bus. Hopkins had alighted there and he sat down but did not look into the view and the valley. After all that had happened he could hardly bear to see it again. He kept his eyes lowered and then, after remaining on the bench for a minute or more, lifted them slowly.

Obediently it lay before him. As it had been before. La Serena.

The house stood square and white-walled, four storeys and a terracotta roof, with different-coloured curtains at each window and the door wide to the Italian summer sun. A frieze of deep green trees was behind it and high above them the mountains enclosed it like a cupped hand.

His eyes followed the dusty path across the open green ground and down to the bent river that, when there was a moon, itself looked like a moon.

There was a compound where he remembered they had kept the circus animals who had been moved many times, each time one step ahead of the war.

Now he imagined they had all gone. The fence looked restored and some cows, who had probably never heard a shot fired in anger nor the screaming fall of a bomb, casually grazed.

The sun that day was still below its zenith, its rays making the shadows of clouds across the sloping rocks of the valley.

Hopkins looked down at the house again, at the centre of the prospect. One chimney had fallen, which was only to be expected, but from the other came a puff of cooking smoke.

Finally, because he could put it off no longer, he pictured her again in imagination, in the white linen dress, walking the path from the door to the river, her hair bouncing gently in the sun and her laughter drifting up the valley. Katherine. Kate.

Now that he was beginning to remember again he had promised himself that he would not become entangled with the memories that would make it too painful. She was dead. He had seen her killed.

Two children, a boy and a girl, came from the house and ran along the pale brown path. Time had gone by and there would be new people.

Then, as if to prove him wrong, he heard the plodding clop of donkey hooves. He could tell by the sounds that there were two donkeys and he knew already who would be with them. Without hurry he turned and saw the old man riding the leading animal with the second towed behind. The old man was probably completely blind now but the donkeys knew the way. They pulled up knowing that someone was waiting. 'What the fuck,' said the Italian.

Hopkins felt a rare grin touch his face. He said quietly: 'La Serena, *signore.*'

'What the fuck,' muttered the old man again. Despite the morning warmth he was piled with clothes, with a pink velvet cloak, which Hopkins remembered, topping them. 'What the fuck' was the only English Signor Albinetto had ever known, or at least said; learned from the soldiers.

From the donkey's back the man motioned for Hopkins to step closer so that he could reach out and with his hand test his height and the breadth of his body. '*Inglese?*' he said.

'*Si, signore.* I have been here before.'

'What the fuck,' said the old man. He nodded in the direction of the second donkey and Hopkins picked up his bag and silently walked back. The donkey appeared to expect him and he climbed on it without trouble. In front the Italian treated his beast to a flat-footed kick and the little procession began to descend into the valley. Towards La Serena.

Chapter One

You could smell the town from three miles out to sea; a place, a sky, a wind full of fish. Only strangers did so, not anybody who lived there or worked with the boats. They had long forgotten the smell.

The trawler was inside the three-mile limit by now, slopping through the water. Hopkins looked towards the land, leaden and low, and sensed the skipper Emrys Prothero turn the wheel to port. Soon they would be back. For Hopkins, his last landing. He was sick of the place, sick of fish.

A convoy sat outside Milford Haven, arrived with a sense of relief from the Western Approaches. It rested solidly, big block-shaped Liberty ships from America, laden with war cargoes. German submarines did not pick them off as they used to. Most of them now arrived.

Gulls came out to meet the trawlers, squawking for their share, whirling around the boat. Hopkins scarcely noticed them. His work was almost done. It was always wet and cold.

The shore lightened and he could see vehicles moving against the shadows of the dockside streets and even the tight yellow light in the van of the canteen where volunteer women worked from dawn. Nobody paid much attention to the blackout now and at this time it was officially daylight. As they moved to the fish jetty he picked up his bag and got ready to go ashore. The other men did the same, leaving the skipper alone and looking unwanted, on his bridge. The fish would be unloaded by different men and gutted by women in the sheds along the quay. The gangway was put in place and the fishermen trudged up its slope. Nobody said goodbye nor did he expect them to. He would not miss them and they would not miss him. It was a hard life and it was not made for friendships.

Without much hesitation he walked up Talbot Street. He had not taken off his seaboots and had only opened the front of his yellow oilskins. He saw the upstairs curtains move at her house and turned in through the gate and up the tiled path. It just gave her time to open the door without him knocking.

'There,' she said with only the touch of a smile. 'Fancy seein' you.'

'Just happened to be passing,' he said. They said the same things every time.

She opened the door almost fully. She was wearing a pink dressing gown. 'Come on in, Davy,' she said quietly. 'You could do with a cup of tea. And a nice bath.'

Without a word he went through the door. She helped him as he peeled away his stiff oilskins. As she usually did, she surveyed him for a moment as if to make sure he was still all there before taking the yellow oilskins into the scullery. She said: 'I'll see to them later, Davy.'

'There's no need, Gwen,' he replied. 'Don't you bother yourself.'

'Mam Rowlands is dead,' she said.

'Oh, when was that?'

'Yesterday morning. Seven thirty-seven.'

The exact time of death was always recited, especially by Welsh people, like the last important piece being put into place.

'She'll be missed,' he said.

'Not so much as she might have been once.' Noisily she filled the kettle and lit the gas stove. 'Taught half the lads in this town about the facts of life, she did. Any one of

4

them from twelve upwards. Except Delmi Roberts.'

'And he had a cough,' recalled Hopkins. 'Sickly.'

'Consumption,' she nodded. 'So they said. But almost all the others. Except you, Davy.'

'I wasn't here at twelve,' he said. He turned his face to her and smiled. 'And after that you taught me.'

'At school, I taught you,' she said primly. 'History, sums and Christianity.' The kettle was boiling and she poured the water into the teapot. 'Fancy. Mam,' she said reflectively. 'Only fifty-two.'

Hopkins grinned a little. 'They should put up a statue. Like reclining.'

When she had been his teacher at the school Gwen was twenty-five and he was fourteen, arrived from another place. Now ten years had gone by. Even on that morning, swathed in her candlewick with her hair sweaty over her forehead, she looked a nicely made woman, decently rounded and with good eyes. He had always enjoyed looking at her and having her look towards him.

Silently they drank the tea until she said: 'Never married, Mam, was she.'

'Never had time for it, I shouldn't think,' he said. 'Too busy.'

Gwen smiled. 'Want a bath?'

'Aye, I didn't just come for the tea.'

'Was the catch good?'

'It ought to have been. Took long enough.'

'Cold and wet,' she said.

'Always is. I'm fed up to the back teeth with it.'

'I'll run the water,' Gwen said. 'Want another?'

He put down his cup. 'No, I'll just have the bath,' he said. She went from the kitchen, moving in her almost graceful way. She had also taught physical jerks. He remembered being entranced by the bouncing of her blouse. The other boys had too. Kenny Johns broke a leg, fell over a stool not paying attention.

He sat in the wooden kitchen chair and wondered how he would tell her. She would take it with her usual shrug but it would show in her eyes. He began to pull off his seaboots. 'I'll do that for you,' she called from the bathroom next to the kitchen. 'You know I'm pleased to do it.'

Almost anxiously she reappeared. 'I've put all the hot in,' she said. Steam trailed her from the open door. Her eyes were bright in the vapour. 'Now for these.' She knelt before him like a supplicant on the lino floor and tugged at the clumsy boot. He moved to help her, first with his hands and then by easing his foot. But she would have none of it. 'Be still,' she said.

It was always a struggle but with a glint of triumph she pulled one long boot away and tossed it aside like something dead. She patted his sock and then, still on her knees, shuffled across the tiles until she was in front of the other boot. Playfully he moved it further to the right, away from her, but with a schoolmistress sternness she pulled it back. 'Stop it,' she said quietly.

'When's Mam Rowlands's funeral?'

'Wednesday. Chapel at eleven.'

'There'll be a few there,' he said. Then mischievously: 'I might go myself.'

She sniffed. 'Well, don't sit among the others, the other men.'

'I knew her.'

'All right. But they *knew* her in a different way. Old Testament *knew*.'

The boot had come free and she bounced it towards the other. Then, while he sat with growing expectancy, although he knew well what was coming, she pulled his socks away, all three layers. 'There's a few darns needed,' she said without lifting her eyes up. 'Doesn't your Auntie Annie ever darn?'

'Not if she can help it. She never does anything if she can help it.'

'She puts her hand out for your wages.'

'Yes, that. But she reckons she did all she was going to do

years ago. She doesn't do much for Uncle Unwin either. He never asks now.'

'They only got you back so you could work. It wasn't out of pity.'

'I've known that for ages. The water will be getting cold.'

She put her warm hand out to him and he took it. 'They get rougher,' she said. 'Your hands.'

'I'm not a shop assistant,' said Hopkins. Gwen glanced at the grate. There was newspaper, sticks and coal arranged. 'I'll light it now,' she decided. 'You can get dry in front of it.' There had never been any shortage of coal. Not in that part of Wales. All through the war they always had coal and fish.

Hopkins was still wearing most of his clothes. She turned when they were near the door of the bathroom, as if they had never done this before, and began to undress him like a boy. He grumbled but only a little. 'Wonder what hymns they'll have for Mam?' he said. 'She had plenty.'

'Don't be amusing,' she said. 'She's dead.'

When they had peeled away his clothes he stretched and she stood back to look at him saying: 'Get in the bath then, Davy. I've got some soft new soap. Palmolive. Bertie had some in the shop. Found it in the storeroom, probably been there since before the war.' She dipped the green tablet into the warm water and smelled it. 'Lovely.'

Familiar with the routine they enacted it carefully. Hopkins climbed into the bath his hands shielding his genitals. She knew he was only teasing and she pushed his hands away. 'Pack it up.'

It was a good-sized bath for a terraced house and he lowered himself into the water, enjoying the rise of it to his ribs. 'It's almost worth being out all night for this,' he said. She leaned over him and began to soap his chest. 'Palmolive,' he said. 'What did we used to say? Put this in your palm, Olive.'

'Not on your life, boy,' she answered laughing. 'We used to have Lifebuoy soap. Cheaper but it didn't niff so nice.'

Once they had entered the game they went about it more slowly, dreamily. When the time came he lounged back in the bath, filling it with his sturdy body from end to end, and she massaged the aromatic soap into her palms. As part of the rules he tried to restrain his erection. But it refused to lie down and she began to rub the suds into his penis. She hummed as she went about it. 'Not too much, Gwen,' he warned.

She mumbled: 'I get warmed to the task.'

There was a picture on the wall, next to the cylinder, of a damp-looking saint, the sort given away in Sunday school. Hopkins attempted to concentrate on that but it did not afford him much distraction from what her hands were about. 'Gwen,' he asked. 'Could we pack it up for a bit now. You know what will happen. Anyway, I've got something to tell you.'

She paused and dipped her hands into the bath to wash the Palmolive from them. 'Funny you should say that, I've got to tell you something too. We'll both have to wait, won't we. It's a pity to spoil it now.'

He stood in the bath, running with suds, his erection standing out like a ramrod. 'Let me help you out, boy,' she said. 'You'll topple over and hurt yourself.'

She held her hands up to him and, smiling at her flooded eyes, he clambered from the bath. 'You're such a fine-looking boy,' she said. 'You ought to get married. But not yet.'

The fire had risen cheerfully in the grate and he stood in front of it while she towelled him. They conversed about various matters and he felt his urgency leave him. They both knew it would come back when needed. As if it were a routine, motherly task, she rubbed his firm white skin, across his chest and muscled stomach, into his groin one side then the other and underneath.

'I'm getting a bit pent up,' she said.

He held her hand into the double bedroom. The bedclothes were pulled back as she had climbed from them. The window was smeared over with morning moisture. As if she knew the whole street was watching she strongly pulled the curtains. 'The moon was shining in last night,' she said. 'So I left them.'

Now she began taking off her nightdress, quickly as if there was an emergency. Her sleepy breasts were waking and her skin was pale. So was his but his neck and face were brown from the sea weather, like the hands that he held towards her as he lay on her sheet and waited.

She climbed above him the way she always did. They had only occasionally managed to get beyond that. 'Same old way,' she commented gently. 'We're used to it now, Davy.'

'You fell off twice, remember.'

'Stop chatting,' she said.

'I like a nice chat,' he teased. 'Fills in the time.'

She arched over him, her breasts hanging down like fruit, and reaching down guided him inside her. 'Never mind the time,' she said quietly. 'Fill me.' She gasped as she felt him move into her.

With scarcely a whisper they made love, not rushing, almost eking it out, until it could not be held back any longer. She gave a short sob at the end.

They lay against each other. 'It's always better every time,' she eventually mouthed against his hard neck. 'Like improving your singing.'

He pretended to sing and Gwen began to laugh against his skin. Then, surprised, he felt the laugh become tears. He eased her away from him. Like a child she rubbed her face with her hands.

'Gwen?' he asked.

'Sorry,' she sniffled. 'But they've found Allan. He's turned up.'

He felt his face change. 'Alive? He's turned up alive?'

'Just about.' She rolled over to his side and clung almost desperately to him. 'They got him out of the water and he's been in Russia all these months. You know what the bloody Russians are. They never tell anybody. Anyway, he's coming home. He should be here by next week.' She regarded him bleakly. 'I can't carry on like this with you with my husband still existing. I wouldn't do it. This is the last time, Davy.'

'I've got something to tell you as well,' he said.

At that season it was often mild in West Wales, in a wet sort of way, and as Hopkins trudged up the hill streets he felt that later it might become a good day, even with some sun, although it might only show itself about sunset. The coast was famous for its sunsets, among the best in the country.

Before the war the town had aspirations to be a seaside resort and a remnant of those ambitions was a palm tree, actually a spiky type of shrub, set in the pebbles that covered the square front garden of his uncle's house. Like all the houses in the grey terraced street it was heavily curtained, nets and, in this case, drapes with an Egyptian theme, for nobody wanted people to spy in. His Auntie Annie's nets could have done with a wash. There was a pot plant in the window which thwarted any looking in at a low level.

The houses were in pairs, each pair graced with a central name tablet dedicated to a Welsh notable. One pair was called Lloyd George Villas named for the famous prime minister, a man of war and women. It was quite a long hill and the council had almost run out of notable names by the end two, which were lamely called Sunset Villas even though they were at the eastern end of the street.

The house where Hopkins headed was one of a pair called Glendower Villas. He knew about Owen Glendower because Gwen had taught them about the famous warrior in the history class at school. He remembered, and indeed they had since discussed, how he could hardly drag his eyes from her woolly jumper while he and the rest recited the proper dates.

He let himself into the narrow passage that led into the parlour where he knew he would see his uncle sprawled in the big wooden-armed chair to one side of the guttering fire. He was always there, in bed, or in the lavatory.

'Long turn?' said his Uncle Unwin. It was hardly a question. The old man knew where he had been.

'Went to Gwen's for a cup of tea.'

'You often do.'

'She makes a nice cup. I'm going to join the army.'

His uncle made the most sudden movement in the chair he had attempted in years. His hands clutched the arms and he rose like a thin balloon before flopping down again onto the stained velvet cushion. 'You're not!' he shouted.

'I am. Next Monday I go. I've got my papers.'

'You don't need to join the army, you bloody fool!' The old man was still shouting. 'You're in the fishing. Reserved occupation. You don't have to.'

Hopkins said: 'I want to go. I'm sick of the fishing. There's no shortage of crew now.'

Unwin continued to look incredulous. 'But there's a war on,' he said lamely.

'We all know that. It's been on for four years and I want to get into the army before it's finished.'

'Think . . .' His uncle tried to think what he should think about. 'Think of the money.'

'You'll think about that, I expect.'

His Auntie Annie tottered through the door. 'What's all the shouting?'

'Him . . .' said Unwin again searching for words and in the end pointing at Hopkins. 'This ungrateful bugger says he's going to join the army. And there's a war still going on.'

'Like the Minstrel Boy,' she said in her bright loony way. She began to sing: *'The Minstrel Boy to the war has gone.'* The men ignored her.

His uncle pointed an accusing finger again. 'After all we've done for you,' he said.

Annie was familiar with the theme. 'All we have.'

'Brought you here, gave you a decent home . . .'

Annie said: 'Out of that orphanage.' It was her turn to look accusingly. 'Bad enough to lose your mam and dad, but to go to an orphanage – well.'

'And we got you out,' said his uncle. 'Gave you a home.'

'You waited until I was nearly old enough to work,' pointed out Hopkins carefully. 'Fourteen. There's timing for you. Anyway I'm going. And I'm going on Monday.' His uncle snorted but now wordlessly. His auntie stood to attention and sang the first lines of 'The Minstrel Boy' again. Unwin told her to shut up.

'Mam Rowlands,' muttered Auntie Annie at the funeral. 'She had a busy life.'

Uncle Unwin had declined to leave the wooden chair even for the dead but most of the other neighbours had put on their hats and turned up. In front were the three Francis sisters who, out of habit and interest, went to at least one funeral a week.

The young men who Mam Rowlands had over the years initiated in her front room, right under the fading photograph of her stationmaster father, most of them now fishermen or home from the armed services, stood in reverence and remembrance. Those who were still unmarried flicked their eyes this way and that to catch a glance of recognition from a fellow initiate. Married men stared straight ahead as Wailing Wally Watkins, a preacher from up the valley, conducted the service.

Hopkins saw Gwen come in late, when they were halfway through the words of 'Cwm Rhonda'. She paused at the door, saw his head and pushed herself into the pew opposite. Her husband was back home, mysteriously reappeared, and all the town knew it. They wondered what she would do now.

The Reverend Watkins wailed well through the service and particularly at the end of his address: 'Mam is not dead,' he said as if he was reasonably certain. 'She still lives among us.' For the first time Hopkins noticed Delmi Roberts, the shortest man in a town of a good number of short men; at school they used to say he was the last boy to notice it was raining.

Outside the chapel afterwards, in the opaque afternoon, the people milled slowly in the circular dance appropriate to such occasions. 'He's back then,' said Hopkins to Gwen under the rim of her hat, a pre-war summer straw painted black.

'Day before yesterday,' she said. 'He's not well, Davy. He'll never go to sea again. I've got him for good.'

'Nice service for Mam.'

'Lots here,' she said. 'When do you go?'

'Monday,' he said. 'Morning train.'

Sudden sadness seemed to sweep over her. She straightened her hat. 'I'll be glad when this war is over,' she said. She regarded him from below it. 'This is goodbye then, Davy.'

'It looks like it.'

He never noticed Delmi on the local train but when it reached Cardiff Central and he changed, there was the thin, small youth sitting in the carriage already.

They shook hands gravely. Delmi had a hand like a child. Hopkins sat opposite him on the war-worn third-class seats with the browning photographs of Weston-Super-Mare and Porthcawl overhead. Hopkins had left to solid indifference from his uncle and a chorus from Auntie Annie, once he had reminded her he was going.

'Where you off to?' Hopkins asked Delmi.

'Army. Called up.'

Hopkins was astonished. 'You passed the medical? What about your . . .'

'Cough?' asked Delmi. 'It was only a cough. It wasn't TB or anything. Christ, man, there was even a rumour I was dead once. They had a small collection for a wreath. Cough? I can't even cough if my life depended on it. Look.'

He attempted a violent cough but scarcely anything came out. 'See, nothing there.'

A woman sitting knitting in the far corner looked up and said: 'Cover your mouth when you cough like that, will you.'

'It wasn't a cough,' argued Delmi. 'Just a demonstration.'

'I'm going to the army too,' said Hopkins.

Now Delmi looked surprised. 'Got you, did they?'

'Reserved occupation, fishing,' said Hopkins. 'But I got sick of it.'

A concerned expression formed on Delmi's face. 'I don't want to go nowhere dangerous,' he said. 'I've told them straight. Not where you can get killed. The cookhouse would suit me. At least you get fed.'

'I'm just going to see what comes up,' said Hopkins. 'Anywhere they want to send me.'

Delmi said: 'I just wanted to get out of that place. See a bit of the world. Women and things. When Mam Rowlands died . . . Well, I'd already been called up then but I was glad to go.'

Hopkins said: 'Oh, Mam Rowlands.'

'My lover,' said Delmi in a proud whisper. The knitting woman dropped a stitch.

He saw Hopkins's disbelief. 'The others,' said Delmi, 'didn't really *do* anything, see. She gave them lemonade and cakes and that. It was me she loved. I used to go around there at night-time.'

'Two plain, one purl,' muttered the woman doggedly. 'You've made me miss count now.'

'Sorry,' said Delmi politely. 'What you doin' listenin'?'

Hurriedly Hopkins said: 'Where have you got to report?'

'Paddington station,' said Delmi. 'Right where we get off the train. There's an office and they tell you where to go.'

'Me as well,' said Hopkins. He took out a wad of papers. 'It says RTO Platform Five.'

After a search of his pockets Delmi found his papers. 'Same place,' he said. 'That's funny, that is.' He reached across and shook Hopkins by the hand again. 'Maybe we'll be together for the rest of the war.'

Chapter Two

From the back seat on the top deck of the bus Small looked to the distant fence of masts, the skyline of the London docks. They were easy to see now, since the bombings of 1940 and 1941 had flattened wide areas, houses, streets, warehouses, yards, providing an open vista like the plain of a low country.

Debris had long been cleared and carted away, the bomb-sites tidied up, but nothing would be built there until the war was over; there were spaces where youths played football, where wild flowers grew and where the exposed grates of first- and second-floor fireplaces were as full and bright as window boxes. By night the spaces were the haunt of feral cats, foxes and sinners.

A scattering of buildings, houses and shops still stood shored up with timbers and buttresses. In places there was only one house standing in a street. The inhabitants who had remained, sheltering in the underground stations, or who had returned, hardly noticed the clearances by now.

Small was glad to confirm that his mother's house still remained on its feet, its emergency timber supports still steady. He picked up his bag and went down to the bus platform. The fat conductress mistook him, in his civilian clothes, for a returning merchant seaman and said: 'Back again then. Been far?'

Small grimaced. 'Far enough.'

'Never mind, mate, it'll all be over soon. I know what I'd like to do with that bugger. Me and my sister.'

The bus slowed. He prepared to get off. 'Your sister a big woman, is she?'

'Big as me,' she said with cockney relish. 'The swine would die in agony.'

He left the bus and it drove off. She hadn't charged him a fare because she thought he had come home from the sea. They waved to each other but a touch wearily. The mateyness of the earlier war years was waning.

There was a front gate to his mother's house which had to be scraped open because the top hinge was broken. They had claimed it as war damage but nothing had been done. The council man said they had to rebuild the City of London first.

The house was done up like a parcel with supports and buttresses all around it and a tarpaulin nailed to the roof. He still had his key and with a growing sense of anticipation he turned it in the lock. It would not open. His mother called through the letter-box: 'Who is it?'

'It's me,' he returned bending towards the knocker. 'It's Stan.'

There were rumblings from inside the door, some of them human, and it was tugged open. She had been aware that he was coming and she wore a clean pinafore and hat, a purple turban as the wartime wives called them. She only had her bottom set of teeth in and she half-smiled and apologised at the same time. 'I can't find the buggers anywhere,' she said.

'Maybe they've gone down the lav again,' said Small.

He walked into her tubby embrace and he returned it genuinely. 'You're 'ome,' she said.

'Right. I'm 'ere. Been all right by yourself?'

He put his bag in the tight hall below his framed granddad and she led the way to the kitchen where she poured a cup of tea, brewed in the teapot that was on the hob all day, replenished with a spoonful of Lipton's in the late afternoon. Her husband, a wartime thief, had been killed by a bomb which demolished the Royal Arms, Millwall, after closing time. He was the only customer left and he had died in the clutch of a barmaid, also a fatality. The question, not always unspoken, this being the East End, was whether their death embrace had commenced before, after or during the arrival of the bomb.

'I been all right,' she said. 'Not too bad, 'cept when the 'ouse wobbles. It creaks in the night something nasty. Sometimes I think it's comin' down round my bleedin' ears.'

She refilled his teacup and he suddenly remembered how the taste of the Lipton's grew more stewy as the day went on. 'I don't like the sound of it one little bit,' she went on. ' 'Specially when the wind gets up and it blows straight from the river these days, now there's nothing in the way – it creaks and it groans and I don't trust these truss things they've put up. Be funny if I got trapped under this lot three years after the Blitz.'

He finished his tea and picked up his bag. 'Same room I 'spect.'

She gave a croak. 'It'll 'ave to be. Unless you want to sleep with the dog.'

'Smelly all right?'

'Still the same.'

He mounted the dark familiar stairs with a half-grin. 'I thought you might 'ave a bit of bunting outside, a few flags like, same as what they did when Bert Wellman came 'ome.'

She sniffed in the dimness. 'Bert Wellman was wounded in action – lost 'is leg. You was only in prison.'

They went into the narrow room. She had made the bed for him. 'Six months, that's all,' he said. He bounced on the bed approvingly and felt the blankets with his hands. 'Anyway I'm back now, 'ome.'

'Not for long,' she sniffed. 'You're getting called up. The papers is downstairs.'

He stared at her and stood up slowly. 'Where?' he asked making for the landing. She followed him down and handed him the brown official envelope. 'I opened it. It looked important.'

'It bleedin' well is. Christ, only I could come out of stir and get called into the army.'

'It'll be a nice change. Anyway, looks like the Jerries are not going to last long, according to the wireless. There'll just be time to do square bashing and you'll be out. Be one of them Bevin Boys.'

He realised. 'But that's . . . that's . . . going down the mines. I'm not going down no soddin' coal mine when I've just got out of the nick.'

She seemed sorry for him. 'You never was very lucky. Run away. Desert before you even get in. You'll never get out of it on a medical. I've never seen you look so fit. I reckons being inside 'as suited you.'

'I'm not scarpering. I've done enough running.'

'Looks like you'll 'ave to go then.'

'Looks like it, don't it.'

The pub, the Coalman's Arms, had never entirely run out of beer during the war and had only closed for a few days when the rest of the street had been blown down, some of the customers never to be seen alive again. Small did not recognise the barmaid, who had sharp eyes and lips and who looked as if she had only just survived any number of events.

Small had a pint of Watney's and carefully revolved from the polished bar to survey the room. There were two Yank soldiers making an old woman laugh in the corner. They were everywhere. There were even a couple in Wormwood Scrubs, who boasted that prisons in America were superior. It was early in the evening and his mother was at home frying ham, egg and chips, the ham stolen. He had given her his ration card and she would be able to go shopping the next day. She would have to conceal the HM Prison imprint with her thumb. Not everyone needed to know. Since his father, the thief, had died there were not so many luxuries around the house.

The only customer in the bar he recognised was a plain-clothes copper. His name was Burton and his nickname was Dabs because he was a fingerprint man. He had been watching Small and when he saw the recognition had been returned he came towards the bar. 'When did you get out then?' he said.

'Today. This is my first pint.'

'Want another?'

Small, after a cautious hesitation, said he did. The detective had a Watney's as well. 'They're even advertising this stuff now,' Small said. '"What We Want is Watney's." I saw it on the posters when I was on the bus. The war must be nearly over.'

'Looks like it. You got six months, didn't you.'

'And time off for being a good boy.'

'Your old man died, I heard. Bad luck 'im getting bombed at this stage.'

Small shrugged, finished his first pint and started the next. 'The bombing was good to 'im up to then,' he said. 'He was a bugger for the lootin' as you know.'

Dabs said he did. 'Got it to an art.'

Small said: 'Sometimes 'e got to the 'ouse before the Germans.'

'It looked like the Jerries was tipping him off,' said Burton.

'As soon as the 'ouse was blitzed 'e'd be in there,' said Small with a touch of admiration. 'And out with the loot before the fire brigade or the ARP got there.'

Burton shook his head wryly. 'I bet you found a few changes at home.'

Small grinned as well. 'Without all the nicked stuff around. And no black-market gear either. Place seemed like empty.'

'So what are you going to do now?'

'That's been fixed for me. I got my calling-up papers. Welcome 'ome present. I'm going in the bloody army.'

'You won't try to dodge it?'

'Don't see any point. There won't be much to do once us

and the Yanks 'ave got across to France. By the time I'm done training it will all be finished. I might learn to drive.'

The detective regarded him over the rim of his glass. 'Keep you out of trouble,' he said. 'You had a knife, didn't you, Smallie. Still got it?'

Small shook his head. 'What a memory you got, Dabsy. No, I ain't got it now. Or the knuckledusters.'

'I was going to ask you about the 'dusters.'

'No, mate. I dumped them before I went in. Dropped them in the river.' He made a dropping motion with his fingers. 'Knife first. 'Dusters next.'

Dabs regarded him quietly. He finished his beer. Small said: 'Want another? I saved up best part of three quid when I was inside.'

The policeman shook his head. 'Got to go,' he said. 'My missus wants to go to the pictures. That Errol Fucking Flynn.' At the door he turned. 'Leave them in the river, son,' he said. 'You'll have a nice time in the army. Learning to drive. Don't let them teach you to shoot.'

Later that evening his mother raised one of the kitchenette floorboards and lifted out a tin of American ham. For a moment she eyed the other unseen contents of the aperture, as if to count them, then carefully replaced the board. 'I don't know if that lot will last the war,' she said.

Small said: 'The old man wasn't to know how long it would go on.'

She turned on the wireless for the news. 'I like this Alvar Liddell,' she said. 'Such a nice voice. I always listen if he's reading it.'

'Wilfred Pickles was the best, they reckoned in the Scrubs. When the news was bad, somehow he cheered it up.'

Minn was a poor cook. She burned the chips and the egg was grubby around its fried edges but the ham looked as good and fresh as when it had been canned in Illinois. She made two cups of tea to go with it. 'Your father's grandmother was a darkie,' she said as if it would make good conversation.

'I know.'

'She came from one of those darkie countries.'

'I know.' His own skin was olive and his eyes deep and dark. 'Women like it,' he told her. 'It looks sort of Spanish.'

His mother regarded him as though she had never really studied him. 'I suppose it does. Not many women in prison, was there.'

'Not in the Scrubs. You had to make them up.'

Despite the raggedness of the meal they ate heartily. 'Won't be many in the army either,' he said, his mouth full of egg. 'You have to look around.'

She dropped her fork but deftly caught it in her fingers as it slipped from the table. He raised his tea mug as if to salute the feast. She raised hers and noisily drank. 'Your father was a right bastard with the women,' she said. 'You know that?'

'I had a rough idea.'

'They made out he was a 'ero when that bomb hit the pub. Died protecting that barmaid with his body.' She wiped a piece of bread across the yolk-stained plate. 'Want some more 'am?' she asked. 'It's open now so it won't last that long.'

Small said he would and held out his plate. She lobbed a generous slice onto it. 'It's funny how them Yanks 'ave all this good stuff. Ice cream and everything. And we're half-bloody-starved.'

She talked as she chewed, as if the food fuelled her. 'Anybody you knew up the pub?' she asked.

'One bloke. And he was a rozzer. That barmaid's new. She's got a face like a chopper.'

'You don't get many in there now,' said Minn. She had wiped the plate clean, but she ran her thumb around the edge. 'Nobody left 'ere to go. They'll never come back neither.'

Small said: 'It'll take years to rebuild all these houses.'

'Right it will. And they've gone to other parts, the country and suchlike with the cows and them sheep.' Absently she took a piece of egged-bread from his plate and put it in her mouth. She ruminated. 'Mind you, it could be in the country around 'ere. You can see for miles from upstairs and there's weeds and grass and flowers all over the bomb-sites. Animals as well. Cats and dogs and in the night you can 'ear wolves.'

'Wolves?' said Small.

'No. I tell a lie. Them others . . .'

'Foxes.'

'That's right, foxes.'

When he had eaten she asked him if he wanted anything else.

'Nah, the beer filled me up. Not used to it.'

He was on the bottom stair and he bent and gave her a kiss on the cheek. She seemed grateful and kissed him back. 'I'm glad you're out,' she said.

'Home,' he corrected.

'Right, 'ome. I been fed up 'ere by myself.'

'I won't be 'ere for long,' he reminded her. 'You ought to get yourself a bloke.'

Even in the dimness he could see she was a little startled. 'Not after your father,' she sniffed. 'Once you've had the best . . .'

He managed a laugh and kissed her again. Once he was in his bedroom with the light turned on he went to the section of skirting board at the side of the scarred wardrobe and with his fingers worked it loose. A piece came away in his hand and he put it on the lino. He grinned when he explored the cavity and came out with the single pair of knuckledusters, five lead pieces on a shoestring. He put them on his right hand and threw a punch towards his reflection in the looking glass.

Chapter Three

Spring tried its best. There were brave daffodils and tulips in the parks, clothing the banks of the air-raid shelters, the gun emplacements and barrage-balloon sites. All the park railings had been removed in the mistaken belief that the metal would be useful for making munitions. Ducks floated appreciatively on fire-brigade emergency water tanks. Some birds, having forgotten the bombing, had returned to the trees.

But London and the people were weary; weary of war, its dangers and its dirt. The great gaps in the buildings were by now part of the scenery, but the buoyancy, the comradeship and the wildly illogical optimism of the early years had waned. The battles would be coming to an end soon, so they thought then, only to have to wait another year; the downcast population and the city, and the country itself, were tiredly waiting for it to be ended.

Neither Hopkins nor Delmi had ever been to London and they emerged from Tottenham Court Road underground station with a sense of relief which neither admitted. 'It's a long way down there, boy,' said Delmi when they reached the grey daylight. 'Like a coal mine.'

'You get used to it,' said Hopkins as if he travelled that way every day. It could not be more strange or dangerous than deep-sea fishing; but at sea you could see further. They each had an army form clutched like a note and each carried a small, worn case. Delmi was wearing his best, shapeless suit with his late father's pork-pie hat, and Hopkins had a new jacket and sagging grey flannels.

'Why get a new jacket to go in the army?' Delmi had said to him on the train. 'You won't be able to wear it. It won't get you promotion.'

'My old one was worn out,' Hopkins had said. 'I wasn't going to go to London in that old thing.'

They had been directed by a grey, fatherly officer in charge of Movements (Paddington) to what they were instructed was a transit camp in Tottenham Court Road. Although they came from the same Welsh streets they had rarely seen or even talked to each other before, not since school. Hopkins had wanted to cut away from his previous life and now here was Delmi with him, like a remnant, asking him questions, seeking assurances, and looking as though he might be there for some time.

'Can't see any camp,' said Delmi looking up and down the gritty street. Many of the shop windows were boarded. 'No tents or anything.'

They were passed by people who all seemed to walk with their heads down as though too fatigued to lift them up. There were black, oddly Victorian taxis, a few civilian cars, some military vehicles and several horse-drawn carts. Moving among them were red-sided London buses. 'Bit miserable, London,' muttered Delmi.

'It probably gets better when you get used to it,' said Hopkins. He was examining the army form in his hand. He put his case on the pavement and studied the writing on the slip of paper. A soldier was going by and he stopped him and asked.

'Fuck off,' said the soldier marching away.

'Norway,' said Delmi looking at the man's back. 'It said "Norway" on his shoulder.'

'He needn't swear,' said Hopkins. They carried their cases along the pavement. Nobody noticed them. There were bomb sites, gaps in the buildings, but no sign of a camp. 'It's well hidden,' grumbled Hopkins.

'A secret, maybe,' suggested Delmi. 'Maybe we'll be doing something dangerous. I 'ope not.'

A bus drew up and three people left it, the third of whom was Small. He put his bag on the pavement and looked about him. Ten yards away he saw Hopkins and Delmi standing likewise. He summed them up. 'You reportin' to this army dump?' he asked.

'We're trying to,' said Hopkins. 'We can't see any sign of it.'

'They've 'id it,' said Small. 'Where you come from?'

Delmi determinedly said: 'Wales.'

'Welsh gits,' said Small but not unpleasantly. 'No wonder you can't find it.'

They were standing by a space alongside the pavement, cracked paving stones cluttered with weed. A large, round, grimy red trapdoor, almost at their feet, began to sound metallically, and as they watched in surprise it opened slowly, pushed upwards by two hands. A man wearing glasses appeared. Unhurriedly he climbed up an inside metal staircase and stood before them in a uniform of tropical khaki, with shorts.

The man blinked as if some sudden sun had got in his spectacles.

'Recruits,' he said. He had two stripes on the arms of his lightweight, short-sleeved shirt. He brushed himself down. 'I wear this because it's bleedin' hot down there,' he said.

It was Hopkins who recovered first. 'We're looking for 307 Transit Unit. TCR. Whatever that means.'

'Tottenham Court Road,' said the corporal. His ginger hair was sparse across his forehead and he did not have a hat. 'You've gone and found it.'

They studied the hole from which he had risen.

'Better come on in,' he added as if he were not that keen. 'Mind the steps.' He pushed the round metal lid to the full extent of its hinges. 'Corporal Blewit,' he said. 'Des. That's me.' Slowly he vanished from view down the aperture. The three youths glanced at each other. Small went first.

They descended into a large chamber lit by dim bulkhead lights, nameless pipes curled around the walls. There were gurgling sounds. Delmi, who was last on the spiral staircase, looked about him fearfully. Their feet clanked on the metal steps as they came down to the deepest part of the chamber where stacks of bunks were lined in rows. Some were occupied by snoring men or others cursing because they had been disturbed. It was seven o'clock in the evening.

Corporal Blewit seemed himself to be hesitant in his navigation between the bunks. 'Some of 'em get nasty,' he said. 'And I don't like bother. Don't want to draw attention, do I?'

There was a rough army desk under an alcove, lit by a bright lamp and looking like an altar. A beret with a dull regimental badge was hanging on the chair behind the desk and, now he was indoors and installed, the corporal placed it on his sweaty head. 'Always bloody 'ot down 'ere,' he said. 'No matter what odds it is up in the street. 'Ot as 'ell. That's why I sport the tropical gear. I only put on battledress when I goes to get my pay from the barracks. Nobody seems to know what I do or that I come up from this 'ole but they don't ask neither.'

'Where . . . ?' enquired Hopkins carefully. 'What . . . is this?'

'You've just come down the fire escape,' said the corporal pointing towards the spiral staircase. 'See it says it on that notice. See . . . "Fire Escape". Normally speaking you come in over there.' He thrust his thumb over his shoulder. 'What we call the front door.'

Hopkins repeated the question. 'But what is it, this place?'

Blewit appeared surprised. 'TCR. Transit Unit,' he said. He prodded a grimy thumb towards Hopkins's piece of paper. 'Like it says there. It ain't Buckingham Palace.'

Delmi was still looking around him. 'No,' he said.

Blewit sat back in his chair. For him it was a familiar lecture. 'It's a plague pit,' he announced with plump satisfaction. 'Well, it was. 'Undreds of years ago, when the Plague was on. They dug it out and chucked the bodies down 'ere. Not long ago they still found bits of bones, shins and that, but nobody's handed any in recently.'

Delmi said: 'Is there anywhere else?'

'Not for you, son. But you sound Welsh. It's only like being down a coal mine.'

'I worked in a grocer's,' said Delmi.

Blewit seemed offended. 'It's not that bad. Bloody safe as well. Right through the Blitz I was down 'ere. Just pulled the lid on myself and stayed put. Bombs everywhere . . . well, you can see up top. But down 'ere all it did was rattle a bit.'

'It looks safer than some of them shelters,' agreed Small. 'Death traps some of 'em.'

'Oh, it is. It is,' beamed Blewit. 'But not many knew it was 'ere. Anyway, it was reserved for the military, so that was that. Sometimes I'd let the girls from the street down if the bombing got bad.'

Small said: 'You been down 'ere all that time?'

'Four years,' said the corporal smugly. 'Before the Blitz really. And I ain't coming out, not if I can 'elp it, until the last bloody all-clear sounds.'

He wiped the top of the desk with his elbow, unlocked a drawer and brought out a khaki-coloured cash box. 'Ration allowances,' he announced. 'For tonight only. And fares.' He looked at the Welsh youths. 'You had your billy-doos right through,' he said. 'Your travel allowance. From your front door in Welsh Wales to upstairs here, including the tube.'

'Correct,' said Hopkins.

Small said: 'I only 'ad a bus fare. Eightpence ha'penny.' He looked with a sort of envy at the others but said: 'I'm a Londoner.'

Blewit asked him if he had his bus ticket but he said he had thrown it away. The corporal wrote on a document: 'Bus ticket missing, believed destroyed,' and passed it to Small to sign. He pushed eight pennies and a halfpenny across the desk and then drew the halfpenny back. 'This man's army don't deal with ha'pennies,' he said.

'Well, make it ninepence,' said Small. 'I walked two stops.'

The corporal shrugged at the logic and added another penny to the eight.

'What man?' asked Delmi. 'You said "this man's army", didn't you. Who's the man?'

'I heard it in a Yankee film,' confessed Blewit. 'All the Yanks say it.'

'Are there many around here, Yanks?' asked Delmi.

'Crawling,' said Blewit.

Small said: 'Every-bleeding-where. Even in the Scrubs.' He looked hurriedly around. 'So they reckon.'

'I'll be glad when they start this invasion,' sighed the corporal. 'There'll be a bit more room around town then.'

He studied them like a father. 'Watch them, the Yanks,' he said. 'And all the other buggers out there. Spivs, deserters, Poles, Maltese. The Malts are gangsters. But just watch out. You 'ave to be in by twenty-three fifty-nine. That's a minute before midnight. Make sure you come back in one piece . . .' He regarded them. 'Well, three pieces.'

'Sounds like the front line,' said Delmi.

'It is sometimes. Worse. But you'll be all right. Just stick together and don't go anywhere shady. They'll 'ave your balls off. Worse, they'll 'ave your money.'

Hopkins said: 'We get ration allowance, you said.'

'For twenty-four hours. Lucky you. Three shillings and seven-pence.'

'Each?' asked Delmi.

Blewit said: 'Each.' He gave Delmi a glance as if he wondered what would happen to him in the army.

'You won't be able to get into the Ritz,' he went on. 'Too many officers. The Savoy ain't that far, but that's out too. Best place if you don't want to be robbed rotten is the Salvation Army canteen just down the road. No booze but it's cheap.'

'How long are we going to be here?' asked Hopkins.

Delmi smiled encouragingly and said: 'Long as possible?'

The corporal looked surprised. 'You don't know?'

All three shook their heads. 'We don't even know where we're going,' said Hopkins.

He glanced at Small who said: 'I don't.'

Blewit puffed out his cheeks and shuffled through some papers. But he already knew. 'Tomorrow at eight hundred hours,' he said. 'Field service marching order . . .' He glanced up and said: 'Except you ain't got any field service marching order 'cause you're still in civvies. But anyway eight hundred hours transport will take you to your next posting.'

'Where?' asked Small.

'Aldershot, soldier,' said Blewit. 'Haldershot.'

When they went out the long, straight Tottenham Court Road was mild in the grey spring evening. There were some split and damaged trees at one corner of a site cleared of bomb debris and, as though to demonstrate something, the stunted branches that had survived were sprouting new leaves.

British Summer Time continued through the winter to increase daylight hours for working and in the true months of summer it was extended so that it was two hours ahead of Greenwich. It was eight o'clock that evening and still light. Some timid lights showed from windows and doorways because it was before blackout time and the strict hours of darkness were not observed as they had been. 'Let's go somewhere for some women,' said Delmi standing up to his full height.

They did not have to look far. Almost at the first corner was a shadowy tart, the red end of her cigarette glowing like an advertisement. The three soldiers in their civilian clothes did a smart, almost military, about turn, and pressed in the other direction. 'Only five bob!' the woman shouted after them.

'Cheap at the price,' mentioned Small to the others. They were letting him lead because he was a cockney and, they believed, familiar with the scene. But Small's upbringing had been a few miles east and most Londoners kept to their own territory especially at night.

Hopkins said cautiously: 'Let's go to the Sally Army.'

'There's bound to be fun there,' sniffed Delmi. 'They might have a rummage sale.'

Another woman, leaning against a damaged wall as if doing a job keeping it upright, solicited them. She was small, almost like a girl, which she may well have been.

'A bit on the short side for me,' said Small.

Delmi said with a sort of wiseness: 'Being on the short side myself I like my girls short.' He glanced at each uncertainly, then said: 'Stunted, even.'

There were people all around them, hurrying or loitering in shadows. The ends of cigarettes showed red. Everybody smoked. Small and Delmi were smoking. Some people were already drunk, shoving their passage through the crowds.

A man in a pale suit and a wide tie appeared from a doorway. 'Gentlemen,' he said. 'Come in and 'ave one. In civvies. We don't get many in civvies. Conchies on the prowl are you, lads?' He was standing back to urge them through the crouching door.

'We're in the army,' said Hopkins regarding him sturdily. 'But we've not got our uniforms yet.'

'I'm a fucking colonel,' said Small.

'Lads, lads,' said the man anxiously. 'No offence. Come in. The beers are on me. My name's Mickey. Magic Mickey they call me. Come on. Meet some girls.'

They glanced at each other and obediently turned in at the

door. The big room was dank and almost empty although there was a clutch of loud Americans in one corner with two squealing females. There was a flashy bar and while they were there two crippled men came in, one setting up a drumkit and the other taking a violin from its case. 'Our orchestra,' said Mickey.

'Three free beers, please,' ordered Small firmly.

'Like you promised,' said Hopkins.

A barman appeared, his bow-tie hanging like a dead bat, and poured three cloudy beers into glasses. At once a squalid woman approached from the recesses of the room and said: 'Ooooh, civvies!'

'We're spies,' said Hopkins.

She turned and laughed coarsely towards the Americans in the corner. 'They reckons they're spies,' she cackled.

The barman forced a grin like an inversion of his drooping tie. He glanced towards Mickey who gave him a shifty nod and he did not ring anything on the till. The trio were suspiciously lifting the glasses to their lips when a wiry young black man in a blue overcoat came in. He joined them as if they had been expecting him and said he was from Bristol and his name was Rumble. He got his own beer and asked if they would like a quick refill. 'Merchant Navy,' he said in a West Country accent. 'Ship's just been paid off.'

'Get that nigger outta here!'

The bellow came from the corner where the Americans were sitting with the two girls. The man who had shouted was already on his feet. He was square and even in the shadows they could see the venom of his face. He began to advance nastily. 'Get him out!' he demanded again. 'We don't want no niggers.'

As if by instinct the three recruits formed a barrier in front of the black man who peered out between them at the American. 'Jesus,' he said quietly.

It was the woman who intervened. 'You sit down, Charley,' she said like an order. ''E ain't one of your niggers, 'e's one of ours. 'E's an English nigger.' She turned to the black man and said: 'Ain't you.'

'Yes,' he said.

'I think you'd better scarper,' Mickey suggested heavily. 'We don't want no bother.'

The American was standing, truculently, legs apart, four feet away. Hopkins thought that Small was going to go for him, but he held a thick arm in the way. 'We was just going,' said Hopkins.

'To somewhere nicer,' mentioned Delmi bravely but quietly.

Mickey began moving them towards the door while the woman ushered the truculent American back to his friends in the corner.

'Thanks for calling in,' said Mickey, his arms and his smile wide. 'Come by again, any time.'

'Bollocks,' said Small as they went out of the door into the Tottenham Court Road night.

Rumble, the black man, stayed with them. 'The Sally Army's down this way,' he said. 'I've been in there before. No booze, no tarts, no worries.'

A double door was open and the blackout curtain inside only half pulled. There was a suffused light behind it and the sound of a pleasant tune. Rumble went in first and ducked below the curtain. The others followed without caution.

It was a homely place despite its size and the stark lighting. A girl in bulky Salvation Army uniform was hovering over a wind-up gramophone. The melody came to an end and she took the record from the turntable, pushed it into a cardboard sleeve and replaced it with another. Then she wound the handle of the gramophone. 'The new Donald Peers,' she announced proudly.

She started the record with a push of her podgy hand and then came purposefully across the floor to them, her tunic bulging almost to the neck. 'Not many in tonight,' she said. She had a pink and cheery face. 'Be more later on. I'm called

Aggie. Tea's a penny, one refill free, and cakes and sandwiches, tuppence and thruppence, depending on what's inside 'em. Once they get the gas going there'll be egg and chips.'

They had sat around a rough wooden table. There were two other groups sitting against the walls. Everyone ordered tea and Aggie said she would bring a few of the older sandwiches which were cheaper. She went away and Hopkins said to Rumble: 'Where you been then? On a ship?'

The black youth half-smiled. 'In the drink mostly,' he said. 'In the briny. Three times I've been torpedoed. The buggers will get me next time.'

'I go to sea,' said Hopkins. Then with a touch of apology: 'Just fishing. Bristol Channel.'

'Same sea,' shrugged Rumble. 'Cold and wet and deep, but it's not so bad as it was. The U-boats used to hang around in packs, just waiting.' He looked around the table. 'Why you wearing civvies?'

Aggie brought four cups on a tin tray and a plate of grimacing sandwiches. 'The whole plate for fourpence,' she said. 'Captain Hennup says. They're dying of old age.'

'Only just joined,' Hopkins told Rumble. We're being posted tomorrow to Aldershot. We'll get our khaki there.'

'You lot are lucky,' said the black man. 'Be finished by the time they get you trained. It's all over bar the shouting.'

Small was eyeing Aggie. Her rounded face was flushed. She saw him studying her, looked away and looked back again. A long grey man in a blue uniform appeared. 'Any complaints?' he joked. 'No booze, I'm afraid. But we don't expect you to say prayers or anything. Only on Sundays.'

'Is there dancing?' asked Small as the man moved away. Aggie glanced towards him and flushed. He had a sandwich in his mouth, fixed below his nose like a white moustache.

'If you like,' she said. He chewed the sandwich into his mouth and washed it down swiftly with tea before standing up.

The other three looked at each other. 'Fast mover, your mate,' said Rumble amiably. 'There's a lot of girl there.'

Delmi nodded sagely. 'Big bum,' he said.

'Quite big,' said Hopkins. He was amazed at how deftly Small had manoeuvred the situation. 'And Salvation Army too.' Rumble passed around a packet of Player's.

Aggie stopped Donald Peers on the gramophone. 'Can't dance to that,' she said privately to Small. 'Bit wet.'

Small eyed the distant captain. 'He don't mind then.'

'Not him. Some of them would but he says God invented dancing like everything else. So it's all right.' She selected a record and took it from its brown-paper sleeve. '"Smoke Gets in Your Eyes",' she said.

Small was taller than she was but half as wide. Her hands were warm, podgy, as he took them on the edge of the holed linoleum floor. 'At least you ain't wearing army boots,' she said.

Small said: ''Aven't got none yet. Only just joined. In the nick . . .' he stopped himself: '. . . of time.'

To his pleasure and surprise she pushed herself against him and rested her puffy face on his shoulder. 'I'm not Sally Army,' she whispered. 'They just let me come 'ere and I wear the coat just to sort of be one of them. But I'm not. Never will be, as much as I try.'

Small moved his sharp body against her. He held his cigarette behind her shoulders. Her breasts were heavy and cheaply scented in his face. 'How come you come 'ere then?'

'They're trying to save me,' she said. 'I've not been a good girl but I *do* mean well and they let me come in 'ere. They're good really, very good. But I don't think I'll ever change.'

A crafty look lit her small eyes. She glanced over his shoulder to search the smoky room, the groups at the tables, two fussy ladies and the uniformed captain. ''Ave a dekko in the banner cupboard,' she invited.

Small put out his cigarette, and held softly by her hand let himself be led in the middle of their shuffling dance from the room and down a dank corridor. 'In 'ere,' she whispered. There was a low door under some stairs. She opened it and climbed awkwardly into the dark interior, her hand still trailing behind her. He went in after her.

'They keep their banners in 'ere,' she said. 'In the dark.'

There was a faint splinter of light coming around the edges of the door. 'Don't need the lights,' said Small. 'I can feel.'

He was already doing so, running his hands up her poly waist to the swellings of her breasts. 'Kiss me first,' she almost whined. 'Don't be in a rush.'

Small said: 'Sorry, I forgot.' He was feeling smug. It was warm in the banner cupboard and her body made it warmer. 'Where's the banners?' he asked.

'They're against the wall,' she said impatiently. 'Get on with it.'

Enjoyably he rolled his hands over her swollen breasts. 'Can you get them out?' he asked, kissing her.

''Course,' she said in a stifled way. 'I needed you to come in tonight.' There were some buttons at the front of the large dress. She began to undo them and he took her fingers away and undid the rest himself, opening the front of the dress. Her breasts were like mounds of snow in the dimness. He plunged in with both hands almost ladling them out.

'They're good, ain't they,' she said proprietorially.

'Among the best I've come across,' he told her.

She pulled away a little. ''Ave you come across a lot? 'Undreds?'

'Not that many,' said Small. Like a greengrocer he weighed them in his hands, the nipples in his palms, before kissing the white skin.

'Oh, that's nice,' she sighed. She paused. 'What's this in your pocket, mate?'

'You know,' he said defensively.

'Not that, silly. This heavy thing.' She felt the knuckledusters.

'Oh, it's nothing. Just a necklace. A sort of necklace.'

'I'd like a necklace.'

'It's not that kind of necklace.'

Her bland nipples had hardened at their centre, pointing like thorns. His busy tongue had just touched them and her podgy hands were massaging his penis when there came the unmistakable smell of egg and chips. His head came up and he sniffed. It was seeping through the edges of the door. Aggie said: 'They're frying up.'

A sneaky knock sounded on the door. 'Supper is ready,' said an apologetic male voice.

Aggie's big body gave a large sigh. 'Never a moment,' she complained. 'I don't know how long I'm going to 'ang around this place.' She was shovelling her bosom away, puffing with annoyance.

'We could come back,' whispered Small.

'When you've had a feed,' she sniffed. 'Oh no, mate. I can't just dish up love like that.'

She shoved the door with her backside and pushed him out carefully.

'They do fried bread as well,' she mentioned. 'The whole lot is only a tanner.'

Small followed her into the corridor and then the room. His companions watched him return. The black man was still with them. 'You must be hungry,' he said. 'It's just coming. Only sixpence each.'

Small still had an erection and had to manoeuvre it aside to get his coin. Aggie was now busy carrying smoking plates around the room singing out: 'Double fried bread ... egg ... and double chips. Plenty of chips tonight.' She came to the table and showing no sign of even recognising Small she said: 'Double of everything for you, I 'spect.'

They devoured the fry-up, except for Rumble who said it

made him feel seasick. He had another plate of bent sandwiches.

'What was it like in there then?' Delmi asked enviously, his
mouth full, his eyes drifting towards the cupboard in the corridor.

'Dark,' said Small. 'Bloody dark.'

Hopkins grinned at Delmi. 'Go and have a look,' he suggested.
They were all smoking.

'I'm afraid of the dark,' said Delmi.

'Banners,' said Small shrugging.

'Like Sister Anna carried,' said Delmi.

'That's right, mate.'

By ten o'clock Tottenham Court Road was filled with heavy
shadows, lines of people moving against each other in the darkness. It seemed threatening. Men were drunk and women
raucous. The pubs were still open. American Snowdrops, military police, were breaking up fights.

Hopkins led the way, keeping clear of what they could see
were the most troublesome areas. Music was sounding through
the dark. There were dullard girls at corners and in doorways,
chewing gum and offering themselves at bargain rates. Delmi,
behind Hopkins in the single file, peered to each side with fascin-
ation and fear. Rumble, the sailor, followed him, trying to hide
his black face, and Small was in the rear.

For an hour they had been in a four-ale bar, conspicuous in
their civilian clothes. Two red-capped military police came in
and looked aggressively around the crowded servicemen. They
asked Hopkins what he was doing there and he told them he
was waiting to join the army. This seemed to satisfy them and
after a further survey from beneath the low peaks of their caps,
they moved out. But their questions to Hopkins gave him and
the others an effective protection. Nobody approached them
or tried to pick a fight.

A clutch of French sailors with red pompoms on their hats

were attracting attention. Some soldiers with 'Poland' across the tops of their sleeves moved in on the Frenchmen and they began to skirmish. One of the barmen bawled: 'Start anyfing and the bleedin' bar shuts.' Other men turned on the two groups and the beginnings of the fight subsided.

Hopkins said: 'I think we ought to get back.'

'Safely,' added Delmi.

The young black man went with them. He had gone without aggravation because there were no Americans. Now, in the street, he crept between the others. The air was gritty as well as dark. Dance music, a popular waltz, overlaid the heads of the moving crowd; slices of light showed.

It seemed they had nearly made their destination when Hopkins was halted by four men who had spread themselves across the pavement in front of him. His three companions stumbled into him. Delmi looked around hopefully but Hopkins said: 'It's us they're after.'

'It's the nigger and his buddies,' said one of the men in front.

'That bastard Yank,' said Small quietly.

'Come on, boy, we're waiting for you,' growled the American. 'Come right on by.'

Rumble said: 'I think I'm going.' He made a rush to one side but one of the big men moved to block his way. 'You ain't goin' nowhere, nigger boy,' said the American.

Hopkins looked wildly about for help. The street and its crowds moved uncaringly about them. No one even turned to look. Small said quietly: 'I'll deal with this cunt.' He stepped forward. The American was advancing jauntily. Small went to meet him.

They heard a metallic crunch as the knuckledusters met the American's face. The cockney hit him again. The man half-shouted, half-screamed and tipped back. He lay on the pavement and did not move. 'Right,' said Small looking up from him. 'Who's next?'

The other men backed away and Small charged at them with Hopkins and the others close behind. The three remaining attackers were stumbling and trying to turn. The American had not moved. Small gave him a kick and jumped over him. The attackers had vanished into the dark crowd. The popular waltz played on. Hopkins and the others ran along the gutter until they reached the round manhole cover, invitingly open. With Delmi now in the lead they crossed the street and scrambled one after the other down into the aperture. Rumble went with them.

Corporal Blewit was sitting in his bed, wearing pyjamas and reading a magazine called *Health and Efficiency*, with chastely nude women, nipples obliterated, on its cover. 'What's going on?' he demanded.

'They tried to lynch us,' Hopkins told him. Small was hiding his knuckledusters.

'And where did *he* come from?' demanded Blewit pointing accusingly at the black man.

'Bristol,' said Delmi.

Chapter Four

About forty miles west of Tottenham Court Road, not far from what was then called the Bath Road, the well-spoken town of Marlow lay beside the springtime Thames. Marlow had found itself only on the periphery of the war. Cossetted in their river valley the inhabitants had watched the burning London sky to the east. The German invasion never turned up and the local Home Guard formed a cricket team and tended vegetables.

Young men had gone to the war and the women had taken patriotic jobs; some of the shops had closed and there was less in the windows of the rest. But there were still some Sunday-afternoon boats on the river and the pubs were busy with American servicemen drinking while they waited to invade Europe.

On a bland evening in early May the sounds floating across the river were those of the Valley String Ensemble playing Vivaldi's tribute to the season.

Kate Medhurst sat in the middle row of hard chairs in the parish hall trying to concentrate on the sight of her fiancé, William, embracing his cello. There were no blackout blinds in the windows; the concert would be over before darkness spread. The loyal supporters of the ensemble, the families and pressed friends of the players, occupied most of the chairs and tried not to scrape them.

William did not look attractive behind his cello. He was a

mediocre player and he tried to compensate for this with an agile performance. The other players, mostly female, turned to face him during his solo passages and he believed that this was due to admiration. He was pinkish and – for wartime – well fed, his fair, sparse hair drifting across his forehead. He tended to close his eyes tightly at intense passages. Kate watched him as his face appeared around the stem of the instrument like a pale sailor looking around a mast. She fingered her engagement ring with doubt. It had belonged to her mother, who had a spare, and was meant as a stopgap for Kate until the war was over.

When the last aching notes of the recital had wandered across the fading evening, Kate waited for William at the back of the hall. He took some time to pack his cello and he did not like to be hurried. When he came to meet her only the caretaker of the hall was there, fidgeting with the keys.

'They were so much better tonight, don't you think?' William asked as he kissed her on her cheek. 'They really concentrated for once.'

'Nearly got it right,' muttered the caretaker privately. He wished them a good night and locked the hall door with a sigh.

'That chap is a bit surly,' said William as between them they carried the cello towards his car.

'He's an old soldier,' said Kate.

'The parish council should be told,' he insisted. 'Surely there is somebody else who could lock up afterwards. He seems to think he's the music critic of *The Times*.'

Kate said: 'People do all sorts of jobs these days.'

The car was a 1937 open-topped MG. The cello went in the seat beside William while Kate sat in the cramped back. But it was not very far. He had an allowance of petrol to cover his duties as a fire-watcher.

They were going to supper at her house, a routine which went unannounced, almost unnoticed, after concerts. Kate closed her eyes as they bumped down the lane towards the river. His hair was thinning behind as well. Outside the front gate William helped the cello out of the car, threatened the dog with his foot, then accepted help from her father who came to the door. The dog was called Rugga. It never barked, never growled, never whimpered, only sounded a low moan. The roses were budding on the trellis and there came a warm smell from the garden. Kate did not want to get married to William.

'Be patient,' her mother had said. 'You never know, he might improve.'

Supper was pea soup and omelette with vegetables. The new potatoes had just been lifted from the garden. It was well stocked and had been since the first Sunday of 1939, the opening day of the war, when her father's immediate response to a world in turmoil had been to turn over a new vegetable patch. He had been proved right; Poland had fallen, France had been consumed, and many thousands had died in the snows of Russia, but the potatoes, carrots and parsnips came up with comforting regularity and the peas seemed greener and rounder every year.

Mary, her mother, had set out the table formally even for supper. They each had a glass of elderberry wine. Her father refused to pour gin when it was only William coming. The dog looked on hopefully and emitted a small moan. William had been known to throw his arms and his food around.

'This country really has to wake up to things,' said William once he had seen the cello safely leaning in the hall. He sniffed over the elderberry. 'It's all getting very weary, don't you think?'

Edward, her father, said: 'After nearly five years fighting a war we really shouldn't wonder.'

'The unions are still lurking,' said William sombrely. 'There's a transport strike in London. Imagine a damned strike when we're preparing for an invasion.'

Nobody around the table really liked him. Kate had been

wondering how to tell him. If she could not, her father, or perhaps her mother, would.

'That's why I'm getting into politics,' said William. They had heard it before. 'Not just collecting for the Conservative Party, not just distributing pamphlets and such. Right *in* there. After the end of hostilities I shall be at the forefront. Making sure we don't lose what we have gained.'

'Good for you,' said Kate's father gravely. The dog moaned.

Kate taught at the junior school and on afternoons she would sometimes pause near the bridge, across the road from the church, at its memorial to a girl who thirty-three years before had been lost on the *Titanic*. She had begun to feel that she herself was drowning. William had announced at their supper, in his best Conservative style, that he had booked the church for their wedding – the first Sunday after the satisfactory conclusion of hostilities. He had a vision, he informed her family, imagining himself and Kate side by side at the altar rail, their two heads shining in the lights newly released from blackout regulations. 'Don't let your headdress be too extravagant, darling,' he had warned his mouth full of omelette. 'We can't have it hiding your hair.'

Kate had said: 'No.'

Walking from the school she knew she would have to say the same word to him again, and soon. He was saving up for his bottom drawer. The previous week he had bought a new pair of socks which cost him two shillings and two coupons. And she would have to reveal that she would shortly be going away. Now she sighed and began to walk along the river bank towards home. She would miss the children although she knew she was not made to be a teacher.

That morning Elsie Manners had arrived in the class, late and panting with excitement. 'My dad's dead,' she announced with juvenile smugness. 'The Germans got him at last.'

The fathers of two boys in the class had died in faraway action and Anthony Johnson's brother, who had played for the town football team, had been missing presumed dead for months.

On her way home Kate had wondered how long it would be before they called her to the women's army. She had volunteered a month before at the Henley labour exchange, travelling to the next town so that she would be unseen. She had told no one, not even her mother.

'They should be calling you up soon then,' said Mary Medhurst when Kate arrived home. Her mother poured the tea.

'You know,' said Kate. She knew she would.

'Mrs Fanshaw from the African Missionary Committee works at the Henley labour exchange and she spotted you.'

'And told you,' sighed Kate.

'Well, it hardly comes under the Official Secrets,' said her mother. 'Information of use to the enemy.'

Kate said: 'I would have told you soon.'

'It's a jolly good thing,' said her mother. 'It will get you away from this place. And from William of course. Run, darling, run. Run for all you're worth!'

Kate laughed a little sourly. 'I felt I was just getting . . . well, engulfed with it all.'

'What about the school?'

'They won't miss me. They're making plans for after the war. I won't be part of them. Some real teachers are even being released from the forces now.'

Her mother had folded bales of red hospital blankets, fitted Mickey Mouse gas masks on frightened infant faces, learned to pump a stirrup pump to douse possible incendiary bombs, and cared for her home and husband. Kate tapped her engagement ring. 'Why do you have two of these?' she asked. They both knew that she would be going soon. It was the time for questions and truths.

Her mother, however, tried a limp shrug. 'It was just a spare one.'

Kate almost laughed. 'Mother, nobody has a spare engagement ring.'

They were in the kitchen. Kate was sitting immediately in front of her as she often used to do when she was a small girl, the warm smell from the stove all around. The dog scratching. 'There was someone else,' Kate said. It was not a question. She sensed there had always been.

'He died in the last week of the First World War,' said Mary slowly. 'He was coming home to marry me.'

Kate knew. 'Father's brother.'

'That's right. Horace. What a name, Horace. Your father married me instead. I was expecting. But I miscarried. He still married me.'

Kate reached out and clumsily embraced her. Mary was bent over in her chair. She seemed to have diminished. 'Your father insisted on a new engagement ring, so I had two.'

She looked damp-eyed at her daughter. 'It's a long time ago now, another war ago.' She began to laugh sadly. 'Now you'll be going away. It seems only yesterday you were a girl at school. You'll be off very soon, I expect. Mrs Fanshaw said they don't take long.'

Almost every wartime night there was a dance in the Thameside towns and villages. Battalions of Americans were encamped and there were air bases patterning the Oxfordshire country-side. Despite their training and their confident uniforms the Americans before D-Day seemed almost like pretend soldiers. They were louche and laughing, and sensed nothing dangerous or deadly approaching. 'I don't know what they'll be like when it comes to fighting,' said Kate's father. 'But they'll probably talk their way through it.'

He came from the bank in Reading every evening on the

train and bus to be met at the gate by Rugga with a fond moan. His car was on blocks in the garage. He read the meagre pages of *The Times*, a folded sheet with one page in the middle, on his morning journey, and did the crossword when he was going home. People told each other that the war would be over by Christmas, as they had said of every Christmas since 1939. Personally he was not so convinced: he thought it could last another five years until Europe was on its knees and the Soviets moved in.

'Your mother says you're going to the dance tonight,' he said to Kate as his wife poured the first cup of evening tea.

'Yes, it's at the village hall. I won't be late,' Kate said.

'No lifts.' It was his familiar warning. 'Not from those Yanks.'

'I'm taking my bicycle,' Kate said. She sounded prim to please him. He grunted. 'They're like kids. Laughing and shouting in the streets. Smoking cigars, for God's sake. Chewing their gum. Whistling at women. God knows how they are going to do when it comes to fighting.'

'They fight every Saturday night in the King's Head in Reading,' pointed out his wife. 'So it says in the *Mercury*.'

'I didn't mean that sort of fighting,' he grumbled. He turned towards Kate again. 'Make sure you take your bike.' After a thought he added: 'Isn't your fiancé going?'

'William's not keen on dancing and it's a something committee meeting,' Kate told him. She suddenly decided to tell him more. 'I've registered,' she said. She saw her mother's half-grin.

He was putting his cup back towards his wife. 'For what?' he asked.

'The ATS,' said Kate doggedly.

'The Auxiliary Territorial Service,' said Mary.

He did not approve of initials and he said: 'Why not call it that? The war is stuffed with letters, ARP, WVS, RAF, FANY and all the rest.' He looked up almost gently at his daughter.

'Women's army,' he said reflectively. 'I'm sure they're delighted.'

Kate was surprised. 'You . . . don't mind . . . object?'

Mary poured the tea and he swung the cup gently across the table. 'It's not up to me to object,' he said. 'I see enough people sitting on their backsides in offices, in banks even, when they could be getting some fresh air. That fiancé of yours for a start.'

'William is saving himself,' said Mary maliciously.

They all laughed.

The Squadronaires, the famous airmen's dance band, had played once in Reading and it was strongly rumoured that Vera Lynn would be singing in the same ballroom before France was invaded, but on this spring evening in Marlow it was an uncertain local band called The Swingers.

They had survived from pre-war times when they sometimes played at local regatta dances. The leader had remained throughout the years staring through his glasses like a man transfixed and the vocalist, who was said to be his bastard son, had a cape of dandruff on the shoulders of his dinner jacket.

'*When they begin the beguine,*' he sang plaintively.

'Christ,' muttered the American Kate danced with. 'This guy needs treatment.'

She was a tall girl and he was two inches shorter and dancing uncomfortably close. She could feel the edges of his medal ribbons through her dress. She managed to ease herself away. 'You've been very brave,' she said cautiously. 'All those medals. What does it mean: "Hell on Wheels"?'

The words were curved in colours on his sleeve. 'Hell on Wheels,' he said as if that was explanation enough.

She insisted: 'Yes, but what is it? It sounds very exciting.'

The American said: 'We drive the trucks. Soon we'll be driving them through French France. Right into Nazi Germany.'

He pulled her quite roughly closer. '*It brings back the night I made you surrender,*' sang the crooner.

She wriggled to disentangle herself. The American looked hurt and turned towards the bar saying something inaudible. Kate left him and crept across the floor in the opposite direction. There were some Marlow girls sipping small drinks in one corner. 'Was he causing trouble?' asked one.

'He could,' said Kate. 'He was just working himself up to it.'

The soldier came twice more to ask her to dance. The first time she refused him firmly but he stood and insisted on the second occasion. 'I'm just getting to like you,' he said. He had been drinking whisky and she could smell it. They danced a waltz and he confided that he did not expect to be on the earth for much longer. He asked her name as if he were going to enter it on a form.

'Kate,' she said. 'Kate Medhurst.'

'You're not kidding – wow! I come from a town called Medhurst in North Carolina. Maybe we were fated to meet.'

She tried to appear quite pleased.

'It's going to be real tough over there in France,' he mumbled. He looked challengingly into her face and his breath came up to meet hers. 'I may not live after the first day. I need somebody to help me. Somebody like you.' He trod on her foot and she excused herself. It was time she went home.

'I'll see you home,' offered the American. 'Every step of the way.'

'I've brought my bike,' she said. 'Thank you just the same.'

The dance still had an hour to go when she left the Memorial Hall. It had always seemed a depressive place with its panels of the dead of a previous war displayed each side of the bandstand. She was not sorry to be going.

There was a glimmer on the Thames and the air was warm for early spring. The sound of the dance music drifted from the inside hall. There were couples who had come out to lean against the walls.

Kate disentangled the bicycle from the others at the side of the building. She pushed it at first and as she was about to get into the saddle she heard his unsteady voice behind her: 'Aw, don't quit now. We're just getting acquainted. You could be my very last lover.' It sounded as if he were consciously trying to order his words and when she turned he was leaning for support against the porch of the hall.

'Sorry,' she said in a voice more firm than she felt. 'I have to get home. My mother is not very well.'

'She's sick? Aw, my ma is sick too. But I can't get to her. She's across the ocean.' The voice became a sob. 'I'm never gonna see her again. This war is going to kill me.'

'I must be off,' said Kate primly. She began to mount the bicycle. 'Goodnight.'

He allowed her to go at first. She went at an unsteady pedal and he started forward and quickly caught up with her. He was broad and strong and he held onto the frame of the bike. 'Hey, wait, wait. Can't you walk a while with a poor soldier?' Kate tried to pedal on but he held the bicycle firmly. She warned herself not to panic but she looked behind and the hall seemed to have moved into a gloomy distance. 'Please, will you let go of my bike,' she said quietly.

'Okay, but maybe you'll walk with me for a while.'

His words were more or less coherent but she could see how hard his eyes were. 'All right,' she said. 'But only as far as the bridge. After that I go up to the road.'

They were almost at the bridge anyway. They began to walk. At first he remained the other side of the bicycle but with a sudden switch, almost like a dance step, he came to her side and slid a thick arm about the waist of her dance dress. She could feel him fingering the top of her knickers. 'No,' she said trying to push his arm away. 'Don't do that.'

He kept his hand there and she could not remove it. She began to pray somebody would come along the towpath but nobody did. 'You English,' he complained. 'You English dames. We come from the States to save you from those Nazis and then you treat us like dirt. We get no cooperation. If the Nazis was here you wouldn't get no choice. You'd have to lie down and enjoy it, for Christsake.'

He pushed his fingers further down the light dress but in doing so relaxed his grip and she wriggled from his hand and slid around the other side of the bicycle. She realised she should have run then, screaming, making for the bridge. But she still had a sense of being foolish, making too much of it. After all he was drunk and he was shorter than her.

Now she manoeuvred the bicycle between them, holding it like a protective gate. He was on the side of the river. 'Okay, okay,' he said. 'Just take a look at this.' Like a man strumming an instrument he opened his fly buttons and produced a pale and erect penis. 'Don't you see,' he said like a plea. 'Don't you see what I've got for you, girl.'

She stared at the object he was displaying through the framework of the bike. 'And there's more,' he said angrily. 'Look.' With a convoluted movement he produced his testicles. She gave him a desperate push.

The movement sent the bike tipping away. 'Holy gee,' he said. 'Don't . . .' With a sort of immobile horror she watched him totter backward. His military hat fell off and he oddly made a grab at it before staggering back onto the bank and toppling off it before hitting the river. There was a loud splash. Kate stared at the river and then guiltily looked around. He seemed to sink quite quickly. In her memory of the scene he floated briefly on his back, still exhibiting his white cock. One moment he was there and the next he was not. The river closed over him.

His soldier's hat was still on the towpath. Carefully and, to her surprise, like someone adept at concealing crimes, she stepped around the bike, and picked up the hat. It still felt warm from his head. She threw it like a discus after him into the current.

Then she picked up the bicycle and attempted to examine the towpath to see if she could detect incriminating tyre tracks. She could see none. She pushed the machine on before mounting and pedalling towards the bridge and home.

Her mother was turning the thin pages of the local newspaper when Kate came down to breakfast and stared at it, as if believing, despite the fact that it was a weekly journal, that her crime would have already made the front page. She still felt shielded by some confidence. After all she had done nothing amiss except push away a man who was exposing himself. The fact that he had fallen in the Thames and almost certainly drowned was after the event. She had decided against confessing to the Marlow police.

Mary Medhurst habitually looked at the clock when Kate appeared. This morning as she did so she passed a buff envelope across the table. 'From the King, it seems,' she murmured.

Across the top was printed: 'On His Majesty's Service'. Mary poured her tea and offered her the toast rack. Kate opened the letter first. 'Next Thursday,' she said. 'I have to report to Farnham.'

Her mother said: 'Oh, that's not so far, dear. They'll probably let you come home in the evenings. It's quite soon, though.'

She had to tell her mother. 'Not soon enough,' she said. Her mother knew her very well. 'What's the trouble, dear? Has something happened?'

Kate took a fortifying drink of tea. 'Better have another,' said Mary as if it were brandy. She poured it.

'Last night,' said Kate. 'A man, an American soldier, tried to assault me when I came from the dance.'

Mary lifted her grey eyes. 'How far did he get, dear?'

'I was wheeling my bike along the towpath and he appeared

and started bothering me. I had danced with him a couple of times and he followed me out.'

'With intent.'

'Yes. He . . . well, he exposed himself to me.'

'Complete?'

'All there was. It was very frightening. And I pushed him and he fell into the river.'

Her mother studied her carefully. 'And he got horribly wet,' she said.

'I think he drowned.'

Mary Medhurst winced but only slightly. She looked at her daughter across the toast rack. 'Don't tell your father,' she said.

On the morning she was due to go she picked up the local newspaper from the doormat. There was no report of an American soldier's body being found in the river. Her mother, as she kissed her goodbye, whispered: 'I will keep you posted, dear.'

She went on the bus with her father to Maidenhead and then on the train to Reading. He sat benignly reading his *Times*, as he always did, only looking over the top of the page as they were nearing the end of the short journey.

Kate thought how downcast everyone was. Gone was the often fierce optimism of the early war days, gone was the stoicism of later. In those middle years there had been slogans painted by Communists on walls: 'Second Front Now!' demanding an early invasion of Europe to relieve the pressure of war on Russia. Now everyone wanted an invasion. They wanted the conflict finished with and done away. Nobody spoke on the bus and the train groaned to itself.

She had to change at Reading for the Paddington train. Her father with his briefcase under his arm walked her to the plat-form. She saw how frayed the cuffs on his suit were. He had two suits, both blue.

They were almost tongue-tied as they awaited the train and Kate told him to go on to his bank. He looked as if he would like to do so but then brought out his frayed wallet and, to her amazement, unfolded a white five-pound note and handed it to her. 'It's like giving you pocket money when I put you on the train for school. Do you remember?'

'I remember very well,' said Kate kissing him sincerely. 'It doesn't seem long ago.'

'It isn't. It is just so much has happened.'

He did not go. She knew the money was half his weekly wage. They loitered among the crowds waiting for the train. In wartime there were always crowds waiting for trains. Eventually it arrived, from Swindon and South Wales, in a rush of yellow steam. 'Your mother asked me to say to you to take care,' he said in his awkward way. 'Look after yourself, please. You have never been away from home since you came out of school.'

'There must be millions like me,' she said. 'Millions.' She kissed him on the cheek and she felt the cheek warm as she did so. She thought he might even be blushing. 'Goodbye, Kate . . . Katy,' he said. 'Keep safe.'

'And you.' Suddenly she felt a sadness, as if she might not see him again. 'You look after Mother and I know she'll look after you.'

Chapter Five

London's sky was grey and the city lay leaden beneath it. She had intended to get a taxi to Waterloo from Paddington but on impulse she took the bus and sat on the upper deck while it made the slow journey through the patched-up streets, alongside the parks lined with military tents and crammed with khaki vehicles waiting to roll to the English Channel ports for the invasion. It must be soon.

She had not been in the capital since the first year of the war, although it was only forty miles from her home. The big stores had been thoroughly bombed and although some were still open others were open to the sky. There were service vehicles in the streets with the coughing taxis but little other traffic except for buses and bicycles. People moved along the pavements as if they were dog tired. She was glad when the bus reached Waterloo.

Carrying her one neat suitcase she walked purposefully along the concourse. She was spotted at once by a broad woman in a tight army uniform and a red cap who looked as though she might have been crying or making love. 'Farnham?' she said without looking at her, her puffy eyes drifting along the platform.

Kate fumbled for her documents but the woman hardly glanced at them. She sniffed as if she had a huge cold. 'Platform eight, Aldershot,' she said still looking elsewhere. 'There'll be transport at the station to Farnham.'

'Thank you,' said Kate.

The woman thrust out an arm on which was a scarlet armlet. 'Listen, lovey,' she warned. 'Don't thank me. Don't thank anybody in this army and especially men. Because they won't bloody deserve it. Platform eight.'

Kate said: 'No, of course not.'

She walked to the platform where an entire battalion of young men seemed to be loading itself onto the Aldershot train. Anxiously she looked for a seat. Soldiers were standing everywhere. They stared at her as if she were another man. Three youths in civilian clothes were in the end seats in one compartment and the door was open. The tallest of them said: 'Come on in here, miss, or it will go without you.'

She heard the guard shouting, and a screech came from the steam engine. 'I will,' she said. He took her case from her and found a place on the rack. 'Sit here,' he invited. He was grinning. 'I can stand. I'm not very good at sitting.'

She sat on the seat and he shuffled along so that he was not standing too close to her knees. She looked up and smiled. 'Off to do your bit, are you?' asked Hopkins.

'Yes. ATS.'

'That's what we're doing,' he said. 'Not ATS, mind.'

They all laughed. His voice was Welsh, his face was strong and so was his smile.

Small had inserted himself into a tight corner seat. When he looked ahead the youth sitting directly opposite looked up at the same moment. A week before they had shared a cell in Wormwood Scrubs. Throughout the journey neither said a word.

The compartment was close and crowded and further soldiers in uniform and more recruits in civilian clothes, one wearing evening dress, appeared and stood between the sitting passengers. Nobody asked the youth in evening dress, with his winged shirt and bow-tie, why he was like that. Each stared privately ahead, their faces swaying to the movement of the train.

It stopped at every station, taking an hour and twenty minutes for the journey. Kate could look from her window for there was no crammed corridor on that side. London went by. Every open space that was not a bombed site was growing vegetables. She saw a horse and cart in a street with a man delivering coal, and another horse and dray belonging to a milkman. Children sat on gutters and a gaggle of housewives gossiped at slum street doors. This is what they were fighting for, all of them.

Into the Surrey countryside the scene softened, well-off houses and aloof churches in untouched villages. But there were military vehicles, some of them big American tanks gathered on the greens and along the lanes. They were properly parked, as if in deference to the surroundings. Latrines had been erected in secluded corners and soldiers were camped in streets of tents that appeared as neat as the pre-war houses. There were camouflaged ambulances on the pathways of the military cemetery at Brookwood.

In Hampshire, an army county, were more tanks, like large animals at rest. Soon they would embark and sail on the war's final adventure.

'Open the window somebody,' called a voice from the rear of the standing passengers. 'It don't 'arf pen-and-ink in 'ere.'

The uniformed soldier standing in front of Kate leaned to pull the window down. His movement gave her a view of Hopkins who smiled at her and she smiled in return. He nodded towards a train loaded with armoured vehicles waiting expectantly at a siding. 'Looks like we're going to be too late for the war,' he said.

'I 'ope so,' said the small Welsh voice of Delmi sitting next to him. 'I don't like the look of them things. Bloody dangerous, I reckon.'

The soldier in the middle, having lowered the window halfway, moved back. Hopkins could still see Kate by looking around the man's thigh.

Delmi said to her: 'They don't let you fight, do they? You don't have guns?'

'I'll probably be sweeping some floor,' she smiled.

'More suited to a woman,' Delmi nodded. 'Much more.'

With what seemed like a personal sigh of relief the train reached Aldershot. The platform was punctuated with straight-backed sergeants already shouting. Hopkins smiled a goodbye at Kate. 'See you after the war,' she laughed.

There was another young woman, looking lost and anxious as a child, who alighted from the train. Kate caught up with her. 'ATS?' she asked.

The girl jumped. 'Oh . . . oh, yes. That's it.' She was short and blonde with a round puzzled face and badly aimed lipstick. 'What d'you think we're supposed to do now?'

'Wait until somebody claims us, I suppose,' suggested Kate.

'Easy to pick us out amongst all these blokes,' said the other girl. 'I come from Bradford. I'm called Dotty.'

Kate said: 'I'm Kate. There's bound to be somebody here.'

'If there's not, I'm buggerin' off 'ome,' said Dotty. 'So far I can't stomach it. I want my mum.'

They were going towards the station exit, surrounded by uncaring soldiers and new recruits. 'I expect we'll all want our mums before long,' said Kate.

The girl looked at her pleadingly. 'Will you . . . sort of keep an eye on me? I'm fair scared.'

In the station yard outside a sergeant-major with a rough face and a bright red sash was lining up the civilian men from the train. 'Three ranks,' he ordered briskly. 'Three lines to you.' He saw the pallor-faced youth in the dinner jacket. 'Christ, are you a crooner or summat?'

They had formed themselves into three rough ranks. The

soldiers in uniform were standing smirking. The dinner-jacketed man said: 'I'm a waiter, sir . . .'

'Not sir . . . sergeant. I am not a sir and I'm never going to be a ruddy sir. A waiter, are you? Well, why turn up in your working gear? We 'ad a clown once, but he didn't turn up wiv a red nose.'

'No time, sergeant,' said the waiter. 'I was working this morning. Anyway this is my best clothes.'

Kate and Dotty stood twenty yards away. 'Here's somebody important,' whispered Kate.

A tall stick of a woman in khaki strode towards them. 'Good, good, good,' she said briskly. 'You've answered the call.' Her face darted to the left and right. 'All we require now is transport.'

The women all half-turned as the male sergeant bawled: 'Right. We are going to *sing*. Yes, *sing*. That's the first thing you learn in the army, apart from keeping yourself and your rifle clean. You learn to *sing*. We will start now and continue on the transport to the garrison.' Abruptly he leaned forward, almost over the top of Delmi. 'Can you sing, little fellow?' he asked darkly.

'Yes, I'm Welsh,' said Delmi straightening up.

'Yes, I am Welsh what?' the sergeant demanded in his face.

'Git?' suggested Delmi. 'A Welsh git?'

Suddenly deflated the sergeant said: 'And you are, son. You are. I require to hear you say: "I am Welsh, sergeant." *Sergeant.*'

'Sorry,' said Delmi bravely. 'I am Welsh, sergeant.'

'Right, now we will break into song,' growled the sergeant. 'We will try "Bless 'Em All". Everybody knows "Bless 'Em All", don't they?' His eyes blazed at them. 'Anybody doesn't know "Bless 'Em All"?'

Everybody did. The sergeant barked: 'One, two three. *Bless 'em all.*'

Shakily the recruits began to sing. He stopped them and started them again. 'Louder!'

'*Bless 'em all,*' they sang. '*Bless 'em all. The long and the short and the tall . . .*'

They continued singing it, untunefully over and over again, and when the khaki truck came for them and they climbed into its metallic back they were still singing as they humped their bags over the tailboard and eventually drove away. The youth in the dinner suit was staring out as if he was considering jumping, but still mouthing the words.

The three women could hear the song even as the truck headed for the station-yard gates. 'It is called humiliation,' sniffed the skinny woman in uniform. 'The army is good at humiliation.'

The youth in the dinner jacket and sagging bow decided to sing louder and better than any in the back of the lorry. 'What's your name, son?' asked the sergeant as they climbed out at the side of a barrack square.

'Angelo, sergeant,' said the young man, apparently pleased.

'Your *other* name. I don't want to marry you. *Surname.*'

'Maroni, sergeant.'

'A Wop. Well, you sing better than that little Welsh git.'

'Louder,' sniffed Delmi to Hopkins.

A small crowd of soldiers had gathered to survey and mock the new arrivals. 'Get some service in!' shouted one.

'I'll fill him in,' grunted Small but made no move. He and the other former Wormwood Scrubs man had distanced themselves from each other.

The sergeant's glare caused the mocking group of soldiers to shuffle off. 'Bloody shower,' he grunted. 'Last week's intake.'

The new group were ushered into a Nissen hut, a black-arched construction, dripping with moisture from overhanging trees. Inside it was only as they had expected, bare and cold, with metal beds ranged down two sides of a concrete floor and a blackleaded stove, unlit, in the middle. ''Ome sweet home,' said the sergeant with a sniff at the damp.

He told them to form a single rank in the middle. 'The section that hoccupied this billet,' he said, ''ave kindly made the beds for you. Army fashion. The first thing you will 'ave to learn. They're gone now, fully trained crack troops dyin' to meet the enemy.'

There were only two wan smiles in the rank and he seemed disappointed. 'Anyhow, they've kindly folded up the blankets and whatnot in the regulation way. Just for you. It was the last thing what they done before they went off to start fighting. I'm not interested, I just train 'em. But they did it, made the beds. Just be careful none of the buggers has put a turd under your pillow.' Still nobody smiled.

He walked along the stark rank, sniffing as he went. 'Singin' is very good for morale in the army,' he said. 'And whistlin' sometimes an' doing the thumbs-up sign, which is what you always see soldiers doing when they get their pictures took, don't they. Sometimes you don't sing or whistle because it wouldn't make sense. When you're doin' silent killin', for instance.' He continued strolling along the rank, then rounded the end and walked behind their backs the other way. 'The regimental barber is to 'ave his leave cancelled,' he forecast. 'Some of your 'air I could tread on.'

He reached the front of the rank again and stood, hands behind back, as if delving into his most remote thoughts. 'Right,' he said eventually. 'Let's practice the thumbs-up.' His voice rose and hardened. 'Squad . . . squad, attention.' There was an ungainly shuffle to close feet. 'Very smart, I must say. Now squad . . . squad . . . thumbs up!' The youths raised their thumbs at random. 'Not good enough . . . let's try it again.' He became suddenly defeated. 'Oh, Christ, don't bother. What's the use.'

He took time to gather his thoughts again. 'Any of you know Mrs Willets?' A few shook their heads.

'No? Well, I'm her only son. Sergeant James – Jim to my few friends – Willets. France, Dunkirk, the Western Desert. I haven't done *any* of them. Nothing. I've been here at good old Aldershot. I am your platoon sergeant. When you need someone to talk to, when things are getting too 'ard for you, *don't* bloody well come to me. Write to your mother. "Dear Mum, sell the pig and buy me out." Well, you can't even be bought out now. We're all here until the war's finished in twenty years' time.'

He smiled at them almost fondly. 'We'll get on fine together, lads. If we don't it's not my fault and don't complain to the fucking padre because he won't do anything except pray.'

Sergeant Willets seemed to be inclined to continue but through the door came a short, sparse officer with an ill-grown moustache. 'Squad . . . squad at-tention!' bellowed the sergeant his voice bouncing on the corrugated-iron roof. There was a shuffling. He flung up a salute so fierce that his arm sprang back with the force. 'Good evening, sir.'

'Evening, sergeant,' said the lieutenant. He flipped up a languid salute. 'Ah,' he said as if he were already disappointed. 'The new men.'

He strolled along the line indolently. 'Why is this recruit wearing evening dress, sergeant?'

The sergeant came to swift attention. 'He's a waiter, sir.'

'Oh,' said the lieutenant. He halted without hurry. 'I am Lieutenant Harvey Goole,' he said. 'Your platoon commanding officer.'

Chapter Six

When the young women were led into the room they saw the beds were ranged in two ranks of ten along each of the walls. Two beds at the end of one row were vacant. Dotty glanced at Kate and then at a redheaded woman sitting on the bed next to the empty two, smoking a Woodbine. Kate took the end bed and Dotty the one in the middle. Dotty said to the redhead: ''Ow many of them do you smoke a day?'

'As many as I can.' The voice was croaky. 'At night the same. You'll be able to see me glowing in the dark.' She took in the squat figure of Dotty and said: 'You smoke?'

'Opium,' said Dotty.

'They call me Ginger,' the redhead said.

'Why's that?'

They trooped to the mess hall, a miserable tunnel hung with steam and fag smoke. They were still only beginning to recognise each other but they went, almost marched, with their metal mugs and their knives, forks and spoons. As they strode somebody began playing a rough tune on her cup with her knife and some of the others joined in.

There was a grubby Union Jack draped over the section where the steam rose from the trays of food. Kate took her meal on a thick china plate, Dotty followed her as closely as she could. It was some form of stew followed by apples and custard. They ate in trepidation and silence.

Reveille, blown by a fat girl bugler, sounded at seven. There were twenty young and chattering women in the barrack room. The walls were yellow brick and the windows glowered. It was not a place to go home to.

'Twenty thousand Canadians less than two miles away,' announced the corporal in charge of the billet. 'All those men and all pent up.' Narrowly she regarded the twenty girls, each one now standing silently at the foot of her neatly made bed. There were two who had never before made their own beds and the others had helped them. Manning, the corporal, sniffed. 'That's why they've put you here. Protection. The walls are thick.' She tapped the bare wall behind her. 'Mind you, those blokes could get through this lot dead easy. They're practising for storming France.'

Corporal Manning walked importantly along the two lines, up one side and down the other. The women wore little make-up, some none at all. 'What's all this?' she asked examining the face of one girl, from a distance of eighteen inches. 'Powder?'

'Aye, corporal,' said the woman. She had a slight stoop too. 'On my chin. It covers up me spots.'

Manning held up her nose between her finger and thumb. 'Get rid of them,' she said. 'The army don't like spots.'

When she came to Kate she came to a studied halt, eyeing her carefully. Kate felt herself blush and blink. 'Where do you come from, soldier?' Manning asked.

'Marlow,' said Kate.

'And where's that when it's 'ome? Marlow?'

'Marlow-on-Thames.'

'Oh, that sounds posh. Is it posh?'

Kate hesitated. 'Compared to some places I suppose it is.'

'Right. You seem a clean, well-brought-up girl, though I've been proved wrong before now. There's a spare cubicle at the end of this barrack room. Down there. It's meant for a corporal but it's empty. So you can move your stuff there.'

'Oh . . . well, thank you.'

Dotty looked anxious. 'Can I move in with her?'

'Not unless you want to sleep on top of her.'

Manning moved on and stood at the end of the room, heavy-bodied with an almost wooden face. 'You'll all have your jabs this afternoon,' she announced. 'Measles and all that. TAB. 'Orrible. You can have half an hour to lie down after you've 'ad 'em, but then you're back on duty.'

She surveyed the walls of the long brick room again. 'You're dead lucky it's this time of the year,' she said. 'In the winter every wall in this place is streaming with water and the bleedin' 'eating don't work.'

The girl with the spots asked: 'What are the chances of getting killed by enemy action, corporal? My mum told me to ask.' There was an embarrassed hesitation. 'And she said I mustn't fire any guns.'

Corporal Manning said: 'Tell 'er you're in the front line.' She grinned at her own joke then said: 'The Germans have 'ad it. They won't start bombing again and anyway you could be bombed when you're safe at 'ome.'

The smallest girl in the room, smaller than Dotty, raised a hand. 'I have been, corporal,' she offered. 'Twice. Bombed.'

Manning studied her. 'I can tell,' she sniffed. She returned to the first girl and said: 'The Auxiliary Territorial Service is not meant for fighting. Unless it's among yourselves or to protect your honour from those randy Canadians down the road. You will not be instructed on using firearms.' She looked towards the questioner again. 'You've got more chance of falling off your bike.'

She paused and drew her heavy body upright. 'But the main event of the day, before you have your jabs, is your medical examination. Then those what get through that, you will be on parade before the colonel. She will tell you what will be expected of you, how you can help to win the war.'

Once they were dismissed Dotty said: 'It sounds important, don't it, helping to win the war.' She glanced uncertainly at Kate. 'But I don't like the idea of you being put in that special room, that cubicle up there. I'm scared already. Dead nervous.'

'Two skirts, two pullovers, two pairs of shoes, brown, three pairs of stockings, lisle, one pair of garters, three vests and three pairs of drawers. Why didn't you two report here yesterday with the others?'

'We wasn't 'ere, sergeant,' Dotty said.

'Quartermaster. I'm a quartermaster sergeant.'

Kate said: 'We only arrived yesterday and they told us to report here today, quartermaster.'

The woman was wide and friendly. 'Right you are. The rest came the day before. Eighteen.'

The corporal began doling out the clothes. 'We got large, small or medium,' she recited. 'Anything needs altering you can take it to the tailors. If you don't like the colour then 'ard luck.'

Dotty put a blouse against her and giggled at Kate. 'Does it suit me?' She stared at the underwear. 'Look at the bloomers,' she whispered. She held the khaki drawers at arm's length. 'Down to the knees!' Putting them against her she said: 'Get a look at me, then.'

Kate was smiling at her. Then Dotty howled: 'No elastic! Ooh . . . missus . . . quartermaster. There's nowt at the waist! No elastic.'

The sergeant marched to the table. 'She's right,' said the corporal as if worried about repercussions. 'They've come without elastic, that size.'

'Elastic, elastic. We've got elastic,' said the sergeant haughtily. 'Get me some, corporal. Elastic.'

Dotty stared at Kate: ''Ave your knicks got elastic?'

Kate's had. She twanged the waists of both pairs.

The corporal came from the rear of the hut with a cardboard spindle. 'Here we are,' she said almost proudly. 'But you'll have to threadle it through yourself.'

'It's our NAAFI break,' confirmed the sergeant. She looked at her watch. 'In two and a half minutes. We have to lock up this store.'

Busily the corporal unwound the elastic. She made a visual calculation of Dotty's waist and said: 'That ought to go around you. Stop 'em falling down.' With a huge pair of scissors she cut the elastic and handed it to the girl. 'If it's too much save it for repairs.'

'Come on,' said the sergeant, checking her watch. 'I need my muffin.'

The colonel was a shining woman. Her face shone, her cap shone, her badges shone, and the pips on her shoulders that denoted her rank shone. She beamed across the parade, young women in stiff uniforms, their shapes and sizes in endless variety. 'All sorts,' she muttered to herself. 'Liquorice allsorts.'

Several new intakes – a hundred women – were arrayed before her. A sergeant-major, who was a man, a matter of some concern to the colonel who believed that women could also shout, called them to attention.

Sergeant-Major Benbow bristled. His short gingery hair stood up on his scalp and thrust stiffly from under his nose. He stretched himself to his five feet seven inches and roared the parade to attention. The response was irregular. He sighed audibly, stiffened his body and saluted so fiercely his arm vibrated.

Colonel Thelma Brandon acknowledged the salute and strode with a sturdy female step towards the rostrum placed in isolation on the barrack square. The sergeant-major received her nod and called the parade to 'stand at ease'. There was shuffling and giggling.

'No laughter!' The colonel on her plinth lifted her chin above the three ranks. 'The army is no laughing matter, young ladies. You have come to be trained to *fight for freedom*. You are unlucky because you will be just too late for the INVASION OF EUROPE.' She shouted the three words. Then lowered her voice. 'Your training will not be complete.'

Dotty whispered: 'I want to go 'ome.'

'I have the honour to be commanding officer of this battalion of the Auxiliary Territorial Service,' the colonel went on. Her buttoned breast rose in the sunshine. 'But I am here not only to command you, but also to help you. I want you to think of me as a mother. Call me Colonel Thelma if you like.'

She went on: 'The ATS will change your lives. It may seem very strange for a while. Many of you will miss your homes and your mothers. But it will teach you discipline and many other things.' There was a protracted pause before she raised her voice: 'And it is important that you value YOUR VIRGINITY!'

The girls smirked in astonishment. Then she ordered: 'Say it aloud. "We value our virginity!"' She held out her arms like a brass band conductor. 'After three. One, two three! "We value our virginity!"'

One hundred girls shouted: 'WE VALUE OUR VIRGINITY!' She called for an encore. 'WE VALUE OUR VIRGINITY!'

The noble words flew across the parade ground in the spring sunshine. Birds flew from budding trees. 'WE VALUE OUR VIRGINITY!'

The sergeant-major had never heard anything like it. He bit his moustache and mumbled to himself. 'Fuck me gently.'

They had their first marching drill that morning. Sergeant-Major Benbow, scarlet-cheeked, had them lined up on the square, taught them how to form a parade, the beginnings of how to march, and simple orders.

For the final ten minutes of the session he marched them around the perimeter of the square. Left, right, left, right, left, right, left. He had never realised women came in so many varieties. Just their legs. He ordered a right wheel and the first three ranks collided. He halted them, remembering where he was and reining in his wrath and language.

As they marched before his nose he heard a screech. He could scarcely believe it.

'Kate!' called Dotty. Kate was striding alongside. Desperately she swivelled her eyes. 'Kate,' pleaded Dotty. 'The 'lastic's broke in my knicks. I'm losing them, Kate, I'm losing them!'

Kate looked sideways. The khaki drawers were hanging below Dotty's skirt and still descending. 'Squad . . . squad halt!' bawled Sergeant-Major Benbow.

Some halted, some failed. They piled into each other. The sergeant-major felt himself trembling as he strode. 'Now what's the matter?' he demanded but trying to be calm. He stood on the spot and surveyed them. 'What is going on?'

'Me, sergeant-major,' Dotty said. 'I've got trouble. With my bloomers.'

Benbow's heart dropped. He took a further step forward. The girls broke ranks and surrounded Dotty like a stockade. He could see her only by peeping through the other girls. He struggled for words and eventually produced some: 'Pull your socks up. Parade dismissed.'

The platoon trooped into the barrack room, Dotty still wiping her eyes. Kate and Ginger comforted her. ' "Pull your socks up",' she snivelled. 'Where's he been all his life?'

It was Ginger who began to chant and the others joined in, laughing and rolling on their beds like schoolgirls as they did so: 'WE VALUE OUR VIRGINITY! ... WE VALUE OUR VIRGINITY!'

In the evening the camp looked as desolate as the moon. New women recruits were not permitted to leave the perimeter until three weeks after arrival and then for no more than a few hours in Aldershot. It was not worth it.

On the second evening Kate walked around the windy edge of the parade ground. One of the sacred laws was never to cross the tarmac square. It was like spitting in church. That evening scarcely seemed like early summer; trees blew irritably and there was an occasional dash of rain. Across the whole military landscape there were few moving people. There were male soldiers on guard at the gate. She wondered if the American she had pushed into the Thames had surfaced yet. She was going to telephone her mother.

The telephone box, deeply scarred, panes broken, was outside the door of the NAAFI canteen, housed in a hut with a curved and corrugated roof and some blind windows. There was a woman soldier shouting into the telephone and another waiting grumpily. Kate went into the canteen.

Christmas decorations still hung above the counter, although it was now May. 'Can't get the ruddy things down,' said the woman serving tea. 'All the men are shut in, or shut out, or on duty or somat. It's this ridiculous ruddy invasion.'

There was a group of four ATS girls sitting at one of the square tables at the end. They had two bottles of Guinness between them and were taking turns at drinking straight from the bottle, without words and with no sense of enjoyment. Two other women, full of doubt, were exploring an apple turnover on another table, teacups at their elbows. Dance music came from a wireless set next to the bar.

'Used to be quite lively towards the end of the week,' said the serving woman to Kate. 'But none of the men, them

Canadians, can come here now. They're cooped up until they go off to fight.'

Kate said: 'You'd think they'd let them have a bit of fun.'

'Once they let them out, half of those blokes wouldn't come back. They're cheesed off. They want to go home and I don't blame them.'

Kate drank the tepid tea. The door of the phone box outside opened. She put the cup down and went out. The woman who had been waiting outside the box was already on the telephone. She had hung a sign saying: 'Out of Order'.

After five minutes Kate knocked on one of the remaining panes of glass and opened the door. 'It can't be out of order,' she said. 'You're using it.'

'I like my privacy.'

'Well hurry your privacy up,' said Kate, surprising herself. 'My grandfather's dying.'

'Mine's already dead,' said the woman over her shoulder. 'Years ago.'

Kate lurked with the door still ajar. The woman suddenly slammed the receiver down and turned. 'Sod it,' she said. 'Get your two-pennorth.' She brushed by and took the sign from the door as she went.

Thankfully it was her mother who answered. 'No, nothing much has happened,' she said.

'Is Dad in the room?'

'Yes, he's in his chair.'

Kate heard her say: 'It's Kate but she can't talk for long. She sends her love and says she is fine.'

'Not in command yet?' She could hear his guffaw.

'Mother,' asked Kate quietly. 'Anything about the American? Anything in the newspapers?'

Mary whispered: 'Not a thing, dear. Are you sure he drowned?'

'Mother!'

'Don't worry, dear. Dad's gone to the lavatory. He goes a lot in the evening.'

'I can't believe it.'

'It's his age.'

Firmly Kate said: 'Nothing in the local paper at all?'

'Perhaps they're saving it for next week,' said Mary. 'The paper is rationed, you know, like everything. It might be secret. So many things are secret. You know, not giving away casualty figures and suchlike. You sound disappointed.'

'Not at all. I'm just anxious. After all, I shoved him in.'

She had uncertain thoughts about the cubicle but she appreciated the privacy; the previous night some of the young women had refused to undress until the lights were out. But some were blatant, a big lowland Scots girl stripping unabashed, lying across her bed flinging her bulging breasts from left to right and laughing. Beside the next bed another girl in long khaki drawers but otherwise naked, did an exotic dance. Others cowered in corners or timidly tried to hide behind the doors of the metal bedside cabinets. Two even went outside to undress in the ablutions, fifty yards from the billet, and ran back in their pyjamas through the dark.

That first night Kate had undressed as sedately and secretly as she could. Since she was eight she had never taken her clothes off in front of anyone and certainly not William. She had flannel pyjamas and had brought a dressing gown from home.

Dotty was the last to timorously take off her clothes. She wanted to join those who had opted to wait until the lights were turned off but decided to try. 'Is anybody looking?' she asked, her eyes swivelling as she began to wriggle out of her stiff new uniform. 'I'm not doing it in front of anybody, excepting you.'

Nobody was. Everyone was too occupied. Some girls were

sitting on their beds waiting for the lights to be extinguished. 'You're all right, Dotty,' Kate assured her. Kate's dressing gown was one of only three in the room. 'We don't have 'em in our house,' said Ginger in the next bed.

Dotty took only her outer clothes off, unfolding a voluminous and luridly pink flannel nightdress. It was of no particular shape. She climbed into it gratefully and hurriedly. Kate smiled at her. 'There,' she said. 'Nothing to it.'

The small young woman looked overcome with sadness and her reply was downcast. 'There's a lot to it. Look at me, I ask you. Bumps and lumps, I am. And this nightie.' She looked down her body. 'I'm like a bloody blancmange.'

On the second night Kate was grateful for the privacy of the cubicle. The walls were a grim yellow and bare, except for the shape of a cross which at some time had been above the bed as if it might have been a nun's cell.

The wall dividing it from the barrack room was only plywood and reached to six feet, leaving an open gap to the ceiling. She could hear the sounds of the girls getting into their beds in the room. Dotty called to her. 'Are you all right in there, Kate? Quite safe?'

'Safe as a castle,' Kate called back although she did not feel it. 'Come and look.' Quickly, Dotty arrived around the partition. 'This lock don't work,' she said at once tapping it. 'And I bet it gets dark in here. You don't have any extra light.' She peered up at the top of the partition. 'It's got to come over the top.'

Kate laughed at her gently. 'I'm not afraid,' she said. 'I'm a soldier.'

Dotty said: 'So am I. Supposed to be. And I'm bloody scared of everything. I wish I was 'ome. Even my 'ome.'

Lights-out was at ten thirty. Kate lay in the enclosed darkness, looking towards the unlocked door. She thought of

William, but not for long, and she thought of the American soldier she had pushed into the river. A great deal had happened recently. She could hear Dotty whispering her prayers.

Her tiredness caught up with her. She drifted to sleep in the narrow bed with its stiff sheets. An hour later the door was pushed open carefully.

The intruders were four women, wearing army dungarees and gas masks. One woke her by pushing a tennis ball into her mouth, preventing her screaming. Then one woman each side of the bed pinioned her arms and another held her legs. Terrified, she writhed and choked. She felt the pyjama trousers being pulled away and then her eyes widened as a shaving brush worked lather onto her pubic rump. The women went about their work briskly. Kate felt the edge of a razor on her tuft of lower hairs. Christ!

With a huge effort she spat the tennis ball out so that it bounced away. She put everything into her scream.

Dotty woke and flinging herself from her bed rushed to the door of the cubicle. Someone heavy was keeping it closed. Some of the girls in the barrack room were awake now. Dotty was screeching and the rest joined in.

Ginger ran to Dotty's side. 'Get on my bed,' pleaded Dotty. 'Can you take my weight?'

Ginger nodded. She climbed on the bed and leaned her arms against the plywood walls of the cubicle. With amazing agility Dotty climbed on her back like an acrobat. She looked over the top of the cubicle onto a confusion of bodies. Someone turned the lights on.

With a ghostly cry Dotty, in her lumpy pink nightdress, flung herself over the top of the wooden compartment. Like a heavy sack she fell on the women beneath. They were trying to get out. As she landed she flung her arms about madly trying to grab some part of them. But they threw her off and she bumped on the floor. Kate tried to clutch her. The door flew wildly open and the intruders, in their gas masks, charged from the tight room pushing aside the frightened women crowded outside.

They ran out into the night, leaving the hut door swinging. Dotty was first after them. She carried the shaving mug and flung it out into the darkness. 'Take that you filthy fucking cows!' she called. Then like a schoolgirl: 'I'm going to tell on you!'

Chapter Seven

There was a shifty sort of moon, the first quarter, lurking among the clouds, and although it was May the odd sniff of chilly wind. It was the first night of guard duty for Hopkins, Small and Delmi, after twenty-one days' training. They had marched and marched again on the parade ground, run in full kit and rifles over rough terrain, shouted as they thrust bayonets into uncomplaining sandbags, and spat and polished their equipment. They were beginning to feel like soldiers.

There were twelve men in the guard that night. They were drawn from all the outposts of the garrison and they only recognised one youth who, on a previous evening, had thrown an enamel mug of tea over a lance-corporal and then burst into tears. It was a chargeable offence but the lance-corporal did not press charges.

Neither had they come across the sergeant of the guard before, thin as a coat-hanger, with an arch in his back and a florid face unusual in such a sparse man.

'I am Sergeant Rankin,' he grunted at them when they were drawn up before the guard duty. He managed to spit out the double-syllable words as if they were single sounds. Swaying backwards then forwards from the waist as though launching a projectile, he bawled: 'And if I 'ear of any of you calling me Wankin' Rankin, as I have 'eard of in the past, taking my name in vain, that man will be on an Army Form 252, which I am sure you know by now is a fizzer, a charge.'

Minutely his eyes went along the front of the two ranks. 'Do I see a smirk?' he enquired, now in a pseudo-shocked whisper. 'I don't think giving me a moniker like that is cause for a smirk. Sergeant Tucker is of the same opinion. Any man deriding us – yes, deriding, that's what I said, *deriding* – any man doing that will be charged with insubordination.'

His probing eyes had reached Delmi. 'You, you soldier.'

'Yes, sergeant.' It was a whisper.

'You. Do I detect a smirk?'

'No, sergeant. I always look like this.'

Rankin studied him from his boots to his cap badge. 'What height are you, son? I thought there was a limit.'

'I'm nearly five feet five inches tall, sergeant.'

'Tall? Tall? Tall has bugger all to do with it.' He continued to glare.

'I've always been like this, sergeant.' Delmi had a sudden fear he could be punished for being short. But Rankin appeared to be mollified.

'Right,' he said. 'One pace forward.'

Nervously Delmi stepped from the rank. 'We can't have you messing up the appearance of the guard,' said Rankin resignedly. 'What will we tell the inspecting officer?' He drew in a deep breath, but it expired softly. 'Dismiss.'

Amazed, Delmi turned, stamped, and strode away. Rankin shook his head sorrowfully. 'There ought to be decent limits.'

The guardhouse was at the gate. No lights showed although it was late in the war and German air raids were not expected. There were six beds for twelve men, a disgruntled six-foot Yorkshireman having been drafted in to take Delmi's place. 'I was just writing to my old lady,' he grumbled.

Each man was consigned to two hours' guard duty with four hours off. Hopkins and Small went on patrol at midnight. 'Trust a bleedin' Welsh git,' said Small. 'Getting off like that.'

Hopkins grunted: 'Well, *this* Welsh git didn't.' The scant moon gave them light enough to see the barbed-wire fence they were to patrol. 'You take that end,' said Hopkins. 'And I'll take this and we'll meet up in the middle.'

'And then do it again,' said Small. 'And again and again.'

'For two hours,' said Hopkins.

'Then two other sods do it,' said Small. 'Bloody dopey, I reckon. There's not going to be any Germans around this time of night.'

Small grunted, groused and rebelled at everything. Hopkins often wondered if he had been in trouble. He also had a set of knuckledusters. He kept them under his mattress. Once they had fallen on the barrack-room floor and Hopkins had picked them up and silently handed them back to him. 'My necklace,' said Small not looking at him. 'In case I get asked to a ball.'

Now Hopkins watched the London youth move off towards the far end of the wired compound. He remained in the shadows, oddly apprehensive, like a boy nervous of the dark. He gave a brief snort to rouse himself and with his rifle held in both hands moved in the opposite direction. He had reached the end of the barbed wire and turned back when a noise, a rustle, stopped him. He backed into the shadow of a wooden building, cocking his rifle as instructed.

He heard the noise again. Then the moon sidled from behind a scrap of cloud and by its faint light he saw a figure. He caught his breath and pulled the rifle into position. 'Halt – who goes there?' he demanded tremulously.

The figure halted and said: 'Halt – who goes there?'

They stood, twenty yards apart, each pointing his rifle. 'Whose turn is it now?' asked the other man. Hopkins thought it was an American voice.

'Christ knows,' he said with relief. 'I'm guarding this bit of wire.'

'Me too,' answered the other man easily. 'You're guarding that side of the wire and I'm guarding this side.' He lowered his rifle and Hopkins did so too. They moved towards each other.

'Sorry, man,' said Hopkins. 'It's my first guard. They didn't say there'd be anybody guarding the other side.'

'They *never* say,' said the man. 'They never tell you anything.'

They had advanced and now they were confronting each other from either side of the barbed barrier. 'Hi,' said the other sentry. His shadow was square. 'I'm a Canuck. Canadian.'

'British,' said Hopkins awkwardly. 'Welsh, that is. I've only been in three weeks.'

'Jesus Christ, I wish I had. This is one bum of a place.'

'It's as bad as that?'

'When you've been here as long as my guys have. Even this goddamn invasion will be welcome. It'll be a change of scene anyhow.'

Hopkins said: 'We're going to miss it, by the look of it. We'll not have finished our training.'

'Thank your lucky stars, buddy. But we always get the ass end of things. They sent our guys to Dieppe, on the raid. Trying to land tanks in the fucking thick of the Nazis. We got massacred.'

Hopkins said: 'I know. On the wireless they said it had been a big success.'

'That's balls. Send the colonials, they said. Churchill said. See if they get wiped out. Well, we did, most of us. And now the rest of us are going to be thrown in at the lousy end again. It'll sure be nice to get home to Canada. If we ever do.'

The guarding fence stretched for five hundred yards. When the thin moon came out it glinted a little on the barbed wire. Small went grumpily towards the distant end and eventually he saw another sentry on the other side of the wire, his cigarette butt gleaming like a glow-worm. The man watched his shadowy approach. When they were twenty yards apart he said: 'Could you use one of these?'

'If nobody's watching,' said Small squinting through the darkness.

The other soldier half-snarled, half-laughed. 'Except for our two buddies up the wire there, every bastard is in the sack.'

Small accepted the Camel cigarette from the offered packet. A match faltered through the wire and lit it for him. He cupped it in his hand to hide the light as the other man was doing.

'Looking forward to visiting Paris, France?' said the Canadian. 'It won't be so long now.'

Small sniffed. 'Not just yet. I've only been here three weeks, mate. By the time we've finished square bashing I reckon it will be all over. You boys will have mopped up. Where're you from?'

'London,' said the other sentry. 'Ontario.'

Small laughed. 'And I'm from London 'ere. Want to get 'ome?' It was hardly a question.

'Oh sure. Like hell.'

'Like the snow and the mountains. Like the Rockies.' Small wasn't sure. 'It is the Rockies, ain't it?'

'It's the Rockies.'

'And the polar bears and penguins . . .'

'And the Royal Fucking Canadian Mounted Police. I miss those bastards,' said the Canadian.

'Had bother, have you? I have too.'

'Done a stretch?'

'Just got out. That's why I came into the army.'

The Canadian shrugged and they began to walk along the wire slowly, each on his own side. There was a separate compound with a square block of a building at its side. A short road came through a gate.

Small said: 'What's this we're guarding?'

'Money,' replied the Canadian. 'Bucks, well pounds, quids. It's the pay office. All our cash is in there. Especially on Wednesday nights, before pay parade on Thursday.'

'And there ain't anybody guarding it?'

They both paused, their steps slowed. 'We are,' said the Canadian.

From the start Small had his doubts. When they met at the wire again, at six o'clock at the start of their next stag, the Canadian suggested that they should not be seen walking on each side of the wire talking together as it might arouse suspicion. His name was Calam; his comrades called him Calamity. Despite his warning he was waiting at the far end of the wire. It was full daylight now and he was not smoking.

'How many times have you been inside?' asked Small studying him sideways.

'Five or six,' shrugged Calam. 'I've been unlucky. Two-timed.'

They had separately surveyed the pay office. It did not look a substantial building but it had a heavy door and a barred window over it. It was in a separate wired compound, adjoining the widespread wire enclosures which they patrolled. 'Next Wednesday,' whispered Calam. 'Can you fix a guard duty next Wednesday?'

Small said: 'I could fiddle it.'

Calam walked towards the corner of the compound. There were still a few soldiers about, a handful of cooks going towards the cookhouse. It was not yet reveille. The sky was pale and early, rooks called in high trees.

'Tell me,' said Small urgently. 'Tell me the plan then.'

Calam looked about them. 'I've got a buddy who can get the keys, okay, copies of the keys. The safe keys as well. Not to the door though. We'd have to get through that window.'

Small looked at the ground and muttered: 'What about the bars?'

'Pull 'em out,' said Calam. 'That building is real easy, jerry-built. One good pull and the bars will come away from the frame.'

'And how do we tug them out?'

'With a vehicle, a jeep should even do it. They're strong, those jeeps. You drive, don't you?'

'Never driven a jeep but I could do it,' said Small who had never driven anything. 'I'll take a look at one before then, there's plenty around.' He began to walk as if guarding the wire with his life.

Calam said in what Small thought was an unnecessarily loud whisper: 'Two other guys will have to take a cut. The guy with the keys for the safe and the guy who's going to hide the money for us.'

'You've fixed all this?'

'Sure, I fixed it a week ago. I just needed help.'

Anything but sure, Small looked behind him at the Canadian. 'And you're not going to be nabbed again. This time I'll be in it too.'

'It's going to be fine. There's no guards, because it's us. Middle of the night everybody else is snoring. We open the gate, pull out the bars then one of us climbs in, opens the safe and throws the money out to the other. Into the jeep and away to where we hand it over to our trusted buddy outside camp through the wire. It's easy. It will be.'

Some soldiers were now moving about on both sides of the wire. Small moved away in a businesslike fashion. 'It's going to be fine,' Calam called softly. 'Just trust me.'

As he moved down the wire Small thought: 'If we get caught then we'll miss the rest of the war.' That did not sound too bad.

By now it was more or less summer. Aldershot sun gleamed over the barracks, across the arid tarmac parade squares, lighting the unending military drabness, shimmering through the smoke of cookhouses. The Hampshire fields altered colour from their stark spring green but sometimes it rained.

Soldiers, waiting for the final invasion command, crouched waiting in their low, damp tents all along the coast, arguing, apprehensive, playing poker, ordered out into the weather to get some fresh air and movement in their limbs by marching along worn-out country lanes, onto roads clogged by khaki-coloured tanks and trucks and gagged guns. It kept the soldiers and the vehicles from seizing up while they waited, and the engines of the machines were regularly turned over. The soldiers were also able to see, during these marches, that they were not the only ones; if they had become isolated in the low enclosures of their tents they could see, while on the march, that there were many others. Thousands, tens of thousands, hundreds of thousands. They would not be alone in the battle.

The novice troops in training could only treat the preparing invaders to sidelong glances, a mix of embarrassment and relief that they were not ready to go yet. When the time came it would be soon enough.

'Don't fancy jumping out of one of those landing barges,' mentioned Delmi. 'Not one bloody bit.' They had been shown a training film. 'Cold water, Germans taking pot-shots at you. All that. Don't fancy it at all.'

'You'd be the first to drown, mate,' said Small. He pointed dramatically downwards. 'Your size. Glug, glug, glug. Under you'd go. There'd be no need to shoot you.'

Hopkins grunted at him, telling him to lay off. Small laid off but he still grinned grimly at Delmi. They were sitting with the others on the flank of a modest Hampshire hillside, drinking mid-morning tea. Angelo, the Italian, always poured it out as he had been a waiter. He ran out of second helpings when Small thrust his enamel mug forward. 'All gone. No more left,' he grunted. 'Now that's a shame.'

Almost despite themselves, they were beginning to feel like soldiers. A tightening of the posture, another dab of bullshit, a smarter marching stride. Even Small was shaping to it. He was strong and neat and he looked as if he could kill if it became necessary. Not that his mind was on the naming-of-parts of the Bren gun or the care of the water bottle. He could not help wondering how long you got for committing a robbery in the army – less or more than in civilian life? The best thing would be not to get caught. How safe was Calam?

Squatting around them on the rough hillside were the others they had come to know. Apart from Angelo there was Williams, who had hollow eyes like a ghost, and Melbury who said he should not be there at all; he was from a good school and he deserved better than all this. He wanted to be an officer at least. But no one in authority would take any notice, even though he wrote notes putting forward his case. Then there was Blake, known as Sexton, and Rabbit, who looked like one.

That morning they had been tramping the lanes, redolent with the smells of flowers, weeds and dung, learning to move across open ground, attacking harmless tree stumps, and now there was an hour on the rifle range.

'This is the best bit,' Small had said to Hopkins, rolling onto his side after firing another regulation five rounds.

'You're good at it,' nodded Hopkins. 'Two bulls and three inners. Don't get too good, son, or they'll put you somewhere dangerous.'

'I'll miss deliberately when I've got to,' said Small. 'I reckon it's a shame just firing at those targets. 'Undred yards, two 'undred, three 'undred. Why don't they make it more real? There's thousands of Jerry prisoners sitting on their arses in the prison camps. Why not get a few of them out and make them run across the range so we can pick them off. That would be more like it.'

Hopkins laughed. 'That's against the rules. The Geneva Convention or something.'

'Rules, rules,' grunted Small. 'All bloody life is rules. I've never 'ad a lot of time for them myself.'

Chapter Eight

'This, gentlemen,' recited the arms instructor, 'is called a grenade.' He held it up as though it had just been invented and he had invented it. 'It can, and often does, blow people to smithereens.'

They were sitting on the modest hill in an hour of sunshine, the countryside spread about them, distant, unawake, unwarlike. Clouds like big hands moved across cornfields. The instructor studied the recruits' faces, holding the grenade between his right finger and thumb, then playing a trick in which he lost his hold then caught the explosive weapon before it hit the ground. 'Just caught it,' he smiled. The men grinned foolishly at the joke and those who had been quicker off the mark returned to their places around him.

'Now, who can tell me why it's called a grenade?'

He had asked the question many times, of many training squads, and had never had an answer yet. This time he got one. It was Rabbit who raised his hand. 'I know, sergeant.'

The sergeant, whose name was Andrews, stared at him with an edge of suspicion. 'I want the *real* answer.'

Rabbit said: 'It was called after the pomegranate.'

There was a round of uncertain laughter.

Andrews looked dumbstruck. 'What's your name, son, and how do you know this?'

'My name is Private Rabbit, sergeant. And I know because my family keep a greengrocer's. We used to sell pomegranates before the war.'

'Fucking hell,' said the sergeant mildly. 'Fancy that.' He looked at the rest of the squad. 'He's right, this Rabbit,' he almost barked. 'The first man to get it right. Ever.' In mid-sentence he began to shake his head and he continued to do so. 'All right, Rabbit,' he said. 'Go on and tell us about it.'

Rabbit looked so pleased he blushed. But he said: 'I'm not sure, sergeant.'

'Pomegranate,' repeated Andrews triumphantly. 'So my small-arms officer told me when I was in training. And it's because it looks like a pineapple, if you take a good look.' He held up the weapon and they leaned towards him to inspect the squared indentations. 'It's got these squares, so that it blows up easier and kills lots of the enemy.' He stared at them with intense eyes. 'What does it do?'

They were used to this by now. 'Kills lots of the enemy,' they chorused.

Andrews nodded as if they had learned a secret. 'Before we get to throwing, or tossing the grenade, we will deal with something even more important – i.e. not blowing yourself to little bits when you are doing it. Hands up those who are in full agreement.'

With slow grins they raised their hands. 'Right. The most important thing about the grenade, from the chucker's point of view, is to make sure when it goes off bang it is among the enemy and not stuck in your muddy hand.' He pointed to a curved piece of metal and a pin at the apex of the object. 'This is the thing you have to hold down with your finger, after you have pulled the pin out. Then as you chuck it the thing flies away and the weapon lands among the enemy where it explodes and kills them. Is that clear?'

The heads nodded unsurely. He pointed at Rabbit. 'You son, Bunny, is it?'

'Rabbit, sergeant.'

'Nearly right. Anyway you come and hold the grenade.'

Rabbit, wishing he had kept his mouth shut, stood and moved towards the crouching sergeant who handed over the grenade and demonstrated to him how it should be held. 'See, this is your throwing hand, whichever one you throw a cricket ball with, and finger across the metal bit.'

Rabbit's face had paled. He managed the correct grip and he showed it to the others. 'Now, ' said Andrews. 'Pay special attention to taking the pin out. And when you take it out, for Christ's sake, keep hold of that metal safety thing.' He took the grenade from the youth and said: 'Then you chuck it. You have to be within twenty yards of your target and, if you've got any common, concealed. Then you toss it overarm, like you see them do at the Odeon. *Don't* throw it like a ball and be careful there's not a tree in the way or it will bounce right back and do for you.'

He looked at them carefully. 'Everybody got it?' There came a series of unsure nods. 'Good,' he said. 'Now we're going over to the grenade range, which is just over that next field, and practise. We'll try a few dummy runs and then have a go at the real thing.'

He smiled at them eerily.

They trooped in single file along footpaths and over the humped fields. There were no animals in the fields for they were left for soldiers. In the distance they could see long lines of slow men, the Canadians, moving across the landscape, practising, practising, filling in the days.

At one point their route took them by an empty farm, wind sighing around its buildings, and a yard with a broken wall. Resting there was a platoon of Canadians who catcalled when they saw the British trainees. The insults were all one-way. 'Get to the war, you bastards.' 'We'll do the fighting, you get the glory, Tommy.' The British soldiers stared at the fighting men but could think of nothing as an answer, only a weak wave, or a weak grin. Delmi said when they finally arrived at the grenade range: 'It's not our fault we're not going.'

Sergeant Andrews sniffed. 'They're brassed off, all of them. Months they've been stuck here. They think everybody English cheats them, the girls, the shop owners, everybody. And they didn't like the way they got chucked ashore and massacred in that fuck-up at Dieppe. They're just pissed off.'

The group had reached a wide trench and he gathered them around it. 'Get fell in 'ere.' At one side, glumly sitting on an ammunition box, was a dusty-looking soldier quietly picking his nose. 'All right, Corporal Smurth, get your finger out and let's get on with it.'

'Right you are, sergeant,' said Smurth wearily. The squad, on Andrews's order, clambered down a ladder into the trench. Smurth opened the box and handed three hand grenades to Andrews who tossed them up like a juggler. He could keep all three in the air at one time. He had practised. It was only when Smurth tossed a fourth grenade to him that he fumbled and the fourth bomb fell to the ground at the feet of the recruits. They all cried out and fell over each other to get out of the way.

'No need for panic,' said Andrews caustically. 'They're all dummies. I wouldn't juggle with the real jobs, would I. We've only got one proper, loaded, grenade. Show them, Smurth.'

Still like a conjuror's assistant Smurth selected a grenade painted with a white cross from the ammunition box. 'There,' said Andrews. 'That's the dangerous bugger.' He leaned forward to examine it more closely. 'That paint's wearing thin, corporal. Give it another dab. We can't have any nasty mistakes, can we?'

As one the squad slowly shook their heads, never taking their eyes from the weapon as the NCO handed it back to Smurth. Andrews selected another one of the dummy grenades and demonstrated again the components. When he took the pin out and let the trigger catch spring away, the men once more stumbled back. As he did so Delmi sat backwards heavily. 'Right, son,' said Andrews as the small man picked himself up. 'What's your name?'

'Roberts, sarge. Delmi Roberts.' He added as he always did: 'I'm Welsh.'

'You can't help it,' said Andrews. He tossed one of the dummy grenades to Delmi, who fumbled it but caught it at the third attempt and regarded the sergeant and then the others with a stiff face.

'I caught it, didn't I?' he said.

'Now you can throw it,' said Andrews. He called Delmi forward and stood him in the centre of the wide trench. 'Over there,' said Andrews pointing beyond the parapet, 'is your enemy. Twenty yards away. All crouched down. Nasty men, ready to kill you. So you take the grenade so . . .' He took the bomb from Delmi's hand and showed him the grip. 'Then you stand side-on so . . .' He moved the small man into position. 'And you take out the pin with your left hand, if you're right-handed that is. You do *not* take the pin out with your *teeth* like you see in these Yankee war films. Use your hand, your fingers. You pull the pin, taking care – and I mean care otherwise you'll explode yourself up – to keep the trigger pressed down.' He passed the grenade tenderly to Delmi.

'Don't drop it,' said Andrews. 'Especially when the pin's out.' His eyes fixed Delmi. 'And remember, we're standing 'ere all nice and peaceful – you might be under fire. All sorts of shit.'

He appeared to check that Delmi was still there.

'Now, sideways on, legs spread, grenade in right hand and . . .'

'I . . . I . . . can't chuck,' moaned Delmi. 'I never could. Even at school.'

'Take the pin out,' ordered Andrews sternly. Delmi did, clutching the bomb in his palm. 'Give it to me,' said Andrews. 'Carefully.'

With an expression of fear and relief Delmi handed the grenade back. Andrews made as if to reach for it but it fell to the ground between them. Delmi shrieked and again threw himself backwards, the rest of the squad only a moment behind him. The trigger bounced away from the grenade but the bomb rolled and lay on the earth harmlessly. Andrews laughed. 'Wrong grenade,' he said. 'Come on, get up all of you.'

When they were on their feet he said: 'But the next time *is real.* I promise.' His gaze went along the line and stopped at the apprehensive face of Rabbit. 'Right, you, Private Bunny.'

'Oh, no,' mumbled Rabbit. His eyes rolled.

'Come on, lad. One day being able to chuck a grenade may win you the Victoria Cross.'

'I'd rather not, sergeant. I don't feel very well.'

Andrews motioned him forward and set him into the throwing position, facing the front lip of the trench. Carefully he handed the youth the grenade. 'The *real thing,*' he said. Rabbit was plaster-faced. 'In the right paw, Rabbit.' Corporal Smurth laughed but nobody else did. 'That's it. Perfect. It will not go off until five seconds after you've released the safety catch. Then you will hear a loud bang – in the distance, you hope.'

Rabbit remained transfixed. Quietly Small moved to the rear of the squad and pretended to adjust his gaiters.

'Right hand across the guard,' said Andrews. 'Left hand on the pin. At the count of three you pull the pin from the grenade with your left hand, forefinger and thumb, remember. Then, smoothly but without hanging about, you draw back your throwing arm and project the missile over the top of this trench and as far as it will go, releasing the guard as you do so. Is that understood?'

Rabbit nodded, his face like wax. The others were transfixed.

'It's no use running for it,' said Andrews. 'Break cover and you'll be exposing yourself to death.'

He turned again to Rabbit who was posed, legs apart, glassy

eyed. 'Right, son,' ordered Andrews. 'Eject pin.' Rabbit's hand went to the pin and he shakily pulled it out. It remained in his fingers. He kept his other hand clenched over the top of the safety guard of the grenade.

'Prepare to throw,' ordered Andrews. He glanced at Rabbit who was drawn back in the attitude of a javelin thrower. 'Release!' barked Andrews.

Rabbit released the safety guard and the metal piece flew away. He still clutched the grenade with his fingers. 'Now!' snapped Andrews.

The stiffened youth, with a sort of choking moan, threw the grenade. It went straight up into the air.

They all looked up. It was dropping like a cricket ball. 'Down! Down!' bawled Andrews. He threw himself forward to the bottom of the trench. Rabbit was below him and the rest tumbled on top. Corporal Smurth, who was on the back lip of the trench, flung himself like an acrobat and landed two yards to the rear. The grenade continued to drop out of the sky.

It struck the rampart of their trench on the forward side, bounding down the earth slope before exploding harmlessly with a detonation that shook the ground. They were showered with mud and stone, smoke curled into the trench.

Rabbit was the first to speak, his voice hushed. 'I didn't get it quite right, did I, sarge?'

The Evangelical church was full on the Sunday evening with soldiers from all over the garrison, some of whom had never before uttered a prayer. It was the only place they were permitted to go outside the wire that contained them, awaiting the invasion.

There was a half-hour of hymns and prayers and a short sermon from a short minister who, as he proudly said, had travelled all the way from Basingstoke. This was followed by coffee and sandwiches, with a few cakes made by earnest local ladies. The cakes were always devoured quickly by the worshippers seated in the early seats in the front row. Some of the ladies attended the service also, although the soldiers, confined and frustrated though they were, only had eyes for the pastries. In earlier days girls from Aldershot and district managed to insinuate themselves into the service but several had been apprehended by a previous minister, fiercely clutching soldiers behind the back wall of the mission, the troops eating their refreshments as they grappled with the females.

Calam had seated himself near the wide door but Small did not recognise him because he had only met him in the dark and topped by a steel helmet. Now the man whistled quietly and Small saw he was bald except for a thin reef of hair around the nape of his neck. He slid in beside him. Calam was taking secret puffs of a dog-end concealed in the cup of his hand. The English Londoner looked carefully about him. He had no experience of churches and he was disappointed in the unremarkable interior. 'I thought there might be some of them angels,' he said to Calam.

Calam had made arrangements, so he said. They discussed them throughout the hymns and the prayers, trying to appear as though they were heartily joining in. The backs of the combat soldiers in front of them shielded them as they spoke, square shoulders, short haircuts, every head turned as the refreshments were eventually wheeled in.

The rotund minister preached a short, earnest sermon, before the largest congregation he had ever encountered, but mindful that this was the only place outside the garrison permitted to the troops who were escorted back, like prisoners, behind the wire at the end of the evening. Even so, many of the men, especially the Canadians who had been confined longer than anyone, eagerly looked forward to Sundays.

'Everything is fixed,' whispered Calam as they bent in prayer. 'You got the guard duty fixed?'

Small said he had.

Calam said: 'Well, I got the guy who makes the keys. One for the gate and the other for the safe inside. It's only a key. There's no combination lock.'

'But no key to the door?'

They were called to their feet then and a thumping piano began to play 'O God Our Help in Ages Past'. Calam and Small pretended to sing from their hymn sheets. 'No key,' muttered Calam between verses. 'We'll need to get through that window over the door.'

'What about the bars?'

'They're just bars. My buddy seems to think they're nothing to worry over. The whole building is flimsy. We'll pull them out.'

'With what?'

'A vehicle. My buddy can get a jeep and some tackle.'

'Your buddy sounds useful.'

'Sure thing. He can get things. He's been here a long time, months. But he can't get too close to the action.'

'That's why you need me.'

'That's where you come in, boy.' He paused to mouth a few more bars of the hymn and Small joined in doubtfully. The volume of praise meant that they could not be heard as they plotted. 'Two of us could clear that safe in a couple of minutes. It's the night before pay parade so there should be plenty of dough inside. And as for the guards – well, like I said, *we* are the guards.'

'I want to take my cut,' said Small lowering his voice well below the singing. 'I'm not trusting some crook to look after it. No fear.'

'We'll have no time to count it.'

'I'll just take a cut. I'll find somewhere to hide it. The floor-boards in the barrack room are loose.'

'Okay,' said Calam. 'Send it home to your mummy in a

package if you like. But don't get caught. If you do, or if I do, we say nothing. Okay?'

'Okay by me. I'd like to be rich when I get out of this army.'

'Me too,' said the man they called Calamity.

It was the right night, so dark you could not see the sky. Small felt a fear and an elation he had not known since he and his late father had robbed a substantial house in Central London only hours before it was bombed.

He was full of doubts now about Calam's plan but there were reassurances. The perimeter of the military area, although heavily wired, was only sparsely guarded, two of the four sentries being himself and Calam. The enemy were miles away on the other side of the Channel, on alert themselves for an attack. It seemed that the barbed wire was more to keep the troops in than to keep any raiders out.

By gone midnight, when he had begun his two-hour stag of duty, the surrounding area had become more quiet, more asleep, than a suburb. He soon located Calam by the occasional red end of his secret cigarette. They moved towards each other, their blotched shapes scarcely distinguishable from the surrounding deep night. Only the barbed wire retained a low inherent glow.

At the end of the week the training platoons would be going on their first brief leave. Small had fixed on a hiding place for the loot. He doubted if he would have any difficulty smuggling even a thick pile of notes out of the garrison in his pack. The anticipation of the invasion was occupying the armed services and, he told himself, nobody would be looking for a few hundred quid in a trainee's backpack. He had mentally repeated the assurances every day since the Sunday at the Evangelical church and, as he patrolled the wire in the deep darkness, he repeated them to himself. He was going to have money; it was going to be easy; it was going to be all right.

93

'Real nice night,' said Calam from the other side of the wire. 'One o'clock we get moving.' Small looked minutely into the dark but Calam did not bother. He glanced at his luminous Canadian army watch and said: 'Forty-two minutes. Then we get the mullah.'

'I want to take my share,' Small reminded him.

'Okay, you'll get your cut. When we've got some dough to cut.'

They knew they were unlikely to be seen plotting. The camp almost snored in the darkness. A farm dog howled somewhere distant but there was no other disturbance. 'The other guys, the guards, should be at the end of the wire, miles away even if they hear anything.'

'If we're going to pull out a window grille with a vehicle then there'll probably be a bit of noise,' sniffed Small. Calam said: 'Don't bring up ways it could stall. It will all be okay. Are you still with me?'

They could scarcely see each other's expressions. Small said: 'I'm with you.' Oddly they shook hands through the wire and turned in opposite directions to continue their patrols. Small still had doubts, big ones.

At exactly one o'clock he saw a movement on the road outside the wire. There was scarcely a sound but a shadow was easing its way towards the gate of the compound where the pay office was innocently standing. He was even more impressed when Calam appeared on his side of the wire, behind him, so close that he jumped. 'This is where we go,' muttered the Canadian. It was not a whisper.

There was a disused sentry box and they both moved towards it, stripped themselves of equipment and put it inside, laying their rifles carefully against the slatted walls.

'Take these,' said Calam handing Small a pair of woollen gloves, the sort that patriotic old ladies knitted for the army.

Small understood and took them. He saw that the jeep was at the perimeter gate. A figure left it and moved to the gate. There was only a moment before it swung open without a squeak. Calam shifted forward and Small followed him, hope overcoming fear. At the gate a soldier stood unmoving and calmly handed some keys to Calam who said what Small thought was an unnecessarily loud: 'Thanks.'

'I'll drive,' said the Canadian to Small's relief. He inserted himself behind the wheel of the vehicle and Small slid in beside him. It was only a hundred yards to the door of the building and it was a downward slope. The jeep moved with scarcely a sound. Small knew what he had to do. He scrambled to the roof of the vehicle taking with him a hook and a rope from behind the seat. The grilled window was almost in front of his nose. He inserted the hook through the grille and tumbled down to fix the other end through the front bumper.

'Get in,' said Calam. Small was still half-ready to run but he got in beside the Canadian who looked about him in the darkness. It was hardly necessary. The camp was still lost in gloom. They hesitated briefly when a sound drifted up to them but it was only a heavy snore.

'Now,' said Calam. Small was beginning to be impressed; it might work. The Canadian put the jeep into reverse and slowly backed away from the heavy door and its iron grated window above.

Small felt the jolt as the rope tightened. He crouched almost against the windscreen. The jeep was halted, then slowly backed again. The engine began to protest. They knew they would have to risk that. 'Come on, come on,' muttered Small. Then they felt it go, felt all of the window collapse and tip outwards.

'We got it,' grunted Calam triumphantly. 'We got the bastard. Get ready to climb, Limey.'

But Small could suddenly see what was happening. The grille was coming out, but so was the wooden wall. All of it. Plaster and wood began to rattle on the bonnet of the jeep. 'Christ,' he muttered. 'The whole fucking wall.'

It came down with a huge crash and a choking cloud of dust. Calam was second out of the jeep, but only just. They ran, heads down through the gate and down the path to the disused sentry box. Frantically they climbed into their webbing equipment and picked up their rifles.

'What the hell was that?' shouted Calam unconvincingly. They began to run back towards the gate, the jeep and the pay office.

'Christ only knows!' shouted Small. He began blowing his alarm whistle as they ran.

Chapter Nine

She caught the train from Paddington, an hour late, and sat in the hot compartment while it clanked through the low, grey buildings west of London. The upholstery was so worn that it no longer had any pattern, the varnish on the woodwork was marked with scratches, and the torn netting of the luggage racks sagged. On long journeys servicemen often slept in them. Below the racks were what seemed now to be ancient browned pictures of how life had been before the war: Henley Regatta, the boats and the boaters and the sunshades; Stoke Poges where Gray had written his elegy in a country churchyard; the bulwark of Windsor Castle, flag aloft.

Kate was wearing her best uniform and looked forward to her parents' reaction. She had seven days' leave and William had promised – insisted – that he would meet her at the station.

As the train moved beyond the damaged streets of outer London the undisturbed green of the countryside gradually moved across the window. Willows and fields, farms and barns, the Thames shifting slow and pale green below the bridges. Everybody thought now that the war was as good as over. The Russians in the east were squeezing the enemy, Italy had surrendered but the Germans fought doggedly on up the length of the country. Soon France would be invaded, resistance swept aside, the war would be over, and there would be no more bombing. Life would flow as peacefully as the Thames. They were fond hopes.

There was still no sense of elation, only weariness and a

fatigue with the whole business. In the hot, grubby carriage Kate thought how much she would have enjoyed a childish ice cream. But there was no ice cream and childhood had gone.

At Twyford two women got in, puffing and grumbling at the height of the step from the platform. They were round and hanging in pullovers as though they expected an immediate return to winter. Even the weather was guesswork; there were no forecasts on the wireless or in the newspapers.

The pair surveyed Kate's uniform. 'Killed anybody yet, 'ave you, love?' asked the first woman. Her hair was rough and streaked with henna. The other woman snorted.

'Not up to now,' answered Kate.

'Plenty of blokes though, I bet,' said the second. 'Pretty young thing like you.'

As though she was not changing the subject the first woman said: 'My boy got killed in Burma. They sent me his last week's pay, twenty-eight shillings – twenty-eight bob for a boy you'd 'ad and brought up. I didn't even cash the postal order. I keep it in a drawer to remind me of him.'

Kate said she was sorry. 'There's lots like 'er,' said the woman's companion nodding sideways. 'Every bloody street. I don't know what it's all coming to. We was quite 'appy before the war.'

The henna woman grunted. 'We didn't 'ave much but we was 'appy. You never 'ad to lock your door but now with all these Yugoslavs around you 'ave to. They're randy buggers.'

Eventually they began to pull their belongings together and prepare to leave the train. The henna woman counted the groceries in her wicker basket. 'I've 'ad my rations pinched before now,' she said.

'Where you getting off, love?' asked her companion as the train reached the platform and they prepared to open the door.

Kate hesitated, then said: 'Maidenhead.'

The woman looked unsurprised. 'Yes, well you would be, wouldn't you?'

An agrarian-looking man holding a garden fork, spikes up, replaced them. 'Goin' to do my allotment,' he said to Kate. 'I used to 'ave this as a weapon, you know, in the 'Ome Guard. Ready to stick it up one of 'em.' He fingered the prongs with some regret. 'But those days is gone. They won't be comin' now.'

She left the train but William was not at Maidenhead station. She was not sorry. The bus for Marlow was in the station yard and it was ready to go. She went upstairs and moved to the front seat. A man and a woman, both smoking vigorously, were towards the rear. The countryside moved across the front windows like a slow film.

Most of the military material had been moved now, no longer lining the roads or cluttering the fields; gone south towards the embarkation ports. The trees were in May-time leaf and the uncertain sun patterned the road ahead. It was almost as it had once been when she was a schoolgirl on her daily journey home.

To her guilty pleasure there was no sign of William at the Marlow bus stop either. She picked up her bag and walked along the lane to the river and her parents' house deep in its garden. Her father's dog, Rugga, doddered up the lane towards her, throwing its tail sideways, and emitting its moan of pleasure.

Her mother was cutting flowers outside and she heard Kate's voice talking to the dog. Looking over the gate she said: 'Rugga must have known you were coming. Didn't William meet you?'

'I think I prefer Rugga,' laughed Kate kissing her mother.

'You look so lovely. So smart,' said Mary Medhurst.

'So do you.'

'Your father will approve,' said Mary. 'He likes girls in uniform. The war has given him a real boost.'

Kate was still outside the gate. Over the top she said in a low voice: 'Any news?'

'About the . . . American? Not a thing. But they are keeping everything so secret that even a drowning wouldn't get in the

Marlow Times.' She broke into a smile and opened the gate. 'You're home now,' she said softly.

'I'm home,' smiled Kate.

'That poor Yank may still be swimming.'

Even after a few weeks, the house seemed a little more worn, the carpet more faded inside the door, the furniture crouching lower, but the May sun pushed determinedly through the old windows and there was a smell of honeysuckle trapped within the living room. Her mother made a pot of tea and put a plate of home-made scones on the sunny table.

'No butter, I'm afraid,' shrugged Mary. 'They've cut the ration again this week.'

Kate reached in her army handbag. 'I've got my coupons,' she said handing over the small squares of paper.

'It *has* worked, this rationing, just about,' said Mary. 'Nobody starves, some people eat quite well with stuff from the garden and what you can charm from the butcher. I've learned to do some wonderful things with old bones.'

Kate smiled fondly at her. 'And Dad?' she asked.

'I mustn't grumble, although he does a bit. He grunts over the newspaper each evening. Thinks he could run the war better. And he doesn't trust the newsreaders on the wireless.'

Mary poured the tea into the white cups they had always used. Kate said: 'Perhaps he would approve if they had some women announcers on the news.'

'I imagine he would,' sighed Mary. 'But it would take more than a war to achieve that.' She looked up from her cup. 'The Rawlings, you know them? Along the river . . . well, they've got a television set you know.'

'Good gracious. What do they do with it?'

Her mother giggled. 'Practise. They bought it well before the war. They sit around it, all four of them, and stare at where the picture would be. Sometimes they have the wireless on at the same time, to make it more realistic. Betty Rawlings told me.'

She looked soberly at her daughter. 'Is it all right, the army?'

'It's fine now. It was a bit sticky at the beginning. But it's fine now.'

'You've made some nice friends?'

'My best friend is a small girl called Dotty, who really is dotty. She's from the north. Worked in Woolworths.'

Mary said: 'All sorts, I suppose.' She added abruptly: 'You're not going to marry that appalling William, are you? He telephoned and said in that awful Conservative Party tone he's got, that he would like to take you to the tennis club this evening, not to play, just for a drink.'

'I'm not marrying him,' said Kate firmly. 'I may go to the tennis club. That will be the time I'll tell him.'

'Indeed,' agreed her mother stiffly. 'Don't saddle yourself with him. Even if he is going to be prime minister.'

In the early evening the tennis club also looked much as it had always done, but the players were generally older and there was a shortage of balls.

But the summer trees, filtering the low sun, still framed the clubhouse and there was no change in the croaking of rooks and the plop-plop of a late doubles match.

'This will never change,' breathed William. He was wearing tennis trousers because he was embarrassed by the thinness of his legs and his bony knees. 'This, for me, is England.'

'You should see Aldershot.' Kate leaned back with her gin and lime.

'I'd rather not,' said William. 'I'm prepared to accept that Aldershot exists but I do not wish to see it.'

'Most of the people there have similar feelings,' she said easily. 'They want to be somewhere else. And they never want to go back.'

'Services social life must be quite lively?' he enquired. 'There must be a lot of chaps around.'

'Guys rather than chaps,' she corrected. 'Nearly all Canadians.'

'The Empire stands by us,' intoned William as though reading a propaganda pamphlet. 'To the end.'

'Twenty-five thousand,' she said. 'All confined to barracks, waiting for the invasion. Cooped up.'

'I imagine they have to be,' said William wisely. 'Otherwise they'd be wandering all over the place. When you come to think about it most of the soldiers in this war do little but hang about. They've been hanging around for years, in camps and suchlike. Waiting for something to happen.'

'And when it does they get killed,' she said. 'That's the trouble.'

William laid his glass firmly on the terrace table. It was a sign that he had terminated a conversation. He had once told her how well it worked, how it demonstrated who was in charge. She kept her glass in her hand. There was only one match on the courts now, the exclamations and the cross-court shots. 'Paddy Penney and Linda Bustard are still as good as ever,' mused William. He sniffed the evening air. 'They won the doubles at the Ministry of Agriculture and Fisheries championship last year you know. At Roehampton.'

'It's fortunate they both work at the Ministry,' said Kate. She still had some gin and lime in her glass and she was tempted to knock it over so it spilled on his cream trousers.

'Ag and Fish?' he said. 'Well, they wangled it. People wangle things these days.'

'I've noticed,' said Kate. She let her finger flick the glass and it fell, splashing his tennis trousers. She smiled and said: 'Oh drat, oh sorry. Could I have another one, please, William?'

He was wearing bicycle clips and she thought how odd they looked around the turn-ups of his tennis trousers. He wheeled his bicycle between them as they walked from the tennis club and along the river bank. He saw she was grinning towards his ankles. 'I know, I am aware,' William said testily. 'But I won't get another pair until after the war. The amount of coupons is outrageous.'

As though making a concession he manoeuvred himself around the other side of the bike so that he was standing alongside her. 'Is that a new tennis sweater?' she asked.

'Good as. I was jolly lucky to find it. Hardly worn. Red Cross sale. I don't really like wearing other people's clothes. They make me itch. You never know where they've been, do you? But this chap had gone off to the services somewhere and, apparently, and unfortunately for him, died. It's an ill wind that does no one any good.'

Kate thought how she truly disliked him. It was him she should have pushed in the Thames. He then said: 'I'm sorry about this, darling, but I don't think I'll be able to marry you after all, not immediately after the war. I've been given the nod that I could be selected as a Conservative candidate in the first post-war election. God knows I've worked hard enough for it.'

She said in a low and level voice: 'William, you never seem to appreciate that there are people dying in this war, at this very moment, while we walk along here.'

'People have always died, war or not,' he said unctuously. 'Always have, always will. The war cannot be stopped now, just to save a few more lives. Personally I was against it from the beginning.'

She could feel her dislike boiling. She said nothing. They were nearing the bridge. The evening was ending. She eyed the bridge and the riverside path sliding ominously beneath it.

'Anyhow, as I said, darling, our marriage will just have to wait. Not too long, I promise you.' He smiled a thin, promising smile. 'Just think, a few years from now you could be the wife of a cabinet minister . . . a prime minister perhaps. It would be worth the wait.'

With a spasm of horror Kate realised she wanted to do it again. It was irresistible. They were almost at the spot where she had pushed the American soldier into the river. It was just a few more steps. This was the place. 'I don't want to marry you, William,' she announced. She stopped and turned to face him. The Thames flowed in a green smooth stream behind him.

William's turn was much slower, more a revolving. 'You . . .' The single word was half-amazement, half-accusation. 'You . . . don't want to marry me? But that's preposterous! This is what joining the silly women's army does to you, is it?'

His voice was raised and little spots of spittle flew from his mouth. Kate could resist it no longer. She pushed out her hands against his tennis sweater and gave a hard shove. The inebriated American had tipped into the Thames with a bemused expression. William went in with a look of astounded anger. He let go the bicycle and staggered back, tipping into the water with a splash and an expletive.

Kate watched with enjoyable horror. He surfaced, spluttering and crimson-faced. She picked up his tennis racquet and tossed it after him and was tempted to follow it with his bicycle. She resisted it. He would need to get home.

She turned and strode away lightly. She could hear him gurgling. A moorhen, overcome with curiosity, was paddling near his head. When she had gone fifty more yards she turned again and he was crawling to the bank. 'I'll keep the ring,' she called back. 'I'll return it to my mother.'

Ten minutes later she gave her mother the ring. Mary Medhurst looked gratified. 'Oh good,' she smiled calmly. 'I'll tell your father. He'll be pleased.'

'Not yet,' said Kate a little worriedly.

'What have you done?'

'I shoved him in the Thames,' Kate said. 'At the same place.'

Her mother giggled. 'You seem to be making a habit of it.'

Chapter Ten

In the first days of June the troops of the invasion army began to leave their camps and to move towards the embarkation ports. The Canadians at Aldershot and their vehicles took more than forty-eight hours to clear their billets. They joined the Portsmouth Road and went south to the boats.

'They don't seem like they're looking forward to it,' said Delmi. The squad had stood aside, scrambling with embarrassment into the summer hedgerows to let the soldiers pass.

'Would you?' sniffed Small as the men moved on. 'I'm glad I'm here, mate. In good old England. Better than charging up some flaming beach.' He abruptly spotted Calam in a jeep now moving slowly by. Calam looking every inch the warrior, his chin straight, his eyes steady beneath the rim of his battle helmet. Perhaps he was a luckier soldier than he was a crook.

'We'll be with them soon,' said Hopkins.

They were balanced among the bushes, standing aside almost politely. The Canadian troops gave them no more attention than they would if they were children playing in a hedgerow. 'At least the war will be a bit more on the safe side,' said Delmi. 'By then. We won't have to jump into the cold water and charge up the sands.'

That morning they had drilled under a close and cloudy sky. There had been squally rain for several days and an edged wind wriggled across the countryside. By now they were drilling like true soldiers, each movement sharp and to time. There was a sense of achievement even among those who were the most reluctant, the most scornful of the army. Boots hit the hardness of the parade ground like a single hammer blow, the right wheels and the about-turns were performed now with the precision of dancers, the cumbersome rifles flew like wands in their hands. And over it all the shouting of the caustic drill sergeant: 'Move, move, one two three, you lazy sods. Left, right, left, right, left, right. Small, have you wet yourself?'

Small knew better by now than to answer. He scarcely blinked, he stiffened his stride.

When the Canadian combat men had gone an odd peace settled over the countryside. There would be more contingents arriving, but for once there was space to move, the air seemed lighter, the sun eventually came out. Along the coast the boats were grimly filling with silent men but only a few miles inland other men wearing white were playing cricket.

'There's going to be a dance!' announced Delmi arriving at the barrack-room door. 'It's on orders! Garrison dance, tomorrow.'

They hurried to see the confirmation he had been instructed to pin to the noticeboard. There it was: *Dancing to the Rascals Band. Admittance sixpence.*

'Women,' breathed Small. 'Crumpet.'

'Bound to be, I s'pose,' nodded Delmi mildly.

'And not much competition either,' said Hopkins. 'They must have waited until the Canadians went off, poor buggers.'

'More for us,' said Small smoothing down his hair. 'Can't bleedin' wait.'

The venue had once been an army slaughterhouse, a shambles providing meat for the Aldershot garrison and, although all the butchers' tackle and hooks had been removed, it still retained the trace of a stench. The Rascals who had taken the name from their badge – the Royal Army Service Corps – were already on the bandstand, led by a corporal with greasy hair and a faded tuxedo. He wagged his baton with what he hoped was professional flair as the band played 'Twelfth Street Rag' trying, and failing, to sound like the American Glenn Miller band.

The squad, all except Rabbit who had tonsillitis, had arrived by public bus, paid their sixpences and prowled like would-be predators into the cavernous place. A sad piece of silver paper hung like a tail over the door and the air inside was already smoky and beery. The strident notes of the band came from somewhere in the indistinct interior. ''Aven't been to a hop in ages,' said Delmi.

Small sniffed: 'Bit of a job finding a tart your size, ain't it?'

Almost as soon as they went towards the bar Hopkins saw Kate. She smiled as she recognised him. 'We met on the train coming down here,' she said. 'Remember?'

'It's the best memory I've got,' he said.

As the band was uncertainly wandering through 'A Nightingale Sang in Berkeley Square', a bus drew up outside and twenty men in bright blue suits with white shirts and red ties stumbled from it, most with bandages, splints and plaster of Paris. They alighted awkwardly and were not charged their sixpence to go in.

'Wounded blokes,' announced Delmi to a small, starched nurse at the bar. 'That's one uniform I don't want to wear.'

Cheerfully shuffling, the injured men went to the beer corner and put their pennies on the counter. They turned and scanned the dancers. 'Not a bad supply of women,' said one.

There were nurses, the Auxiliary Territorial Army girls, some sturdy members of the Women's Voluntary Service, and a group from the fire station. One wore her helmet. 'Something for everybody,' said his companion.

Small approached one of the blue-suited men. 'Who did for you then, mate?' The man had a sling on each arm but had enough movement in one to lift a tremulous half-pint of beer.

'Can't manage a pint,' he explained. 'Too 'eavy. Artillery, son, that's what did this.'

'Italy?' asked Small.

'Nah, Farnborough. Artillery centre forward. Big bugger. Caught me full on. The ref sent 'im off.' He painfully lifted both slings at once. 'I won't be keepin' goal for a bit though.' He nodded across his shoulder to one of his bright blue neighbours. 'If you want to know about Italy. Eighth Army. Bert was there.' He raised his voice over his beer. 'Wasn't you, Bert?'

'Wasn't I what?'

'Italy. That's where you caught your packet.'

The man seemed glad to share his wounded self. 'Cassino,' he said moving towards Small. Delmi's nurse surveyed him professionally. 'I've been keeping out of his reach,' she said. 'Ward Four.'

The slung man grinned at her. 'Monte Cassino,' he went on. 'Trying to get up to that bloody monastery. Don't talk to me about religion. All the poncey monks was down in the cellars. Christ, we threw everything at it. And we 'ad Yanks, New Zealanders, all sorts, even some fuzzy-wuzzies from Africa. And casualties . . . you should have seen.' He waved his twin slings. 'This is nothing . . . nothing.'

He was enjoying the attention. 'There was even a Jewish brigade. Fierce bastards they were. They frightened us, I can tell you. We kept out of their way.'

A nurse asked him to dance. He was surprised and flapped his slings. 'There's nothing wrong with your legs,' she said. He grinned. 'Come on then, love. Let's do this one.' He moved against her uniform and she put her hands to his waist as if she were holding him up. 'No groping,' she smiled.

The big room was getting full. Girls had come in from the town. There were young airmen, soldiers from Norway and Denmark.

'I don't know your name,' said Kate as she danced with Hopkins.

'Hopkins,' he said. 'Davy, but I'm always called just Hopkins.' He grinned and recited his army number. 'Three four one five eight six four seven'

She was dancing six inches away from him. 'Would you like to know mine?' she asked.

'Not your army number,' he said.

'Don't be silly, my name.'

'Yes, I would.'

'I'm Kate, Kate Medhurst. I'll spare you the number. I can tell you're from Wales.'

'West Wales. I was in the fishing.'

'You should be in the navy, shouldn't you?'

'Not if I can help it. I've had enough of the sea. Nasty cold wet stuff. Where are you from?'

'Marlow. On the Thames.'

'There's posh, isn't it?'

'Some people seem to think so.' She came to just below his strong jaw. 'I'm learning to drive.'

'That's handy. Wish I could. God knows where we'll all end up. I reckon we've just missed it. It will all be over in a couple of months. There won't be anything for us to do.'

'I want to see some action,' she said.

'It doesn't seem fair,' she said. They had left the hall and were walking on the dusty road next to a small park and a regimental war memorial. 'All those Canadians, confined to camp for so long, and the minute they're off to invade France they put on a dance.'

They were walking a foot apart, almost shyly. 'It was getting very hot in there, stifling,' she said.

There were nondescript buildings on one side of the road. One had a notice: *Army Book Warehouse*. Another had been gutted in a fire, its windows like ranks of open mouths. Together they turned into the small park. It was a light summer night and the white stone war memorial stood out against the dark bushes of the park.

There were couples in the bushes. There was rustling and grunting and one or two sobs. Hopkins took her hand. 'It sounds busy.'

'Let's sit on the steps of this,' she suggested turning to the memorial.

He led her towards it and they squatted on the second step from the bottom. Hopkins turned and said: 'At least it's useful.'

She rose and walked gracefully up the six steps until she was almost at the inscription. She leaned forward. 'Boer War and World War One,' she said. 'They'd all be fathers and grandfathers by now.'

She returned and sat by him, suddenly and to his pleasure, laying her head on his shoulder. He leaned his cheek against her hair. 'Are your parents still in Wales?' she asked.

'Oh, my mam and dad? No, they're both gone, dead. Before the war.'

'When you were a boy then?'

'Right. The old man was in the fishing and was drowned in the Bristol Channel. Accident. And my mam died the next year. Cancer.'

'Brothers and sisters?'

'Never had any.'

'So what happened to you?'

'I got shoved off to a home, an orphanage. I'll tell you about it one day.'

'Please.'

'I had an uncle and auntie in Wales and as soon as I was old enough to work they got me out of the orphanage.'

'Like out of storage.'

'Just like you say. So I lived with them until a few weeks ago, until I came into this mob. You don't have to join up if you're in the fishing, but I wanted to clear out.'

'You're on your own then?'

'On my tod. And I'm glad of it.'

Kate stood. 'The air's getting a big damp, don't you think? We ought to go back to the dance.'

As they stood they heard a moaning squeak from the far side of the memorial. 'We've got neighbours,' said Hopkins.

They crept away from the plinth. 'It seems it has its uses, apart from being a memorial,' she agreed.

They walked, holding hands now, towards the entrance to the small park. They could hear robust music coming from the dance. They turned to each other and kissed, carefully at first, but then he enclosed her to him. They kissed again, more deeply. 'Thanks, Hopkins,' she said quietly. 'I'm glad we met.'

'So am I,' he said. 'Could we go to the pictures one night?'

'Yes, of course. Next week?'

'Wednesday,' he said. 'Farnborough Forum. See you outside. Seven. I can get off by then.'

'I'll be there. Seven. They change the programme on Wednesdays.'

Boots burnished, brasses bright, creases almost bisecting his trousers, his cap set at the correct fractional angle on his forehead, Hopkins reported at the guardroom. There was only one evening bus to Farnborough and he could not risk being turned back.

'On the town, the bright lights are we, soldier?' the duty sergeant said. He sneered from one corner of his mouth. 'And what has Fancy Farnborough got to entice you on a Wednesday night?'

'Pictures, sergeant,' said Hopkins. He caught sight of himself in the guardroom mirror and knew he must pass muster. There was another mirror on the floor, used when Scottish Regiments were inspected before leaving camp.

'Pictures? What's on?'

'Errol Flynn, *Objective Burma*,' said Hopkins. 'Starts tonight.'

'Errol Flynn! That ponce! Never done a day's fighting in 'is bloody life.'

'I've got a date,' explained Hopkins. The bus was due in three minutes.

'Ah, crumpet, that's different. Back row in the dark.' He sniffed as his eyes ran up and down Hopkins. 'All right. And don't get stains on the front of your trousers. They're a bugger to get off.'

'No, sarge,' said Hopkins.

'All right, soldier. Get going. Twenty-three hours fifty-nine. Back here, pronto. No blaming the tart or the bus.'

Hopkins thought how he would enjoy punching the man in the face but turned and strode in a military way towards the bus stop. The green bus came promptly and Hopkins climbed aboard. As it set off again he waved from the window to the sergeant who was watering geraniums in the guardhouse window box.

The journey took only twenty minutes. Other soldiers got on and a couple of giggling girls who worked in the canteen.

'Christ, did you see him eat it!' spluttered one.

'*All* of it,' joined the other. 'If 'e knew what we done to it!'

There was a stop outside the cinema. There were several prospective viewers of Errol Flynn's Burma exploits already waiting. He joined them. At ten minutes past seven he was still standing alone. She had not arrived.

He stood for another ten minutes. A small army truck drew up and a young woman's head appeared from the passenger window. 'Are you Hopkins?' Dotty called. He moved quickly towards her. 'Kate can't come,' she said. 'She says sorry. We're being posted tomorrow and nobody can get out. I was lucky to be sent to do something.' A small arm projected from the window. 'She sent a note,' she said handing it over.

'Thanks, thanks very much,' he said taking it from her.

Dotty said: 'I'll tell her you got it. I like that Errol Flynn.' The vehicle drove off fiercely.

Hopkins walked to a seat near the bus stop and sat down to open the envelope. '*Dear Hopkins*,' the note said. '*I'm so sorry but*

I can't come. We're being posted (military secret!) but I hope we meet up again some day. You're a good chap.'

He stood and looked back at the poster above the cinema. He was not going to watch Errol Flynn on his own.

Chapter Eleven

For the training squad, that day in June looked set for another routine: reveille, physical training, shit, shave, shower, breakfast, parade-ground drill, NAAFI break, weapons training (the Bren gun), cookhouse, lecture on citizenship (Army Bureau of Current Affairs), more drill, field exercises (three-mile march to the field and back), finish for all except those on guard duty, bulling hour, cookhouse, NAAFI if you had the money, bed, lights-out ten thirty.

But through the previous night they had heard the passage of planes like a non-stop train in the sky and at early dawn it intensified. The day had come: the invasion had started.

They were on the parade ground for physical training, in vests and shorts, under the instruction of a sergeant who had to shout above the roar of the planes. Eventually he gave up and called them to a halt. The vested parade stood and as a man looked up at the pale summer sky. Above them, a pattern from one horizon to the other, were hundreds of aircraft, high and droning, spread out, the sun on their wings. The soldiers on the ground stared at the gliders, hanging behind their tow planes like children holding hands. Then an interval and a grunting force of bombers, then another break and more gliders; all pointing due south.

The physical-training sergeant was staring up with the men. 'Come on, lads,' he abruptly cried. 'Let's give 'em a cheer . . . after the count of three . . . squad . . . Cheer!'

They cheered. Delmi almost jumping with the force of his, Small yelling like a hooligan and Hopkins cheering with the lines of others, but thoughtfully. How long would it be for them?

Now, suddenly, inland across the counties of Southern England an odd peace came about. The invaders had gone.

Cottages, which had been darkened by the shadows of military vehicles, tanks and armoured troop carriers, mobile canteens and lines of latrines, blinked as though in surprise in the June sunshine. The roads away from the coast became quiet and supplies of coffee and beer were obtainable. Children ran out of chewing gum and young women, some of them justifiably worried, wondered when, if, the Yanks would be back.

Like all those left behind, the training troops listened as avidly as schoolboys to the news bulletins. It seemed unreal to be playing at soldiers across stubbled fields, hiding in harmless woods, crossing rivers under imitation gunfire. But every day they felt more like real warriors. The practice bayonet thrusts were accompanied by warrior-like shouts; everyone knew how to read a map, how to take a gun to pieces in a hurry and how to put it back together quicker; they knew now how to cover open country quickly and how to know whether a man was alive or dead.

But they also knew it was nothing like the real thing. There was almost guilt about fighting a close skirmish and breaking off for NAAFI tea, about having meals in the mess hall, about being spread on the grass looking at the sky, when pretending to lie in ambush. In the evenings they could leave their billet and go to the canteen, or with a pass even out of the camp. They would march to the canteen smartly, however, boots bright, belts Blancoed, brasses glinting, like men going forward to occupy a position. Beer was sixpence a tankard and a mug of tea was a penny. They ordered in gruff warlike voices.

A week after D-Day some of the squad made for the canteen, six of them with enough money for three pints between them. They could play darts for buttons and the Gaff, the camp cinema, was showing a romantic comedy.

Two abreast, they marched properly, unselfconsciously, from the billet, skirting the now deserted Canadian camp. The last Canuck to leave had left a door open and it had been banging for a week, like a reminder. The place looked ghostly, row on row of bleak-eyed windows, huts where men who were now fighting had lodged. Some were already dead.

They reached the main camp road and as they were striding like a proper patrol up the slope to the open canteen door, with dance music, the Andrews Sisters, bouncing out, a military ambulance passed them and pulled up. All six men stopped.

The rear double door was opened and a figure in the bright blue uniform of a casualty appeared. He straightened his coat and his red tie and began to stroll towards them.

'Bugger me,' breathed Small. 'Calam.'

'Did you get shot?' asked Small searching for signs of a wound. Calam had refused to disclose anything until he was seated behind a NAAFI table with a pint of beer before him.

'Shot? Sure,' said the Canadian easily. 'A shot of syphilis.'

Nobody could say anything to that. Calam said: 'I knew I'd gotten a dose but I didn't want to leave my buddies to go into action without me. I wanted to be with them.'

'You would,' said Small caustically. Hopkins shook his head and Delmi said: 'Natural.' Rabbit eyed the Canadian with what could have been admiration.

'But when we got on the landing ship in Portsmouth,' Calam said, 'we had to stay there for two whole days, rocking about in that fucking tub, and plenty of the guys were sick even before we set sail. I was too and it brought on a fever. Really bad fever, delirium even, and then I had to tell them I had the pox. I was sweating and sick and they decided to unship me, send me back. And here I am.'

'Pox,' muttered Delmi. 'Pox. How do you get the pox?'

'It's been no fun,' said Calam. 'I've been in that fucking hospital for days with not another goddamn soul. I had the place to myself.'

'With the nurses,' suggested Hopkins.

'Forget it. They don't want to know a genuine sick man. They're waiting to drool over wounded soldiers. There's some guys being taken in right now. I still got a whole ward to myself but they'll be moving me out soon to some hospital in London. They got a new drug for pox.' He reached for the coat pocket of his vivid hospital suit. 'I even wrote it down. I'm going to be one of the first to get it. I guess I'm kind of a guinea pig but I can take that, I'm strong enough.'

He showed them the single word on the scrap of paper. It said: *Penicillin.*

In a strange way their bleak billet had become almost homely; the soldiers looked forward to returning there at the end of the day's drills and field exercises, clanking in wearing their bulky boots, quickly thrown aside to ease aching feet. They had showers, went to the cookhouse where the quality of the food had improved since the invasion. It was rumoured that an entire store of Canadian rations had been acquired.

An hour was spent on bulling their boots, webbing and brasses. Rifles were cleaned with an oily four-by-two-inch piece of cloth on the end of a cord. They tended them inside and out, the stocks and butts polished. The men on guard duty had already gone to muster and the others sat and smoked and looked at the war news in the papers; a few read battered books and the wireless set in the corner gave out jazz and dance music from the American Forces Network. There was a British Forces programme, and a Home programme also, but the soldiers preferred AFN.

Someone forgot to switch off the set when lights-out sounded and they settled to sleep in their beds, thirty men, soon snoring or grunting, scratching their testicles or dreaming of home and girls. The music had dropped to softness and it sounded like a distant lullaby. Then, at two in the morning, some were woken by a deep throaty drone, intermittent, low and threatening.

Hopkins woke and thought it was someone snoring. 'Stop that flamin' row!' he shouted. Then the air-raid siren wailed. There had been no serious air raids that year and only spasmodic attacks before that. The soldiers sat up abruptly, staring about them. They did not know what to do. Delmi got underneath his bed. Then an explosion shook the whole surroundings. It rattled the walls and sent dust cascading from the roof. 'Bloody 'ell,' shouted Small in disbelief. 'The sods are bombing us!'

For all their intense training no one had thought of air-raid drill. Now the soldiers panicked, running around in their issue pyjamas, rubbing sleep from their eyes, opening the door to see. A corporal in a steel helmet appeared and bellowed: 'Put your heads under the pillows!'

Men were getting dressed in the dark, hurrying into their boots. Some instinct made them get out of the building and crouch against its walls. In the distance anti-aircraft guns suddenly began to fire. There was another explosion, closer.

The corporal came back to them, his eyes wild in the night. He ran across the forbidden parade ground. 'Squad, to the shelters!' he shouted. 'Get under cover. At the double!' Someone began wildly blowing a bugle.

Angelo remembered where the air-raid shelter was. With him in the lead they clattered half-dressed over the square. Other shadowy soldiers were doing the same, some running in the opposite direction.

Their designated shelter was outside the perimeter wire, a surface shelter, an oblong of brick walls and a six-inch-thick concrete roof. Angelo still led the way shouting with unaccustomed importance: 'Come on, men! Come on!' Inside it stank. They turned in through its dark door as anti-aircraft guns began to fire again. Each man was pulled up by the dank smell but then bundled in by those behind. Someone found a dim light that worked and they stood round-eyed and wondered what to do next.

The busy corporal turned up at the door. 'Make yourselves comfortable,' he said. 'It could be days.'

There were slatted wooden benches along the length of the shelter. There was a dead rat in one corner and Delmi carefully eased it aside with his foot. They sat on the benches. 'I thought the Jerries was finished,' said Small.

'Somebody's been lying to us,' said Delmi.

Sitting impotently, waiting for more explosions, now they did not feel like soldiers. The guns had fallen silent. 'Somebody's coming,' whispered Delmi as if it could be the enemy.

They sat upright and stared towards the dark entrance. Through it came a policeman wearing a steel helmet. 'Ah, somebody is in here,' he said cheerfully. 'Well, I've got company for you.'

The company followed close behind him, a stumbling group of civilians, mostly women and children, who came in with shouts of disgust. 'What a whiff!' 'What a pong in 'ere!'

They pulled up short when they saw the seated troops and regarded them accusingly as if they might be responsible. 'You'll need to share,' the policeman said ushering in the final people. They included a fat man and an old man. Most had pulled on random clothing – an overcoat, a jumper, a pair of trousers. The children were mostly in their nightclothes. The fat man was in huge and grubby striped pyjamas. He clutched two blankets. 'Their street shelter is flooded,' said the policeman. 'Nobody kept it properly.'

'Nobody told us,' grumbled the fat man. He was younger than he looked. A woman who appeared to be his mother told him to shut up. 'We thought the bleedin' war was over,' he continued. 'Good as.'

Some of them sat on the benches. The women stared at the sheltering soldiers as if wondering why they did not do something. Standing next to Hopkins, although those around her had slumped to the benches, was a girl of about fifteen, white-eyed and shivering in a creased nightdress.

'You all right, love?'

'Cold, bloody freezing,' she said.

He turned and took a few paces up the shelter to where the fat man was arranging the two blankets around himself. 'Could I have one of those, mate?' he asked. 'There's a kid up there who needs one.'

The man's watery eyes regarded him belligerently. 'Who?' he asked. 'Who wants it?'

'The girl,' said Hopkins sensing trouble. 'The young girl there.' He pointed.

'Them?' said the fat man. 'That lot. I'd never get it back. They 'aven't got a blanket between them in that 'ouse.'

The woman who was his mother sat nodding. 'They 'aven't got a bloody stick.'

Hopkins said quietly: 'She needs a blanket. She's shivering.'

'Give 'im the blanket, Cedric,' sniffed the mother. 'Make sure we get it back.'

'No bloody fear,' said Cedric. He confronted Hopkins, his fat face hard in the lamplight. He pushed it closer. 'I'm on munitions, I am, mate. Munitions. Not poncing around like you lot, playing fucking games. I'm doing a real job.'

'You've been off for a week,' pointed out the mother in a dull voice. She looked at Hopkins. ''E's 'ad a cold.'

'Give me the blanket,' said Hopkins. He felt Small moving somewhere behind him. Small was slipping on his knuckledusters.

'What if I don't?' said the fat man. He was half a head taller. Hopkins said: 'I'll make a hole in you.'

The man shifted forward a few inches and said with a sniff: 'Try it.'

As he said it there was a huge explosion nearby. The people cowered, some screamed. Dried cement and brick dust showered from the ceiling. The fat man was coated, and so was Hopkins. 'Give it me,' said Hopkins trying not to cough.

'Christ,' choked the mother. 'Give 'im the blanket, Cedric.'

Cedric, dust and debris falling from his hair and eyebrows, handed it over.

By the morning the wireless news was full of the attack. Pilotless German planes, loaded with high explosives, blind flying bombs, had been launched against London and Southern England. They fell at random. Two hundred and six had fallen during the night and two hundred and twenty-one people, mostly civilians who had confidently believed that air raids were finished, had been killed.

At Aldershot a parade was called on the barrack square at ten o'clock. Two hundred men in the training battalion, some who had only joined the army the previous day, formed up. A dais on wheels was trundled out with some ceremony and an officer who had been tapping his cane on his leg mounted it and peered over them as if he wondered where they had come from. None of the soldiers had ever seen him before.

He was sharply turned out, wearing a leather Sam Browne belt and a service revolver in a burnished holster. His pointed nose peeked from beneath his pointed cap. Nobody in the ranks knew his name and he was never announced. 'In the night,' he began in a high and high-class voice, 'you may have noticed something distinctly fishy going on.'

It was meant to cause a snigger but nobody did. The officer seemed displeased, but raised his voice another notch. 'Jerry decided to throw in what might well be his last hand. The things you heard were flying bombs, literally explosives with wings. No pilots, just a funny engine at the arse, which eventually runs out of juice and sends the thing to the ground. Needless to say it is not aimed at anyone in particular, but the general direction of London and the south of the country. Quite a lot of the blasted things came down last night and there were casualties.'

Two hundred faces, serious beneath their berets, were turned to him. He was a captain in the Veterinary Corps, pressed into service that morning, and he had never had the attention of so many soldiers before. 'At the moment the powers that guide us are working out ways to combat this thoroughly unsporting weapon. You can shoot the blighters down or knock them down with fighter planes, but they crash anyway. That's Jerry's object. It seems that we're going to have to suffer this inconvenience until our ground forces in Europe can reach the launching sites and put them out of action.'

He paused again to ascertain the effect of his words. All he saw were the ranks of set faces. 'Right,' he said uncertainly. 'That's the information. As much as we know, that is.' He eyed them as if privately he knew a good deal more. 'As much as I can tell you, that is. Your officers and non-commissioned officers will instruct you how to act when one of these contraptions appears. . . .'

As though it had been awaiting the cue one of the contraptions appeared at that moment. It was grunting like a pig and jolting in the air at no more than two hundred feet across the parade ground. A collective shout went up and, as one man, the soldiers threw themselves flat on the asphalt. The officer stood and watched the flying bomb abruptly losing height. He seemed transfixed, the last man on his feet. Then he half-stumbled, half-fell from the dais. Around him a small clutch of junior officers and sergeants were already hugging the parade ground. The weapon dipped and swooped and with a huge explosion landed behind the NAAFI canteen. Smoke and clods of earth flew in the air. The officer scrambled to his feet and began shouting: 'Attention! Parade attention! On your feet! What are you doing, for God's sake? Get up, get up!'

Some men half-rose. Then there was a blinding red flash and another explosion that demolished the vehicle workshops at the edge of the square. Again black smoke billowed with an eye of fire at its centre. The soldiers fell to the ground again. The officer tipped sideways but scrambled back on the dais and began to shout hysterically: 'Up! Up! On your damned feet! Parade att-ention!' He turned to the sergeants and junior officers. 'Get these men on their feet, for God's sake. What is this? Charge these men. Charge them!'

Two hundred trainee soldiers still lay disobediently flat, or crouched, hands over heads, eyes squeezed. 'Bollocks,' muttered one of them. 'And more bollocks,' grunted another. 'Bollocks . . . bollocks . . .' The word was passed around. 'Bollocks . . . bollocks . . . bollocks . . . bollocks . . .' It spread like a chorus. 'Bollocks . . . bollocks . . . bollocks . . .' It came from every-where. Two hundred men all muttering 'Bollocks'.

The officer stood whey-faced, helpless. 'Stop them, stop them,' he sobbed.

Three sentries armed with bulbous motor horns were stationed at the extremities of the garrison at night with orders to honk the horns continuously at the sight of approaching flying bombs. They could be seen from miles away, hanging low in the sky, each one with its lit engine glowing like the end of a celestial cigar. Like many in southern Britain during those few weeks it was a case of the soldiers snatching sleep when they could. The air-raid shelters, damp and smelly, were quickly aban-doned. Often the flying bombs were merely observed as they flew over on their way to London, a passing show. If an engine cut out and the cigar light was doused as the weapon descended then the motor horns would honk and the soldiers would seek whatever cover they could, at night below their beds.

There was sometimes a pause in the raids in early evening – it was presumed during the German launching crews' dinner break – and many in the training battalion snatched a few hours' sleep. At the end of their training they hoped to be transferred to the north of England out of the range of the bombs.

At three o'clock one morning the motor horns began to honk and ten seconds later there was a big explosion. Creeping from beneath their beds, or taking their heads from under their pillows, the men went out and saw a glow in the summer sky no more than a mile away. Five minutes later two sergeants drove around the square in a covered truck bellowing for men to get into the back of the vehicle. Another followed closely.

'Don't like the sound of this,' said Small. 'Sounds like action to me.'

'I'm reporting sick tomorrow,' said Delmi. 'I've got a dose of fear.'

'Let's get on with it,' said Hopkins.

Wearing their steel helmets and pulling on their clothes they climbed into the back of the first truck. It turned swiftly, throwing around the sleepy men in the dark back as it rushed through the garrison roads and out onto the main highway. In ten minutes it braked noisily and the tailgate was flung down.

'Out! Out!' shouted the sergeant. 'Sharpish. Move!'

They moved. They were formed up into a ragged squad in the road. The second truck arrived just behind them and more soldiers piled out. An officer, the officer of the guard fully attired and alert, called them to attention. He was calm. 'One of Jerry's flying jobs has landed on the railway across there.' He pointed towards a glow over distant buildings. 'Trouble is, it has set the end of a train on fire. And that train is parked against military installations, including unfortunately the main Royal Ordnance Corps depot.' His neck seemed to elongate. 'Which is full of what?'

'Ammo,' suggested a voice from the ranks.

'Well done, that man. Ammo indeed. If the train continues to burn then the whole jolly lot is likely to go up. There's no other means of moving it except to pull it away, tow it, and that is going to be our job.' He smiled at them in a grimly pleased way. 'We'll be at the front end of the train, so our end will not be burning.' His bright eyes snapped up. 'Any questions?'

'How far, sir? How far will we have to pull it?' It was Rabbit.

'First-class question. No more than say a hundred yards, so I'm told. There's a gradient and once we can get it on the downward slope the jolly thing will roll on by itself. It will end up on fire in a siding and everyone will be happy – and safe. But if the flames set off that dump there will be a nasty bang. And the ammunition is important because . . . well, because it is.' A fifteen-hundredweight army truck appeared slewing alongside the two bigger vehicles. 'Got the ropes, sir,' called a man in the darkness.

'Excellent,' said the officer sounding genuinely impressed. 'Right, sergeant. Single file. Let's get into action.'

'Definitely going sick tomorrow,' moaned Delmi. 'That's me.'

They loaded themselves into the trucks once more but it was only for a few minutes. 'This is as far as we go,' shouted in the sergeant. The burning railway wagon lit up the field. 'Don't forget the ropes.'

Behind them the second truck pulled up and shadowy men tumbled out, their sergeant giving orders. There was no sign of the officer.

They were familiar with the field for it was used for training exercises. It was flat and hard with a couple of half-demolished buildings at its fringes. Hopkins and Small ran together. 'Last time I did this I was going to nick some coal from the sidings,' panted Small. Delmi called from behind: 'Wait for me. Don't leave me by myself.'

They waited while he caught up and almost carried him along with them. The embankment rose above the far edge of the field and on top of it, burning like a pyre, was the guard's van of the train. Flames lit the sides of a brick building beyond it. 'Stuffed with ammo,' muttered Delmi. The officer was there, pointing towards the other end of the train. He stood out quite valiantly against the red and yellow flames, his cane held out like a sword.

'Other end, chaps!' he called. 'By the engine. It's cooler down there.'

'Come on,' said Hopkins. They scrambled along the rough embankment almost at the head of the crowd of soldiers.

The ropes were slung between them as they panted until they were alongside the small engine. 'Round the buffers, lads!' ordered a sergeant poking his head almost comically from the cab. 'I've got the brakes off. All we have to do is pull!'

The ropes were attached to the buffers at the front of the engine. Six wagons back down the line was the guard's flaming van. 'Come on, pull!' called the sergeant in the cab and they began to pull. Two teams, like tug-of-war contestants, tugged at the ropes, spreading themselves on the railway line, feet against the sleepers. 'Pull! Pull! Pull!' sang out the sergeant. Nothing happened. Then, making a groaning noise, the train began to move, edging forward, an inch it seemed at a time, then a foot, then two.

'She's coming, she's moving,' gasped Hopkins. It was like hauling in a gigantic fishing net. They felt the whole train crawling forward. The upper accent calls of the lieutenant came across the roofs of the trucks. The sergeant in the engine pleaded: 'Another fifty yards, come on boys, another fifty . . .'

The soldiers sweated and tugged. Then, like a miracle the train began to shift by itself. 'Get out!' shouted the sergeant. 'She's moving. She'll knock you over!'

They staggered and flung themselves aside. Some fell down the embankment. Hopkins and Small tugged Delmi to his feet. 'Scarper!' bawled the sergeant. 'The whole bloody lot will go up!'

They were rooted with shock. Then they realised and began running frantically across the field. The sergeant who had been in the engine overtook them. 'Get a move on,' he panted.

Behind them they could hear the train now rolling down the slope towards the siding. As they reached the half-demolished buildings they had used in their training there was a single, huge, ground-shaking explosion. Every man jumped a wall or fell into a welcoming hole. They cowered while a succession of enormous eruptions lit the air and shook the protecting stones. From three hundred yards away they felt the earth move under them. Suddenly everything went quiet. There were a couple of small punctuating detonations but then they could hear the growing roar of the flames. The sergeant, with great care, lifted his head above the truncated wall. All he said was: 'Just in time.'

'You didn't tell us all the trucks were loaded with ammo, sarge,' complained Delmi mildly.

'Forgot to mention it, sonny,' said the sergeant. 'I had a lot to think about.'

Chapter Twelve

They sat more or less safely in the open fields and watched the chugging flying bombs come from across miles of English countryside. The soldiers knew when to take cover in ditches or trenches because the engine of the machine would cut out and it would begin its silent descent. And they would count in unison . . . one . . . two . . . three . . . every second until the distant explosion. Sometimes it was less than twenty. A spiral of black smoke would curl into the June air a few miles away.

The attacks continued for weeks. Schools broke up for an early summer holiday; watchers armed with warning hooters were posted on roofs. Few people went to the long-disused air-raid shelters. Sirens were confused. The British carried on with their lives, ready to run at any moment.

Over the English Channel was the only place where the pilot-less planes might be safely intercepted. Fighter aircraft were awaiting them and destroyed them either with gunfire or by deftly tipping the wing of the weapon so that it curled away into the sea. But it was an inexact science and seaside towns, having cleared their beaches of mines and barbed wire, in anticipation of a good following summer, found they were under bombardment. The bombs were aimed towards the London region and, although some fell short, many reached their huge and easy target. There were deaths, almost all civilians but including three hundred and seventy servicemen and their families when a flying bomb hit the Guards Chapel in Knightsbridge during a Sunday-morning service.

'Sooner we get to the front line, the better,' grumbled Delmi. 'It'll be safer there.' They were trudging back to the camp, through villages hung with roses, alongside fields bulging with corn. 'Won't be long now,' said Hopkins. 'At least we'll be able to fight back.'

It was not long. 'We're on the draft,' said Small coming into the billet. 'I just got told by a bloke in the orderly room. We're going to Liverpool.'

'Liverpool?' said Delmi. 'What we going to Liverpool for? You don't go to Liverpool for France.' They sat with their kit packed ready for the troop train from Aldershot.

'Far East,' guessed Hopkins. 'Bloody Burma.'

'Nice and warm,' suggested Delmi hopefully. 'Sunny.'

'Wet and dangerous,' said Small. 'Up to your arse in swamps, Japs picking you off.'

'I know where it will be,' said Rabbit. 'A landing on the west coast of France, round the back of the Jerries.'

'Italy,' said Calam definitely. 'That's where you're heading. I've been told.'

He had been standing on the station platform when they arrived in the trucks, his bright blue suit and red tie standing out in the sunshine. Small briefly detached himself from the others. 'You know then?'

'I can find out anything. In that hospital they gossip all the time. Yap, yap, yap. The doctors and nurses, the guys with their balls shot off. Gossip, gossip, gossip. You can bet it's true.'

Small dropped his tone. 'Did you hear anything? About our little picnic?'

'Some picnic,' grunted Calam. 'Nothing. Not a question apart from the stuff the Snowdrops asked us because we were the guards. I guess everybody was too busy with the invasion.'

'Lucky for us. But we got fuck all.'

'Less than that,' said Calam. 'I had to square the guy for the vehicle and the keys.' He looked at Small as though he thought he might like to contribute. Small turned his eyes back along the platform towards his platoon.

'So where are you off to now, Cal? The Savoy?'

'Not too far away, they tell me. It's a new pox hospital. When I'm cleared up they'll ship me home. There's plenty of room right now, going west across the ocean.'

Small could see a sergeant taking a roll call. 'I've got to go,' he said holding out his hand.

Calam shook it confidently. 'Canada, after the war,' he suggested. 'In a few months, it will be wide open for all kinds of activity. There's bucks to be made, a lot of bucks. Maybe sometime we could work together again.'

Small turned as he said: 'Good idea.' But as he went back along the platform where the train was steaming in, he muttered to himself: 'Not bleedin' likely.'

They clambered into the worn-out train. It took fourteen hours to reach Lime Street, Liverpool; its staggered progress across the country a normal wartime journey.

The train was reserved for troops. More got on at Reading and more again at Rugby until the engine wheezed with the weight. They were travelling out of the range of any random flying bombs. The men, jammed in the wooden carriages among their equipment and rifles, in thick uniforms, had trouble even breathing. The windows were thick with steam and the section that was supposed to open, would not. A Scottish soldier, mouthing a silent obscenity, smashed it with a rifle butt and some air filtered in as the train plodded on. At Rugby packed rations had been loaded aboard, corned-beef sandwiches and heavy urns of tea. The men, with their enamel mugs, queued in the corridors.

They reached Liverpool when it was almost dark. Rolling from the train, cramped and crumpled, they were formed into threes and marched in tired columns to the docks. They arrived in time to see the dark outline of the troopship against the dying Mersey sky. As they clattered up the gangway some men turned to take a final look at England, at a bombed and blacked-out city.

There were tannoy orders blaring on the decks. Hopkins, Small and Delmi kept together and joined a line of plodding men snaking through the darkness, to a low deck where they chose their bunks. Delmi was given the bottom bunk of three because otherwise he would have to climb. 'No being sick on me,' he said.

Another order booming across the tannoy told them to form up at the mess and they clanked up the metallic steps to the open deck to join another queue. Few of the men spoke. One was having a snivel because he was already missing some woman, but no notice was taken of him. The rumour was that they would be sailing by three in the morning.

They were shuffling in the queue for almost an hour before they reached the mess-deck, a hold lit by bulkhead lights and thick with the stench of food. They each collected a tin plate from a pile and moved along the counter while a sticky-eyed cook doled out some lukewarm stew. There was a mountain of bread and more tea was poured into their mugs from a huge jug. They turned and sat down at one of the long wooden tables. 'At least it's not rocking yet,' said Delmi gazing morosely at his plate.

'Wait till we sail,' said Small.

But they were still in the dock the next morning. The soldiers had used the orange life jackets for pillows and now they rolled from their bunks and queued for the latrines, then queued again for breakfast. They were ordered on deck and at eight o'clock the ship cast off her cables and began to move off through the Liverpool morning. There were a thousand men and twelve women aboard.

Hopkins sniffed the sea air, so familiar to him once. At nine they were near the mouth of the river and two naval vessels appeared through the early light, their escorts, moving like pieces of tin, low in the water.

They could still see the silhouette of Liverpool, the Liver birds, the city's mascots, standing above the shadowed buildings. The ship and the water around it were both shabby. 'Nice of the navy to turn up to see us off,' said Small as they stood at the rail.

'They're staying,' said Hopkins. 'In case of U-boats.'

'There's always something to spoil it,' grumbled Delmi. 'I was looking forward to the cruise.'

The tannoy sounded for lifeboat drill. They found themselves in sections lining the decks, their orange life jackets stuffed under their chins and facing the sagging lifeboats. 'This is the ship's commanding officer,' came a glassy voice. 'I am Colonel Gerald Furnley-Hiscock. Welcome aboard.'

Some of them mumbled what could have been a response. 'By now,' the voice went on, 'most of you will be aware of our destination. It's supposed to be a secret, of course, but everybody knows a secret in war. We are not joining in the fun and games in France, and we are not en route to Burma either – for which we ought to be thankful because it's ruddy awful and the war is going to continue in the Far East for years by the look of it. No, we are sailing for Italy, land of opera, pasta, wine and beautiful women. You may recall that, not long ago, we were at war with the Italians, but now they've swapped sides and we've got our old familiar enemy, the Germans. They have to be turfed out of Italy and we are going to do our part in that turfing out. Some stupid bloody woman Member of Parliament said the other day that our forces in Italy are "D-Day dodgers" – that's what she actually called them. Well, like a lot of women, she knows nothing. I've been in that theatre of war and the only bit of dodging you do is from bullets . . .'

He went on, with the loudspeaker throwing his voice. Hopkins let his eyes wander down the deck along the lines of orange lifebelts, each with an uplifted chin and angled eyes above it. He suddenly saw that the section next to them, at a right angle caused by an indentation in the deck space, was of women. They scarcely looked different from the men in their khaki trousers, berets and lifebelts.

She was third in the rank. Suddenly, astonishingly, he saw her. Her eyes and chin were elevated, and she did not see him. Kate.

'Auxiliaries, girls, ladies . . . attention if you please.'

The woman wore a bulgy uniform, tight around her middle-aged middle, and bursting forward at the bust. She was an officer and her voice had a squeak. In the close wardroom, with its ceiling only just above their heads, the twelve young women turned to her. She was not very tall and she had to stand on a small box. Kate thought the woman might be happier taking tea in her country sitting room. There was not much space to move forward but they did their best. 'That's right,' she encouraged. 'Gather round.'

Dotty glanced up and towards Kate as she always did in uncertain moments. Kate grinned at her.

'I am Captain Delia Carne, and you may call me madam,' said the officer. 'To my face, that is.' She smiled conspiratorially and some of them smirked politely. She appeared to sum up the reaction before she continued.

'We are here, just a small group of females among a great many males,' she said. 'Which to some might seem an enviable situation.' Her eyes swept about. 'But a ship is a tight place, even a big ship like this. We are a small group of women and there are something like a thousand soldiers aboard.' Her tone changed for the worse: 'Other ranks, that is. It is important, in the circumstances, that we keep ourselves separate from these other ranks. I'm sure that the majority are good chaps but in certain areas this could cause trouble. So you will be kept apart from these fellows. You need never come across them on the ship. They will eat and sleep and move about in their designated areas and you will be in yours.

'You will find it not uncomfortable. This wardroom and the officers' wardroom adjoining will freely be yours and you already know where your sleeping and eating accommodations are. Please keep to them.

'If there is any interference from the other ranks then it must be reported immediately. Any questions?'

It was Dotty who asked. Kate was amazed. 'What if we have interference from the officers, ma'am?'

The officer stared at her as if in shock. 'What's your name, auxiliary?'

'Dotty, ma'am.' She knew it was a mistake. 'I mean Dotty Bright, ma'am . . . I mean Auxiliary Bright.'

Captain Carne studied her for a moment as if marking her down. Then her military bust swelled visibly. 'There will be no interferences, as you put it,' she asserted. 'These officers are also gentlemen. Dismiss.'

The last they saw of England was the Bishop Rock lighthouse at the end of the outriding Isles of Scilly. Down the Irish Sea the ship had made cumbersome and uncomfortable progress and it was the evening of the second day before the beam of the lighthouse waved them goodbye. On deck many of the men stood in uncertain silence in the pale grey light.

Small said: 'I reckon we could climb up to that deck and take a butcher's at the tarts through those skylight things.'

'If we're spotted,' said Hopkins, 'we'll be doing the rest of this trip in the brig.'

'Not if we keep low. There's them life rafts in the way. They'll 'ide us.'

'You're for it then?'

'Course, mate. You'll only bugger it up on your own. I'm used to climbing on roofs and looking through fanlights. There's no real guards. Just those sailor blokes ploddin' around the deck every now and then. Nobody will spot us and you can see if you can get a look at 'er. That's if it is 'er.'

'There's no doubt it's Kate,' said Hopkins. 'I saw her. Even if she had a life jacket up to her ears.'

'All right, we'll have our nosh and try it out when it's a bit darker. If we get nabbed we can say we felt seasick and came up for air.'

'We'll give it a try,' said Hopkins.

It was ten o'clock by the time daylight had fully faded and the ship was ploughing on darkly through the sea, heading with caution towards the deeper Atlantic before turning back into the Bay of Biscay. The western coast of France was still occupied by the Germans; there were submarines and torpedo boats in the Brittany ports.

There was nothing to prevent them going up on deck. There were some men talking in a group by one of the hatches, the points of lights showing from their only half-concealed cigarettes, but the air had turned colder and there was an ocean wind. Most of the soldiers were below in their bunks and a man was playing a piano accordion badly in the canteen.

'Let me go first,' said Small. 'I've worked it out.' He kept his voice down.

They were wearing gym shoes and they went silently along the deck before Small, with a quick turn of his head both ways, decided it was clear. He climbed lithely on a rail and slid over the top, then up a short run of steps. He curled his finger to Hopkins and Hopkins followed. Twenty feet ahead were the fanlights of the officers' wardroom; they were blacked out but not very thoroughly and there were gaps showing a yellow light.

Music came from within – soft, peacetime music – and the sound of social voices. Small moved forward on his stomach. Hopkins crawled after him. Army training across open fields had come in useful.

The Londoner reached the low wall and its roof. He edged himself closer and put his face to a fanlight. There was just room through the careless blackout curtain to afford him almost a full view of the room below. He crooked his finger again and Hopkins crawled to the next fanlight. There was a gap in that curtain too. Scarcely breathing he looked down into the warm scene: twenty or more people conversing, raising and sipping from glasses, their faces caught by the comfortable light. The music warbled low behind them.

There were ATS women in the room but at first he could not see Kate. Then he saw the small shape of the girl who had come to give him the message outside the cinema in Farnborough that night. He saw her jovially enjoying the attention of a chunky young naval officer. Her head scarcely came up to his chest. Then he saw Kate. She was further into the room but as he peered she and two army officers moved across the room and directly below him. It was almost as if she knew he was there.

She looked beautiful in that light, her hair reflecting it softly, her eyes sharply. The two lieutenants were admiring her, one leaning forward so far he almost had his nose in her glass. She moved away a fraction. Then Hopkins felt water swilling around his legs.

Small let out a stifled squeak and began to crawl backwards. Hopkins got to his knees and shuffled after him. Two crew members were below washing the roof with a hose. They were talking and paying no attention to where the hosepipe was pointing and they moved away and out of sight. Small and Hopkins, soaked to their waists, climbed down and wetly moved back towards their place on the troop-deck.

They squatted morosely on Delmi's bunk, the bottom bunk, towels around their middles. Men were moving in the wan troop-deck light. Some were in their bunks, already asleep, others reading with difficulty or writing letters that could be posted when the ship called for a day in Gibraltar. 'How can I get in touch, for God's sake?' grumbled Hopkins. 'She don't even know I'm on board. She could be in another country.'

'In purdah,' said Delmi smugly. He had just read about purdah in a women's magazine.

'Purdah, any bloody country,' said Small. 'They keep them from us like we 'ad the soddin' mange.'

'Concert party,' said Delmi suddenly. And again: 'Concert party.'

Hopkins asked: 'What about it?'

'Auditions,' said Delmi. He laid down *Housewife* magazine after carefully marking the page. 'They're asking for volunteers. It's on orders. You're supposed to read orders on the noticeboard.'

'What's it say?' asked Hopkins.

'They want volunteers for the ship's concert,' said Delmi. He looked as smug as a small boy. 'Auditions in the officers' wardroom.'

Hopkins said: 'That's good. Very good. But what can I do?'

'Us,' corrected Delmi. 'What can we do? Sing, boy, that's what. They're having auditions. Every bugger can sing a bit – even Small 'ere. If we all sing together it will hardly notice. And if we get chucked out it won't matter because we'll have got into the wardroom and you may see your lady friend.'

'You're a genius, Delmi,' said Hopkins.

'I know,' said Delmi.

Spruce in their newly pressed uniforms, with hair clipped and brasses gleaming, they reported to the wardroom. 'Drinks,' muttered Small as they went under the threshold. 'Don't forget the drinks. We're entitled.'

It was eleven o'clock in the morning and they were offered coffee. Small made a face but they took it. An infantry sergeant was on a low dais reciting 'The Green Eye of the Little Yellow God' and they stood awkwardly in their group, trying to balance their cups in the unaccustomed saucers. The sergeant had a slight harelip.

There were a dozen people around them in the room, but Kate was not there. A busybody corporal with a clipboard was studying the auditioning sergeant without enthusiasm.

'Can you do jokes?' he asked as the man stepped down. The sergeant said he did not.

The corporal regarded Delmi in the front of the trio. 'All right, short-arse,' he said. 'What do you do?'

'Ventriloquist's dummy,' said Delmi flatly.

The corporal said: 'Smart-arse.'

'Short-arse, smart-arse,' reflected Delmi. He looked at the man steadily. 'We sing. We are a Welsh trio.' Small said nothing.

Small looked sideways at him as they moved forward to the dais.

'Piano?' asked the corporal. 'Do you want a piano?'

'I play Jew's harp,' said Small to the surprise of the others. They had never heard him play it. He took the tiny instrument from his tunic pocket and played a few notes next to his mouth. 'No piano needed.'

They stood on the platform, Delmi at the front. He whispered: 'One, two, three,' and they were about to launch into 'Nellie Dean' when Kate walked through the door, the rays of morning sun dropping in stripes across her khaki blouse.

As the ship lumbered south-west the air became warmer and the sea flattened. The moon flooded the ocean, outlining the escorting destroyers and some other vague ships travelling with them.

'Hopkins . . . Hopkins.' He heard her low call as he loitered on the aft deck. There was a free-beer evening (one per man) in the canteen with a lance-corporal pounding a piano so no one else was above the hatch except a lone, shadowy soldier, at the very stern of the ship playing a sad guitar. The thoughtful melody drifted on the ocean air. 'Hopkins . . .' she called again. 'Up here . . . on top of the lifeboat.'

He went through the shadows of the deck almost on tiptoe and stood below the lifeboat. He was not sure it was the right one. 'Kate . . . are you up there?'

Her face, even in the slight light, appeared briefly, mischievously. 'Up here. There's some steps.'

Cautiously Hopkins glanced about him. Only the guitar player was there. From the hatchway came the sounds of raucous singing now and the thud of the piano. Hopkins climbed the steps.

She was lying on the tarpaulin which stretched across the open boat. She was wearing her tropical army skirt and her legs were gracefully arched to one side.

'Hello,' he said in his awkward way. 'I wondered if you'd remember.'

'I've been remembering,' she said. 'Come and lie down. I've sorted out these life jackets. It's a bit rough otherwise.'

Carefully and consumed by gratification he lay down beside her. 'Are you comfortable?' she asked seriously. 'There's no means of standing up.'

Hopkins said: 'I'm very comfortable.' He moved against her and her slim English arms edged around his broad neck, an inch at a time at first but then sliding the full way. He turned his head a fraction and kissed her forearm as it went by. 'Are you?'

'Comfortable? As much as I'll ever be in a lifeboat.' She smiled close to him. 'Fancy this, meeting up again.' They kept their voices to whispers.

Hopkins said: 'I couldn't believe it when I saw you. Small, that's my mate, and me climbed up and spied through the little openings at the top of that wardroom. You were right underneath us. Talking to that officer.'

'A terrible twerp,' she told him softly. 'Some are all right but he's a twerp. Kiss me now we're up here.'

He moved against her feeling her breasts pressing his army shirt. They kissed, each tenderly, testing the territory, then deeply. 'God, that was delicious,' she said, her voice sincere. 'It's a long time since I've been given one like that.'

'It's a long time since I've been given any sort,' he said. 'I'd almost given up.'

'Don't you have a girlfriend? In Wales?'

'Sort of and not sort of. I joined the army to leave home.'

'Put your hand on my breast. The left one, it's nearest.'

'Any one. I don't care,' he said. It filled his palm. He stroked it and she shifted so he could then stroke the other. 'Careful with the buttons,' she said.

He was undoing them with care. He opened her military shirt and saw that she wore nothing below. 'Try again,' she said.

He pushed his mouth against the curved skin, firm and soft, and then caressed it with his teeth. 'Lovely,' she whispered. 'Oh, that's simply lovely.'

The troopship eased its way lethargically through the dented sea. Around them the moonlit wind was soft and scarcely blowing. Their bodies were entwined now. She smelled sweet and he could hardly breathe. He kissed her again, a long kiss, and then they were drenched with cold water. They exclaimed as they pulled apart. He put his finger urgently to his lips. 'They wash the deck,' he whispered. 'Every night, they wash the bloody deck.'

'Oh, hell,' she said.

There had been a U-boat warning although no submarine appeared. But all on board were ordered to wear life jackets all the time, even in their bunks, which made sleeping irritating in the unaired deck. The weather was getting warmer and as they turned back from the Atlantic into the Mediterranean it burst into full summer.

On the night of the concert party many of the troops and some of the ship's company crowded to the aft of the ship where the stage had been set up on a hatch cover. The vessel proceeded at an easy wallow.

The ship's off-duty officers and their army counterparts had deck-chairs next to the women alongside the stage while the soldiers crowded close to its edge. Their room was decreased by the life jackets thrust up under their chins.

The master of ceremonies was a sweating quartermaster sergeant who had been everywhere the British army sent him for over twenty years. Boldly and badly he sang:

> *'They say there's a troopship*
> *Just leaving Bombay,*
> *Bound for Old Blighty's shore.*
> *Heavily laden with time-expired men,*
> *Bound for the land they adore.*
> *There's many an airman just finishing his time,*
> *There's many a twerp signing on.*
> *You'll get no promotion*
> *This side of the ocean,*
> *So cheer up, my lads*
> *Bless 'em all!'*

Every man knew the chorus:

> *'Bless 'em all!*
> *Bless 'em all!*
> *The long and the short and the tall*
> *You'll get no promotion*
> *This side of the ocean,*
> *So cheer up, my lads*
> *Bless 'em all!'*

In the British army it was an anthem, a battle hymn, a rite of passage. Each of the soldiers had been permitted only one bottle of beer to be consumed after the performance so that abusing the performers was eliminated. But their faces were youthful and bright as they turned them to the stage. Introduced as Three Boys from Wales, Hopkins, Delmi and Small sang 'Nellie Dean' as best they could and to muted appreciation. Then the sergeant announced: 'One of the lovely ladies aboard. The pride of the ATS. Miss Kate Medhurst!'

There was wild applause. Hopkins stared and swallowed. Delmi nudged him from one side and Small from the other. Her skirt was slim and her face was calm. The performers had been given seats at the side of the stage and he was almost below her, at leg level. She smiled at him.

She was not nervous. She announced: 'I would like to recite "Pippa Passes" by Robert Browning.' Silence dropped over the audience, the officers ogling from above, the other ranks ogling from below. She drew in a slight breath and spoke in her Thames Valley voice:

> *'The year's at the spring,*
> *And day's at the morn;*
> *Morning's at seven;*
> *The hillside's dew pearled.'*

She raised her eyes as if to ascertain they were all listening.

> *'The lark's on the wing;*
> *The snail's on the thorn;*
> *God's in his Heaven –*
> *All's right with the world!'*

There was a moment of stunned silence. Then Kate performed a brief bow and there was pandemonium. The shouts and cheers and applause might have been heard in North Africa. Men jumped up and down.

Then they fell to silence again. She remained on the stage, blushing, and said: 'I learned that at school.'

The shouts and cheers erupted again. And the big, grey ship lumbered on towards Italy, ever nearer the war.

Chapter Thirteen

They entered the Bay of Naples on a scenic morning, islands and mountains trailing mist, the sea unmoving.

'Just like the New Theatre, Cardiff,' said Delmi. They were standing at the ship's rail. Hopkins was wondering how he could see Kate.

'Pantomime,' continued Delmi still in his reverie. 'Every year different, *Aladdin* one Christmas, *Dick Whittington* the next. *Snow White and the Seven Dwarfs.*'

'You could have been in that,' said Small.

The ship began a circular movement. The scenery revolved around them. Vesuvius shifted. Delmi was still remembering: 'Every year they had the same scene. Just like this. Didn't matter what panto it was, same scenery.'

Small pointed high towards the horizon. 'The war's not finished 'ere by the look of it. Look up there, smoke. Air raid, I 'spect.'

'Vesuvius,' said Delmi smugly. 'All the time it does that.'

Some units were already on deck, their kit humped around them, facing the curve of the bay and the city of Naples. Hopkins looked intently for the ATS group. 'They make 'em like secret bleedin' weapons,' sniffed Small. 'The common tommy don't even get a butcher's.' Hopkins had not seen her since the night of the concert; their only touch the briefest brush of his hand on her shirted arm.

It took a further hour before the cumbersome troopship was

moored alongside a jetty. As she moved in, pile upon pile, the ruins of Naples took shape. The port had been cleared but the water was grey with debris.

There were still fears of air attack although the Germans by now were many miles north, and the troops wore steel helmets. 'See Naples and die,' said Delmi. He was unsure what it meant.

They watched the khaki men, huddled beneath their packs and their metal hats, and with their rifles slung, go carefully down the gangways to the dockside. Military policemen, red faces beneath red caps, were shouting orders and directing the disembarking men. Then Hopkins picked out the small clutch of girl soldiers. He saw Kate at once, taller than the others, almost tripping as she turned and looked back towards the rails. He called and waved but she stumbled again and did not see him. The women were conducted by a show-off policeman to a separate truck. That could be the last he would ever see of her. The army, the war, would swallow her up. And him too. He put his hands to his face and muttered: 'Sod it.'

The units still on the deck were thinning and at last the number of their troop-deck was called and they went below to collect their kit. Resignedly Hopkins heaved his pack on his back and followed the others to the hatch and up onto the deck with Rabbit, Angelo and the rest. Angelo was saying he was going to look for his auntie in Naples.

Small said: 'Bollocks.'

They could see that some of the ancient city had been reduced to powder by the fighting. But roads were scraped clear, the dock area brought into working order, and some rough cafés and bars and even a few optimistic shops opened, their summer blinds hanging like freedom flags.

From the ship they were directed to a transit camp in what

had been a Roman amphitheatre, ancient stone seats in a half-moon around a flagged stage. Few of the soldiers paid any attention to it. Looking at the ancient ruins Small said: 'Been some fighting around 'ere.'

There were huts inserted among the stone remnants, some for billets, some for stores, two for cookhouses and one, in a bashful corner, for the treatment of venereal diseases.

'You lot won't be 'ere for long,' forecast the corporal who conducted them to their quarters. The hut was shared by twenty men.

'How long do you think, corp?' asked Hopkins. He was wondering where Kate had gone.

'Couple of days at the most,' said the man. He was languid and deliberately moving, like a soldier who has arranged to see out the rest of the war in comfort and safety. 'They'll get you north, towards Florence. Heavy fightin' up there. The Teds are digging in.'

'Who's these Teds?' asked Delmi.

'Teds? Tedeski – Germans.' The corporal studied him. 'You've 'eard of Germans, I s'pose?'

Delmi said: 'Oh, yes. I've heard of them. Several times in fact.'

The NCO regarded him sideways as if he were not to be trusted. 'Anyway,' he decided as if they were expendable. 'You're only in transit.'

'What do we do till then?' asked Hopkins. 'Admire the ruins?'

'You might learn summat,' said the corporal. 'But you won't. You'll be paid and then you'll be on the town tonight. Until twenty-three fifty-nine. It might be your last chance to have a bit of a good time. For them that's goin' to exercise the elephant don't forget your Frenchies. The women 'ere could give you distemper.'

'At least we'll get out on the town,' said Small. 'Find a bit of action.'

'You'll have enough action before long,' grunted the corporal. 'All you'll want.'

As they left through the gate an hour later Hopkins immediately saw her. She was aboard a jeep against the opposite pavement with four American soldiers. She sat on the lap of one. 'There he is!' she called happily. 'Hopkins! Hopkins, I'm here.'

She climbed over the side of the jeep, her good legs slipping from below her military skirt. 'Thanks, chaps!' She blew kisses to the Americans as she crossed the road.

One called: 'What do you see in that guy?'

Standing transfixed Hopkins had to jump back as a motorcycle dispatch rider snorted by. Kate embraced him and the Americans cheered and started the jeep forwards. 'Thanks again!' Kate called to them. She fell into his arms.

'How did you know where I was?' he laughed as he kissed her. 'I thought I'd never see you.'

She pulled a little away from him. 'Easy,' she said. 'We're posted to the Movement Office. Just for now. But as soon as we got there the manifest from the ship came in. All the names and where the men had been sent. I found your name right away. Those nice Yanks gave me a lift.'

He looked at his watch. 'This time,' he said holding her again, 'we've got six hours.'

Kate said: 'All to ourselves.'

In a street at the back of the port, a place of sharp shadows and rubble, a woman in black was standing expectantly by three tables with red-and-white checked cloths. A parrot of many colours paced grumbling in a cage. The woman straightened one of the cloths and brushed it with a ragged feather duster as they approached. '*Buena sera, signore e signorina.*'

'Our first date,' laughed Kate. She led him by the hand and they sat down.

Hopkins said: 'I hope it goes on and on.'

'Hopkins,' she said seriously. She leaned over the table to him. 'It *is* going on and on. We'll always know where the other one is.' Her smile broadened with confidence. 'And when the war is over we'll get married and have a house and children.'

He grinned. 'You've got it worked out.'

'Every last moment,' she told him. Their hands met across the table and they had to part them when the woman wearing black came from the inside dimness with red wine in a grubby bottle and two glasses which she polished on her apron. Without asking she poured two glasses and then, with a brief, old-fashioned curtsey, withdrew.

Their hands came together again. 'Listen, Hopkins,' she said softly. 'I've come to the conclusion that we're in love with each other. Do you feel that as well? I expect you do.'

He grinned again. 'You've made up your mind.'

'I have. While we've been on the ship. I've thought about you. I liked you before. Even when we first met on the train I liked you.'

'I'm glad,' he said slowly, honestly. 'I've never met anyone like you. You're like nobody else. You're very . . . well . . . you come as a bit of a surprise.'

'I'm a bit definite about things, I know. I've pushed a man into the Thames.'

The parrot, which had been paying minute attention to them, cocked its red head and began to squawk: '*Santa Caterina! Santa Caterina!*'

The woman reappeared. '*Santa Caterina*,' she said pointing to a damaged church across the street. '*Santa Caterina*,' said the parrot. The church had been on fire; its roof was missing and its four columns were broken and brown with smoke, standing like cigarette stubs.

'Caterina, Katherine,' laughed Kate. 'Kate. That's my name.'

'*Caterina*,' nodded the woman.

Kate lifted her glass. The red wine curled around it. 'Cheers, Hopkins,' she said. 'To us. You and me.'

'*Santa Caterina*,' the parrot said again.

Hopkins looked across the table and said: 'I've never had wine before. Never tasted it. Just beer up to now. And a drop of whisky when you could get it.'

Kate drank. 'God knows what it is,' she said tipping the glass and studying it. 'But it's worth the risk.'

Hopkins sipped carefully, grimaced, but then drained the glass. 'Not too bad,' he said.

Three unkempt men wearing bits of cast-off uniforms came along the street and insisted on shaking hands with them. They spoke volubly, with a little English, about how they had thrown the hated Germans out of Naples. There was arm waving and the pretence of firing weapons. Vigorously they shook hands again and marched on slapping each other on the back.

When they had gone an ancient man appeared and sat at another of the three tables. The woman appeared unasked and poured a glass of wine from the same bottle as before. The old man studied them quietly before he lifted the glass to them and drank. They lifted theirs. 'Those men,' he said almost in English. 'Those children, boys. They tell you how they beat the Tedeski.' He laughed sourly. '*Now*, they beat them. *Before*, they hide. Shoot? They cannot piss straight.'

The woman came out and understood what he had said because she motioned him to shush. Then she said something to Hopkins which he did not understand.

He said to Kate: 'She's trying to sell us a camera, by the sound of it.'

He motioned to the woman. 'No camera.' She seemed hurt.

Then the man at the other table said: 'Not a camera. A room. *Camera* is Italian for room. She asks if you would like a room.'

Their expressions met across the table. It was a smoky evening, late sun shadows cut into the back street. 'There's no time like the present,' said Kate.

'*Santa Caterina*,' shouted the parrot.

It was a surprising room, undamaged, undisturbed it seemed, the old brown furniture in careful place, the heavy curtains complete and keeping out the rest of the daylight sun, and a crucifix lit by a candle over the bed.

'Christ,' said Hopkins. He performed a short apologetic bow to the crucifix.

Kate laughed and said: 'It's only pretend.' She looked around. 'But after all the blasting Naples has had this is a bit different, isn't it? Not a shell-hole anywhere.' She peeped briefly into the street through the gap in the curtains. 'Pity about poor Santa Caterina.'

They were, oddly, standing each side of the huge bed, now looking happily at each other. 'This is our time,' she said quietly. 'Do you want me to come over there?'

'Please,' he said. He could feel the moment swelling within him, a promise, an expectancy, a scarcely muffled joy. She looked at him for several moments and he could see in her face how loving she was going to be. 'Come on over,' he said.

'I'll just move Jesus,' she said firmly. 'We don't want *anybody* looking. Even Him.'

The crucifix was only hooked on the wall and she blew out the candle and lifted the figure aside. Some plaster came with it. 'Looks like He was about to fall down anyway,' she said. She regarded the image pensively. 'The descent from the cross.'

He smiled at her. 'Are you coming over here?'

'I'm on my way,' she said. She moved around the foot of the brown, carved, heavy bed, stepped to him and raised her slim arms about his broad neck. They kissed deeply. She said: 'We're going to enjoy this.'

They did. They undressed each other slowly, putting their

lips to the intimate parts as they became exposed. She tapped his erection playfully like a music teacher with a tuning fork. 'Ding,' she said. Then she knelt and quietly put her mouth there. He closed his eyes with the deepest pleasure.

Her arms encircled his thighs and she pressed her mouth closer. He closed his eyes again with the sensation but then eased her to her feet and lifted her onto the high and voluminous bed. Dust came up in clouds. They began to cough.

'Wait, wait,' she gasped. Laughing at the pantomime of it she slid over the side of the padded counterpane. He shifted onto his back, watching her over the edge of his own penis, and she eased the quilt onto the floor. It subsided like a balloon. She patted the sheet below. No dust rose. 'That's more like it,' she murmured. He eased himself to accommodate her slim body and she slid half beneath him. He moved gently above her and bending over kissed her pubis and then below it. 'Hopkins,' she whispered. 'I'm going to explode in a minute.'

'Me too,' he said sliding himself into her.

'Can you hold on for as long as you can.'

He waited and waited again before easing himself fully into her, feeling the interior warmth of her. He pressed and retreated carefully. Then advanced again. They kept the experience going. There was no unseemly hurry at the end, either, just a gentle conclusion.

'That was a real joy, Hopkins,' she whispered as they lay beside each other, warm with the room and their entanglement. 'How many times do you think we'll do it?'

'I've got to be back by twenty-three fifty-nine,' he said.

She giggled. 'I meant in the whole of our lives.'

'Lots of times,' he said. 'Hundreds, I expect.'

Delmi and Small sat at a small round table, two pale beers before them. 'We ought to see if they've got any nosh,' said Small. 'I'm starving. They must have spaghetti or something.'

'Spaghetti?' asked Delmi. 'In a Heinz tin? With tomato sauce?'

Small said: 'It won't be like that for sure. Maybe they've got egg and chips or something.' The woman who had brought them the beers appeared appropriately at the door.

'*Volete mangiare?*' she said. '*Bene.*'

'If you've got some, missus,' said Delmi.

'Egg and chips,' said Small making signs, two round shapes with his fingers and then a whole hand of fingers laid in a row.

'*Si, si,*' said the woman. She went back into the room.

'Think she savvied?' asked Delmi.

'Egg and chips is international, mate.'

They waited over their beers until the woman reappeared with two steaming plates of spaghetti Napoletana and sat dumbly while she put the plates in front of them.

'*Bellissima,*' she said turning and going.

'Fuck me,' said Small.

'We could try it,' said Delmi sniffing. 'It don't niff too bad.'

'If we can't stomach it we'll bugger off without paying,' said Small. 'I wanted egg and chips.'

They began to eat the pasta and kept eating. They ordered more beers and then more pasta. Two loose-looking women came and sat at the table opposite and stared at them. 'Don't like yours,' said Small, spaghetti hanging from his lips.

'I don't like yours either. Or mine,' said Delmi.

'You have the one with the hairy mole,' sighed Small. 'I'll have the one with the big conk.'

'I don't think I'll 'ave any of them.'

In the morning they were paraded and told to be ready to move from Naples that day. Angelo, Rabbit, Blake and the others, the men who had come together at Aldershot, were posted. They went with a wave and they never saw them again. Hopkins, Small and Delmi stood close together.

They found themselves marching to the station with a

hundred other men, every one a stranger. Some weary-eyed, unspeaking, New Zealanders returning from rest to the fighting front, and some black French African troops. The British soldiers had never seen so many black men, eager and fierce. Delmi said: 'I'm glad they're on our side.'

They boarded a train for Rome, sharing a scarred carriage with three soldiers from a grave-registration unit. 'You mean,' said Delmi hesitantly, 'that you have to see the . . . dead? The actual dead, like corpses?'

The men, two Scots and a grim youth from Lancashire, regarded him with surprise. 'We canna do this job with our eyes shut,' said one of the Scots. 'When a man's dead all he's got left is his identity discs. We collect them.'

The Lancashire youth said: 'If we didn't do our job this war would be a shambles. Nobody would know who'd been killed.'

Beyond the dirty windows the countryside was mockingly sunlit. But few trees or buildings were left upright; people trudged the partly cleared roads, their backs bent, their steps small. Once into the hill areas the desolation softened, even the sky seemed to be clearer. There were rivers and patches of green and people working in fields. But the villages were broken and holed, houses held up precariously, and roads cut deep with tank tracks.

'What do you reckon you lot will do in Rome?' Small asked the grave-registration men.

'I'm going to inspect the catacombs,' said the Lancashire youth. 'Too good to miss.'

The journey, stopping and starting along the damaged track between the rubble of stations, took ten hours and it was early evening before they drew into the main Rome terminus, the locomotive wheezing as if it could go no further anyway. Trucks took them on the last stage of the journey, open-sided so they could see the miraculously undamaged city, not a building out of place, umbrella-decked cafés and shops open, people busy on the evening pavements. 'Looks like the war went the other way,' said Small.

At the transit camp the discipline was informal. There were hot showers and decent beds and they unrolled their best uniforms and pressed them in an ironing shed. The men in the camp seemed to come and go as they pleased. 'But you've got to be back by the morning,' said a soldier in the ironing shed. He paused with the steam iron poised. 'Or they'll come and get you.'

There was transport to the city: a bus left from directly outside the gates to the Via Repubblica. It was evening and still light. They stopped at a bar and sat with three beers. Soldiers moved all around them, many of them Americans. The city looked miraculously untouched by the battle that had extended up the breadth of Italy for more than a year.

'Prostit-toots,' said a riven-faced American, slumping into a chair at the next table. 'This ain't the Holy City. It's a city of prostit-toots.'

'How long have you been here?' Hopkins called to him.

'In Rome, four days. In Italy for fucking ever. Since Salerno anyway, which seems like for ever. I want to go home, man. I want to go to Bowling Green, Kentucky, and I want to stay there.'

'What chance of that?' asked Delmi regarding the American solemnly.

'Maybe in a box,' said the American. 'I don't know. If they can make a deal to keep Rome with no bombs or shells, why can't they just arrange the whole goddamn war the same. Jesus, before Cassino there was so many dead men on either side they was blocking up the battlefield. Imagine that. You couldn't see the enemy because of the piles of dead. You could hide behind them, there was so many. Just guys. Then, for Chrissake, they call a truce so that both sides, us and the Huns, can get the corpses out of the way. So we can get on with the battle. And there was our guys and the Huns clearing up the bodies and then talking a few words to each other and passing cigarettes and beers, just like they was buddies. What sense is there in the whole fucking business? Why can't they do that all round?'

He fell to silence, drinking his beer by the sip. 'And Rome,' he said eventually. He waved his hand about. 'You got to keep Rome okay because it's a Holy City, my ass. The only ruins here are the ruins that have been here for ever. None of it makes sense.'

He finished the beer and refused another. Then he rose. 'Prostit-toots,' he repeated. 'The Holy City is full of Prostit-toots.'

Chapter Fourteen

By now the battle lines had moved north of Rome to the folding mountains of Tuscany and Umbria, the fighting fierce on the coastal roads before Florence. The new soldiers were moved up the country by train and fatigued combat men were withdrawn to the rear. The autumn, with its rains, was ahead. It was going to be a long, muddy winter.

The rail journey was tortuous for the track had been heavily fought over and even as the train progressed gangs of men were filling in craters and rebuilding precarious bridges. From the dusty windows the new men could view the countryside that had a few weeks before been a battlefield. Nature's swift greenery had covered many of the rural places but every village and much of every town had been reduced to brown rubble.

Only a couple of hours into the journey, at the town of Terni, the train sighed to yet another stop and the men were told to get off. They stood on the only platform of the railway station that had space to stand and then formed into a column and marched through the desolation of the place. There were close on five hundred soldiers, new and untried, and as they marched their eyes moved sideways and saw what a battle could do.

Hopkins, Small and Delmi kept together. They marched in the forward formation along a roughly cleared road; hunched Italian people watched them before turning their backs on them as if they needed someone to blame.

The sun was cutting ragged shapes through the damaged walls along the street, shapes like dragons and strange trees. They marched on, wondering what was coming for them, what dangers were in store. They did not know the men around them, only that they were bound in the same dangerous direction. Hopkins kept thinking of Kate. He wanted to run but, like the others, he kept marching.

There were no sounds of fighting, no explosions, no smoke on the horizon, only the hard and mocking sun that had seen it all. A woman had set up a stall by her fallen house and was pathetically trying to sell a few melons. As the soldiers marched before her she held out a big melon but then pulled her hand back as if she knew she was wasting her time.

It was not a long march, no more than a mile, although enough to make them sweat under the weight of their weapons and equipment. Their steel helmets were heavy but shaded their foreheads from the sun. The cleared road petered out at what had been the edge of the town, against some growing hills, and they wheeled to the right and entered what had once been a ploughed field but was now a dustbowl. A sergeant-major who had marched alongside them, a puffing veteran, gratefully called them to a halt and then formed them into three lines facing away from the sun. After five minutes standing easy they were ordered to attention and an American jeep carrying a British officer, erect as a statue, came from the road.

The officer was sharp but his face was stained and strained.

'What a God-awful fucking place,' he said to the sergeant-major as he surveyed the open area.

'Good description, sir,' agreed the sergeant-major. He lowered his saluting arm.

The officer, a major, spoke to the driver and the jeep was manoeuvred so that it halted at the middle of the parading men. 'Stand easy, sergeant-major,' called the officer. The NCO shouted the order, raising a flock of pigeons hiding in a clump of stunted trees. The soldiers stood easy, the sweat glistening on their faces.

'Apologies for keeping you out in this, chaps,' called the major. 'If there was any cover big enough we'd be under it. So I'll be brief. My name is Brian Willows, Major, Royal Armoured Corps. I've been in this country since we invaded Sicily and frankly I'm pissed off with it.'

There was a brief sign of a snigger. 'The quicker we get the rest of the Teds out of Italy the quicker this war will be over and we can all go home again. You have just arrived and you will have an important part to play immediately. Our friends the Yanks are meeting strong resistance about twenty-odd miles north of here, the Teds well dug in and showing no inclination to be shifted. So we intend to go around by the back door. We are going to attempt a minor amphibious landing to drive a beach-head behind the bastards.' He paused. 'We'll give it a try anyway.'

After a night in rough tents on hard ground they were sent on a pointless march through the damaged countryside before being taken to a cookhouse and badly fed. 'Like animals,' complained Delmi. 'My uncle treated his pigs better than this. Who knows what else might be coming?'

Hopkins said: 'What was? For the pigs?'

'Slaughterhouse,' said Delmi.

Small was polishing his knuckledusters. They had seen him toying with them sometimes. Hopkins asked: 'What you going to do with them, son? Punch a German tank?'

Small almost fondled the knuckledusters. 'You never know when they might come in useful,' he said. He slipped them over his fingers and punched the air. 'Whoosh. Bang,' he said.

'Ouch, more like it,' said Delmi. 'You could hurt yourself with those things.' They were allowed to lie in the sun that afternoon, stretched out in the heat, their equipment sprawled around them. Delmi crawled on all fours below a ragged patch of trees.

'Be nice to do this all the time, wouldn't it?' said Hopkins. He imagined lying in the sun with Kate. Where was she now? 'Just stretching out like this in your bathing cossie. One day I expect people will again.'

'On Barry Island,' said Delmi. 'We won't be in Italy, the likes of us. Barry Island is about all we'll manage.'

Confidently Small said: 'I'll come back 'ere, to Iti-land. With a couple of tarts maybe. Sitting drinking champagne and that while the wop waiters dash around.'

'Where's the money coming from?' asked Hopkins.

'I'll pinch something,' shrugged Small. 'Something big. Nick it. It's the only way the likes of us is going to get rich. Nicking things. You ought to know that by now. It's the buggers sitting on their arses in offices at 'ome. Right now, this minute. They'll be all right. We're just the mugs they send out to do the scrapping, getting killed, or ending up on fucking Barry Island.'

A staff car and a convoy of trucks had arrived on the road beyond where they were lying. 'I feel scared,' said Delmi quietly. 'Bloody scared. I didn't think all this was going to turn so serious so soon.'

Small said: 'You can always desert, mate. They'd take a month of Sundays to find you in this country. Hills and all sorts. And when they catch you all you say is you took a wrong turning and lost your way. Or report sick. Get the shits.'

'I already got them,' said Delmi.

'Like all of us,' said Hopkins. 'But they've come for us and we've got to go. Better get on the way.'

All around them men were reluctantly standing and buckling on their equipment, checking ammunition packs and sliding the bolts on the cumbersome rifles.

'It looks like I've lost my housewife,' said Delmi searching his small pack.

Hopkins said: 'You're not going to be darning any socks.'

'But when we get to kit inspection they'll make me pay for it.'

'A needle and thread,' mocked Small. 'The next thing you lose, mate, could be your bleedin' life.'

Delmi was suddenly distracted. 'Look . . . look at this. I found a tortoise,' he said in a pleased way. 'Look, it was just by 'ere.' He reached down and picked up the creature from the rough growth. It kicked its legs. He stroked the shell. 'Just like a Jerry helmet,' he said. He made room in his small pack and dropped the creature gently into it.

'You're not taking that thing, are you?' said Hopkins.

'Why not? He's got nowhere else to go. He'll be company.'

'Maybe we could eat 'im,' said Small.

A hoarse-voiced sergeant was calling them to form up in front of the vehicles. They trudged with the others up the slight, sunlit incline to the road and formed up in rough threes. An officer, a captain, opened a roof in the staff car and he stood inside and poked his head through. 'Gather round, chaps,' he said. 'Gather round.'

There were about a hundred men. His face was ragged and his eyes set into holes. 'Benning is my name. Just to put you in the picture,' he said. Then he paused. 'What I understand to be the picture at the moment. This being the army it could change any minute and they'll tell us it's off and we can all go home. But I don't think so.'

He surveyed the apprehensive faces. 'A lot of you are new, I know,' he said. 'Just arrived. Sorry to rush you into things.' He lifted his chin. 'How many have seen action?' A dozen men raised slow hands as if they feared some added peril.

'Well, that's a few,' said the captain. 'Any amphibious experience, anywhere?'

A sole hand went up. 'Anzio, sir,' said the man without enthusiasm.

'How was it?'

'Terrible, sir,' said the soldier. 'Not to be recommended.'

'I heard,' said Captain Benning. 'Lots of casualties. Very little gained.' He tried a jagged smile. 'But this is not going to be Anzio. This is much smaller, much more localised, much less risky.'

He appeared to be trying to think of some excuse. 'When you and the other units involved get to the landing craft you'll get a last-minute briefing. They've got the maps and suchlike. And then it's an hour on the boat and the sea is nice and calm. Any questions?'

Hopkins was always amazed when Delmi raised his hand. He did now. The captain pointed a finger at him. 'Are you coming, sir?' asked Delmi.

'What's that sticking out of your small pack, son?'

'A tortoise, sir. I just found him.'

'Ah, I see,' said the captain. 'A tortoise. Anyway, in answer to your question I *am* coming with you. I've been here two years and I'm due some leave. But it's got to wait.'

'Thank you, sir,' said Delmi. He firmly pushed the inquisitive head of the tortoise back into his pack.

'Good luck, chaps,' said the officer. 'Last one on the beach is a cissy.'

They slowly climbed into the lorries. Delmi said to Hopkins: 'I'm scared.'

'So am I,' said Hopkins.

Small said: 'I'm crapping myself.'

It was fully dark when they reached the coast. They climbed from wooden benches on the cramped trucks onto a cobbled harbour with the shapes of a clutch of landing craft fidgeting offshore. To the north the sky was flickering with flashes and distant detonations.

'Looks like a storm,' said Delmi.

'Gunfire,' said Hopkins. 'We're nearly there.'

Small said: 'I think I'll bugger off. Make a dash for it now.'

'They'll catch you and put you in the boat right at the front,' forecast Hopkins.

'We might be in it anyway.'

All the soldiers were directed towards what looked like a warehouse on the quay. It was lit with oil and filled with the smell of fish. Hopkins remembered the stench. He wished he were back there.

Soldiers, laden with weapons and equipment, trooped in. When two hundred or more men were in the building someone shut the double doors but the officer who had briefed them earlier climbed onto a fish trolley, held at each end by a soldier so that it did not overbalance, and ordered the doors to be reopened. 'I don't see why we should stand in an aroma like this,' he called. 'It's fucking disgusting.'

Dutifully some of the men laughed. But only briefly. The captain turned his deep-lined face towards them. 'Right, chaps,' he said. 'This is chapter two.' A lieutenant was fixing a large sketch map on an easel. 'It's upside down, lieutenant,' pointed out Benning without emphasis.

The junior officer looked to make sure and said: 'Silly old me,' before turning it up the right way.

'Cunt,' said Benning to himself.

Out loud he said to the troops: 'This is a section of the coast about eight miles north of here. That's where we will be going ashore.' The light was dim and he called for two men to hold oil lamps each side of the easel. He pointed with his cane. 'This is Abbe del Mora, a town of about three thousand who, if they've got any sense, will have cleared out by now. The Italians are not keen on noise. Each side about two miles each way are two villages, Santo Augustino to the north and Picca Violetto to the south. There is a road running from due south through all three places and behind them is the River Loppe.'

Despite the lamps each side of the map the men's heads were straining forward. 'Our objective,' went on Benning, 'is to secure Abbe and the two villages and hold them until an armoured column can get up the road and relieve us. Any questions?'

A man at the front raised his hand. 'How long will that take, sir? The armoured column?'

'Any *other* questions?' asked Benning looking across the faces. Then he said: 'Will the chap who was at Anzio come forward, please.' There was a shift in the crowd and the soldier emerged. Benning climbed from the fish trolley and invited him to take his place. He climbed up and balanced, the two corporals still supporting the sides.

The man was a lance-corporal. Benning said: 'This is going to be the shortest briefing ever given on amphibious warfare.' He nodded to the squat man who seemed unsurprised. 'What advice would you give to a soldier going ashore from a landing craft?'

There was little hesitation: 'Keep out of the way of the bloody thing,' said the man. 'Once the ramp goes down, don't charge off ashore, because you'll fall into the drink and the landing craft will run over you and you'll be drowned dead.' He stopped.

Benning said: 'Thank you, sergeant.'

'Lance-corporal, sir. Acting, unpaid.'

'Sergeant,' repeated Benning. 'Promotion in the field. You're the only one who'll have any idea what he's doing.'

The men trooped from the building into the warm and dark night. Gunfire was still going on to the north, flickering along the edges of the mountains. A cookhouse truck had arrived and was dishing out soup, bread and tea.

'Do we get lifebelts, like on the troopship?' asked Delmi as they clattered down the metal ramp into the boxy metal hull of the landing craft. He looked around him fearfully. Sitting there already was a Bren-gun carrier, two men perching on its turret.

'That thing will sink like a stone,' commented Small.

'Thanks, mate,' said one of the Bren-gun crew.

There were wooden seats down each side of the interior of the landing craft and transverse seats at the rear. At the stern, set above them, was the navigation bridge. Hopkins looked that way. There were four heads and a steering wheel.

They unhooked as much of the heavy equipment as they could. Some men pushed their steel helmets from their heads but were ordered to put them back in place. 'You'll be needing that on your napper before long,' said a sergeant walking along the tight space between the rows.

They sat dumb and apprehensive in the darkness while the craft rolled gently beneath them. They could hear sounds from other landing barges. Then came some shouted orders from the shore, the engines were started and they moved away.

'Is that officer on this thing?' asked Hopkins.

'Didn't see him. Up the front if he is.'

Delmi said: 'He'll be the first one to jump onto the beach. I'll be the last.'

Small said: 'That tortoise of yours is sticking his ugly head from your pack.'

'He's 'ungry, I expect,' said Delmi. 'I got no idea what to feed 'im on.' He sniffed speculatively.

'They got a galley back there, under the bridge,' pointed out Hopkins. 'Go and ask them.'

Delmi climbed out of his cobweb of equipment and left it spread across his seat, taking the tortoise from his pack and carrying him legs flailing through the silent and silhouetted soldiers. The galley was small and smelly, enough for serving the crew of the craft. 'What you want?' asked a greasy soldier looking into a pot.

Delmi said: 'I've got this tortoise.' He held out the kicking creature.

'Can't, mate,' said the man, his face still over the pot. 'No time. You 'ave to boil 'em for three hours.'

Delmi regarded him savagely. 'I don't want him bloody boiled,' he said. 'I want to feed him.'

'What does 'e eat?'

'I'm not all that sure. I only just got him.'

'There's some spud peelings over there,' said the soldier nodding sideways. 'I 'eard they likes to crunch up snails but we ain't got no snails.'

Delmi took one curling piece of potato skin from the pile and offered it to the tortoise who bit at it avidly and jerked it into his mouth. 'Aye, that's all right,' said Delmi. 'I'll take a few of these.'

The greasy soldier nodded. 'Can 'e swim?'

'Dunno.'

'All I can say,' said the man, 'is that 'e'd better learn bloody quick.'

Delmi looked worried. 'I'm not much good myself.'

'Better climb on 'is back then,' said the cook.

Delmi stumbled back along the narrow passageway between the men. No one spoke. They were only faces, dark faces, glistening on the cheekbones and noses. Then a whisper started and made its way along the seated men. 'Half an hour to go.'

Hopkins moved along to make room for Delmi. 'Get anything?'

'Spud peelings, but he eats them. The bugger in there said they take three hours to boil, tortoises.'

'I bet they taste all right,' sniffed Small on Hopkins's other side. 'Why bring 'im, for Christ's sake? 'Aven't you got enough to lug ashore?'

'Poor thing was lost, that's why,' said Delmi.

Hopkins said: 'He might have been safer if you'd left 'im.'

'Nobody seems to reckon this is going to be all right,' grumbled Delmi. 'Maybe the Jerries have pulled out.'

'You've got more chance of pulling your dick out,' grunted Small. 'And that's none.'

Delmi climbed into his webbing and pushed the tortoise into his pack with two long pieces of potato skin. The twenty-minute warning was passed along the line. The soldiers stared ahead like stone men.

'Nobody jumps until I shout.' It was the man who had been at Anzio, the new sergeant. 'Anyone who does will get run over by this thing.'

They felt the craft lurch slowly. The night was close around them. Then, as if a secret door had been opened in the sky a low aeroplane appeared above. 'Jerry!' shouted somebody. 'Get down! Get down!'

There was no room to get down. The men curled up, heads almost between their legs. Nothing happened. The plane roared away and slowly, with relief, they began to straighten. But then it came back meaning business, its cannons firing like hammers. The boat heeled away like an animal. Another plane dropped a straddle of bombs across the sea and a tall tree of flame shot up as one of the other craft was hit. Men were crying out, screaming. Some tried to get to their feet but fell back. Then the landing craft began to describe circles. It lurched to starboard and kept going until it was facing the way it had come, and then turned back again. 'Steering's gone,' said Hopkins.

'Maybe it will take us back,' muttered Small. 'I'm going to piss off the first chance I get.'

The new sergeant's voice bawled over their heads. 'Anyone who can steer this thing? The crew have 'ad it.'

'I can try,' said Hopkins almost to himself. He rose, hung on, and staggered towards the bridge at the back.

The sergeant saw him coming. 'Can you do it, soldier?'

'I'll have a go,' said Hopkins. One of the planes came back, guns belting, and they ducked as far as they could. It was gone in a second but men were sprawled dead all over the deck now.

The sergeant, his face like a devil, said in almost a whisper:

'Get up there. Get up and see what you can do.' Hopkins made for the short metal ladder, the sergeant behind him. 'Stop it going around in rings!' His voice leapt to a shout. 'I'm getting bloody giddy.'

Hopkins reached the bridge and shrank back at the scene of horror. All the men up there were dead, five of them including a major he had never seen before, spread-eagled across the metal deck, one propped up in a corner. The man who had been at the helm was hung across the spokes of the steering wheel. Hopkins made himself move forward. The sergeant was with him. 'What a nasty mess,' the NCO muttered mildly.

Like shifting a heavy sack they manoeuvred the steersman's body aside, letting it fall with an ugly thud against the bulkhead. Down below them, in the well of the landing craft, a tangle of men were crouching and crawling. The vessel lurched in its mad circle.

Hopkins looked up to see if he could spot Delmi or Small towards the front of the troop-deck but the light was not strong enough, the huddled and moving forms hardly distinguishable one from another. He took hold of the wheel.

'Can you handle it?' asked the sergeant.

'Yes, I think so. But we'll need to cut speed.'

'Just stop us going around. We're disappearing up our own arse,' said the sergeant.

A man crawled along the bridge towards them. His face was agony and he was clutching something under his arm, against his ribs. Hopkins saw it was a cushion or a pillow, thick with blood. 'I'll do it.' It was all he could manage to get the words out. His hand went to the controls and he pulled at a lever. Immediately the engine decreased and the vessel lost momentum.

'No more than that,' spluttered the man. 'She'll cut out. This cow always does.'

He slumped over the cushion hugged to his chest. The

sergeant eased him away and put him against the bulkhead with the others.

'Please God,' muttered Hopkins. He got the feel of the wheel and began to bring the landing craft on course again, turning after the other boats that were now half a mile ahead in the morning light. From the shore heavy gunfire began, fountains were thrown up in the dark sea. Then the planes came back, screaming above them, only a few feet it seemed, banking and firing their guns. Hopkins tried to stay behind the wheel but he felt the gunfire hitting the metal deck around him. The sergeant fell backwards but reached up and pulled him down beside him.

'We're for it now,' he said.

The planes turned away but came back again for another run, killing men trapped on the deck below them. Hopkins and the sergeant again toppled back but regained their feet as the aircraft swerved away. 'Missed again,' grunted the sergeant. 'What's your name, by the way?'

'Hopkins. And you?'

'Sergeant Doyle,' said the man almost formally.

'Let's . . . Let's . . . try and stay alive,' said Hopkins. He realised he was stammering.

'I'm going to,' said the sergeant. 'I've got some leave coming.'

Now that its course was straight Hopkins increased the engine power and the craft urged itself forward. Gunfire continued from the shore. 'We're going to come last in the race,' said the sergeant. 'Which may be no bad thing.' He pointed to the left. 'Get her in there. There's a gap. Put her as steady as you can onto the beach. Where did you learn this?'

'Fisherman,' said Hopkins. 'Bristol Channel.'

'Went to Ilfracombe once,' said Doyle. 'On holiday.'

Now they were almost at the beach. Tracer bullets were flying from the shore like comets through the sky. Hopkins, concentrating on guiding the boat, tried to glance towards the bow of the troop-deck. It was lighter now and he saw Small. He was waving towards the wheelhouse. Hopkins waved back. Then he spotted Delmi on the fringe of the crush of men waiting to leap ashore. They wanted to get off quickly now. Delmi had something held with one hand above his head, his tortoise, almost like a second helmet. The other hand clutched his rifle. Hopkins shouted but there was no chance that the small Welshman would hear him. Nor any opportunity as the craft, with a massive shudder, came into the shallow water before the beach and slewed half-sideways. Hopkins cut the speed back and Doyle, who knew what he was doing, operated the ramp so that it fell forward at the right moment.

'Done it,' he whispered to himself. Then aloud: 'Good luck, boys!'

The men in the bow were already ashore. Some concealed machine guns to the left, abruptly burst into life. Some of the landing soldiers fell as soon as they touched the beach. Hopkins cut the engine. All at once, exhausted, he tumbled forward against the steering wheel, his rifle propped in front of him. 'I'd better get going,' he groaned, grasping the weapon. 'Get with my pals.'

Doyle reached and stopped him. 'You're not going.'

'But . . . my butties . . . my mates . . .'

Doyle said firmly: 'You're staying right here, son. We may need to get this bucket out of here again.'

A slash of machine-gun fire flew over their heads and brought down the radio antenna, which had miraculously survived, and both men fell to the deck. Carefully Doyle looked up. The other craft were disgorging their men; the invading party was already high up the beach. All around the firing went on. 'I think I could do with a cup of tea,' said the sergeant.

'Me too,' said Hopkins. 'Strong with three sugars.'

Chapter Fifteen

Quickly the soldiers who had landed on the beach contrived to get into the scrubby sand hills a little inland. 'Fear,' sniffed Doyle. 'It makes you move like shit.'

The firing continued and the German planes came back but left the stranded boats now, screeching low across the hinterland. Gradually the explosions moved forward from the landing places until the sounds became duller and there were only the flashes against the morning sky. Then the neutral sun came up. It was a beautiful day.

Forty minutes later Doyle went ashore leaving Hopkins sitting on the hull confronted by dead men. No wounded seemed to be left. After half an hour the sergeant came back and said the landing had gone well. 'They're across the road and into those villages,' he said. He looked about him at the bodies. 'Somebody will be coming to clear this lot up,' he said. 'Why don't you get some breakfast?'

'Sarge,' said Hopkins, 'I can't just eat ruddy breakfast when my butties are up there. I should be with them. I've always been with them. I went to school with that Welsh midget.'

Doyle sighed and repeated: 'Get some breakfast. They're brewing up down the beach. Three boats down. Bacon and eggs by the smell of it. I'll come and get some myself. I'd better stay in charge until somebody comes for the casualties. They're never long. Best-organised unit in the army, the blokes counting the dead.'

Hopkins grunted. 'All right.' Stepping around the grotesque forms on the deck, trying not to look at their faces, he went along the beach. There were bodies lying in a rough pattern on the sand and three medical teams were kneeling by some wounded. From the third barge along came the sound of Bing Crosby. Hopkins could see men holding plates and mugs, standing in an orderly queue or sitting around the deck as if they were at a sombre picnic.

They had the dull glaze of weariness and they ate slowly as though having to think about each mouthful. Even raising the steaming cups to their hard mouths was taken in stages. Their faces were stained. No one spoke, no one even nodded as he reached the deck from the ramp incline to the beach. Only the man doling out the fry-up watched him arrive and grunted: 'Nice morning.'

He piled eggs and bacon on a tin plate and Hopkins put a metal cup under an urn gushing hot tea loaded with sugar. The food was always good after a battle.

There was plenty of space on this deck. The casualties had been quickly removed. A pool of new blood lay across one area and he carefully avoided it. Hopkins looked at the parties on the beach, tending to both the dead and the wounded. Innocently the sun was spreading across the sand as if it were a holiday place. He saw Doyle almost strolling towards the ramp; he passed by as if he had never seen him before and went to the man cooking the breakfasts. He collected his wordlessly and came and sat down by Hopkins.

The food was congealing on Hopkins's plate. 'Listen, sarge,' he said quietly, 'I want to go and find my mates. I ought to be with them. They'll think I legged it.'

'Son,' said Doyle folding a fried egg and pushing it entirely into his mouth, 'let an old sweat give you some advice. Stay as safe as you can. Don't get shot and especially don't get yourself killed.'

He munched on the egg and spoke through it. 'Nobody ever remembers that you're a hero, nobody even remembers whether you were a good soldier. Nobody cares in the end. At the end of this bleeding war you'll be just another bloke in a demob suit looking for a job.'

Hopkins said: 'I'm talking about *now*, sarge. How I feel right *now*. I ought to be with them.'

'Bollocks,' said Doyle, mild as a mention. He forked a piece of bacon and let the fatty end dangle. 'Listen.' He leaned forward and Hopkins could smell the fat. 'You know I told the officer at that briefing that I'd been at Anzio. Well, it wasn't all that true. I was there and I would have had to take part in that bloody awful business, the landing, the getting stuck on the beaches, the big slaughter. But the day before I fell down a flight of hard steps on the troop transport. Complete accident. But I broke my ankle. Sort of thing you do playing football. So I couldn't go. I stayed on the deck keeping my head down and watched the others, poor bastards.'

'You couldn't help it,' said Hopkins.

'Right you are, but when this war started I made a promise to myself that I was going to come out of it alive and so far I've kept that promise. Christ, just by telling that half-fib to that officer I got made up to sergeant. Fully paid.'

They went back to their own beached barge. Hopkins sat feeling guilty and useless on the side of it while the death parties continued their work on the beach. He almost felt he ought to go and help them – go over there anyway – but he knew what he would be told to do. The dead men lying there in the sand looked like sunbathers.

The fighting had quickly retreated over the horizon. 'They've got control of the road now,' called Doyle as he trudged through the sand. He reached the barge. 'Taken both villages and the town, whatever it's called. Proper job. Now they're dug in and waiting for the reinforcements to come up the road.'

He had gone to the forward headquarters, which had already sprouted among the deeper sand dunes. In the next dune a tented hospital with a red cross on its roof had appeared. 'You've got to hang around here,' he said to Hopkins. 'That's orders from above. They haven't got enough blokes to sail these bloody tubs and they may be needed. Anyway you're stuck with it. Take it easy on the beach, I would.'

Hopkins said: 'Can I wander up to the hospital tent, sarge? I'm still worried about my butties.'

Doyle said: 'Good man. Go and have a dekko. Just don't get in the way.'

'I'll watch it,' said Hopkins. He levered himself upright and went down the ramp to the beach. There was an eerie peace over the place, almost a lassitude; the only sounds were the small grumbles of the unconcerned waves.

At the entrance to the hospital tent he paused uncertainly. The air was heavy with what he thought was the smell of chloroform. From inside he could hear a lone voice calling out for a mother. A dopey-looking medical corporal wandered in and said: 'What you want then? Ingrowing toenail?'

'Not yet,' said Hopkins. 'I've come to see if you've got any of my mates in here.'

'Get left behind, did you?'

'Sort of.'

He said: 'Lucky you,' then he decided to be helpful. 'Well, we've only got the beach casualties in this place. The blokes inland are in some farmhouse.' He took a thought. 'We've got some stiffs outside. You could shuffle through them if you like. They're not all that pretty some of them.'

As Hopkins was trying to make up his mind it was done for him. A lanky orderly came in. 'Blimey, corp,' he said. 'One of them stiffs is wearing knuckledusters. Never seen that before.'

In death Small's expression remained one of good-natured insolence. But his eyes were blank as if half of him had gone elsewhere.

Hopkins approached the body timidly. It was lying with others as if resting. The Italian sun streaked across the ground but Small was in the shade. Hopkins bent over him and touched his face. He could see no sign of any wound. He was suddenly engulfed with sorrow. 'Oh, Christ,' he muttered.

'Your mucker?' asked the medical orderly who emerged from the tent and walked along the lines of inert men.

'My butty,' muttered Hopkins without looking up. 'One of the best.'

'That's what they always say,' said the man, but not unkindly. 'Why is he wearing the knuckledusters?'

'To fight,' said Hopkins as if the orderly ought to know. 'The Germans.'

'He won't be needing them now. Why don't you take them? Like a keepsake. I've seen blokes take a watch from a dead man's wrist.'

Hopkins said: 'Yes, I will.'

'Want a hand?' asked the orderly. He seemed to think it might need an expert touch.

'All right,' said Hopkins. 'Thanks.'

'Right you are.' The orderly bent and slid the lead-and-leather band from Small's dead hand. 'Heavy,' he said weighing them in his own. 'Wouldn't like to get a swipe with those.'

Dumbly Hopkins held out his hand and the man passed them to him. He glanced at Small once more. 'What happens to him now?'

The soldier looked surprised. 'Well, he's . . . like buried. A medico comes and gives them the once-over and then they take them off and bury them.'

'Here?'

'Just for the time being. Later they'll take him home, if his people want. Otherwise he'll be buried here. Like a lot of others.'

Conscious of the weight of the knuckledusters, which he placed with care in his trouser pocket, Hopkins mumbled: 'Thanks. Look after him, will you.'

'We do our best,' said the man.

Hopkins went back into the tent and, not looking towards the wounded men, and trying to cut out their sounds, he almost stumbled into the bleak sunshine and took the ragged road back towards the beach. A military car drew up alongside after he had walked only a few sad yards. A woman's voice said: 'Want a lift, soldier?'

It was her. Kate.

'How in Christ's name did you know where I was?' he asked. They sat in the rough front seat of the vehicle. The windscreen was layered with dust.

'Thank God I did,' she said. 'Dotty, you remember my friend, she's still at Movement Control, told me you'd come up here. It takes a little while but not all that long if you want to find somebody. Thank God you're safe, Hopkins.' She studied his face. 'It was terrible, was it?' She leaned and kissed him on his sweat-run cheek.

'I've just been to see the body of Small,' he muttered. 'My mate. Got killed after the landing. You remember Small?'

'I think I do,' she said. 'Terrible, terrible. What about Delmi? I remember Delmi.'

'God only knows,' he said. 'He wasn't back there.' He nodded back towards the hospital. 'I just hope. There's nothing else I can do.'

'And you are here,' she said solemnly. 'Thank God.'

Slowly, almost woodenly, he turned and kissed her on the cheek in return. It was brown and clean. Her eyes took him in. 'I'm serious about you, Hopkins,' she said simply.

'And I am about you,' he said. He found he was weeping.

'It's just this whole bloody business. You can't believe how terrible it is, not until you find out. And I can't believe how you just found me, just like that. In this whole mess. What are you doing?'

'They've shifted me over from Movement Control now and I'm driving this for a lieutenant-colonel. But I've still got Dotty and my other friends there. I'm so sorry about your pal. I bet it was frightening.'

'I was scared silly and I didn't even get ashore. The men on the bridge of the landing craft were all knocked out, five of them in a minute, and I was the only bloke who knew how to steer a boat. So that's what I did. I managed to get it to the beach and saw them all charge off. I felt bloody ashamed, I can tell you.'

His tears had not stopped. She held his roughened head.

'There's no need to be ashamed. You do whatever comes up in this war. Sometimes you're lucky, sometimes not.'

'You've been promoted,' he sniffled touching her arm just below some sergeant's stripes.

She dried his eyes with a clean khaki handkerchief and said: 'There. I can drive and I look like a nice girl,' she said. 'So I'm chauffeur to Lieutenant-Colonel Irvine, Scots Guards.'

'And it's all right, you can just come up here, like that?'

'This is the only road open and Movement Control thought you might be here. I've had to bring him in this direction anyway, to Terni, and then we're going on somewhere inland, into Umbria.'

He put his tired arm across her and, silent for a moment, they each looked through the dust-grimed windscreen. 'Where is it going to end?' mumbled Hopkins. 'All this crap and thinking about being safe and able to live.'

Kate said: 'They reckon it will be over by Christmas.'

'They've said that about every Christmas since it started. Here it is.'

She stopped the jeep and he leaned towards her again to kiss her cheek, then stopped and looked about them. 'Insubordination,' he said. He managed a smile across his wet face.

She got out of the jeep and walked towards the landing craft with him. The parties tending the bodies had moved up the beach. Some soldiers looked over and because he was with a woman called from the next vessel, askew on the sand, but he merely waved at them. There was no sign of Doyle.

'We need an escort,' she said casually. 'My boss needs an escort.'

He did not realise what she was saying. 'All that's arranged, I expect,' he said.

'Not yet. Do you want the job? The colonel will say it's all right, I know. He's a decent man. And it's up to him. He could get you on detachment. You could come to Umbria with us.'

Hopkins stared at her as if she were taunting him. Then he said: 'Can your mates in this Movement Control place find out if Delmi is safe?'

Chapter Sixteen

Umbria is the silent heart of Italy. Green mountains stand like tents. Some have single white towers at their summits; there are rising woods and deeply incised valleys with white-foamed rivers, villages clustered in clearings and a few red hilltop towns. Today, in the square at Spoleto, is a stone bearing the names of the Italian partisans who died in 1944 fighting against their one-time allies, the Germans. Below it, children today eat ice creams.

Hopkins sat, Sten gun across his knees, in the rear of the jeep. He had never fired a Sten gun but he knew how it worked and was not going to tell anyone now. Kate sat upright in the driver's seat, a service revolver looking big and odd at her waist, and beside her the round figure of Lieutenant-Colonel Stanley Irvine who was already sweating although it was early.

Irvine had said they could have used another escort soldier. 'But the Italian partisans run this part of the country, now the Germans have moved north, most of them anyway, and we more or less have to fit in with what they say.' He half-turned and glanced at Hopkins over his shoulder. 'So you'll have to be two men at once, son.'

Hopkins said: 'Yes, sir. I'll try.'

'How strange that you two people have met before,' mused the colonel. 'Hundreds of thousands of troops about, the whole country in ruddy turmoil, and you just run across each other as if you were in a street in England.' He sighed reflectively. 'I wish I were in a street in England, don't you, Hopkins?'

'Yes, sir. Well, Wales, sir.'

'Yes, of course. Wales. These partisans are going to rendezvous with us at some place en route. We are heading initially for Assisi, where I'm told St Francis kept his animals. They'll drop in on us on the way and after that they'll guide us. Which means they'll be in charge. I hope they have a few bottles of Chianti left.'

It was not long before they realised how enclosed the land was around them. Peaks, round-topped, with trees dropping away like skirts, formed close about the curling road. They sometimes passed an isolated house, or two or three together, houses that seemed to be undamaged although unoccupied. 'Doesn't seem to have been a lot of heavy fighting hereabouts,' said Irvine.

'No room to manoeuvre, sir,' suggested Hopkins. He realised how helpless they would be if they were ambushed on the tight bends of the road. He surveyed both sides of the way; a whole army could be concealed there. They approached a feeble-looking bridge and he insisted on stopping and going forward to check it. 'Good chap, this,' said the colonel to Kate.

'I think so,' she said looking straight ahead.

'How come you know him?' asked the officer mischievously.

'Oh . . . well, sir, we met on the train to Aldershot when we were both joining up. Then we saw each other at a dance and we made a date to go to the pictures. But I didn't turn up.'

'Got cold feet, did you?'

'Posted, sir. On a driving course.'

'Amazing,' said Irvine carefully. 'You seem fated.'

They could see Hopkins crouching and moving below the bridge looking for explosives. He emerged on the other bank of the narrow river and walked across the bridge to them. 'Seems to be clear, sir,' he said. 'I think that you and the driver should get out and I'll take the car across the bridge. I can drive a bit.'

The colonel said: 'Get in, lad.'

Kate said: 'I'm in charge of the vehicle.'

She drove tentatively for a few yards, then made a dash for the bridge. Hopkins stopped her with his hand on her shoulder. 'Gently does it,' he suggested. She smiled and cut the speed. As they crossed the bridge they saw there were figures at the side of the road a few yards further on. A man with a wide-brimmed hat and a German sub-machine gun around his neck came to the centre of the road.

Hopkins slipped the Sten gun's safety catch off and the man heard it and told him in English to put it back. 'This morning no shooting,' he said putting up his hand.

The man was young and burned deeply by the sun. He had dark, violently crossed eyes and disarrayed teeth. He saluted the colonel as if swatting a mosquito from his brow. 'Good morning, officer,' he said. 'Good morning, soldiers, lady and gentleman. My name is Nico and I speak good English as you can almost tell.'

He climbed in the back beside Hopkins and sniffed at the Sten gun. 'Is this all they can give you to fight?' he asked. 'We have good guns. German, Russian and a bazooka we stole from Americans.'

'Do you want me to drive on, sir?' asked Kate a little frostily but directing the question to the colonel.

The colonel said: 'Better ask this bloke.'

'Sure, sure, drive.' Nico waved the machine gun like a hand. 'These people . . .' He pointed to the gathering in the next bend in the road. 'They are safe and okay. On our side. We will go to their village. I show you nearly the way.'

'Your English is interesting,' remarked the colonel.

'My father, he had a restaurant in London. A place called Finchley. But the British smashed the windows when we made one little mistake and went with the fat dog Mussolini into the war on the wrong side. They put the old man in some camp in England and he is still there for everything I know. But I lived in the restaurant, in Finchley, London until I was twelve. I wanted to play football for the team they call Queen's Park Rangers. They had nice shirts. But my mother came back to Italy before the start of the war and so I didn't play. After that my eyes went crazy, like they are. Here is the place now.'

Nico led them along a crooked pathway. The land rose deeply green to the blue sky on their left and dropped away into a crater on the right, tangled trees giving way to bulky rocks and then to the banks of a tumbling and almost hidden river. They could hear it gushing.

A straggle of people, some listlessly carrying flags, was awaiting them. An old woman carried a Russian flag but the hammer and sickle were upside down, and a small boy had a Stars and Stripes which, as he watched them approach, he draped across his head like a scarf. No one seemed over-glad to see them although an old man with a pitted face performed one or two hollow hand claps. He stopped when nobody joined in. They had seen so much in so little time.

Leading them on, with the colonel at the lead, Kate in the middle and Hopkins with his Sten gun behind, Nico, the cross-eyed Italian, vocally pushed people aside and marched through. The pitted old fellow showed an interest in the Sten gun Hopkins carried and put his hand out to touch it; then he sniffed it and finally spat on the ground.

Nico led them further along the path to where the land broadened. There was a wooden building. Part of the roof sagged and the door was held up with tree trunks. He led them in under the low roof. Some men, guns dangling about them, sat on a bench behind a table. There was some food – fruit, bread and a few eggs with cracked shells – but not much else apart from a couple of dusty bottles of wine.

'Don't eat their food,' warned Nico turning his fearsome eyes on them. 'They don't have much food. Wait and it will be better.'

He took them and introduced the gun-hung leaders casually, almost dismissively. They never heard their names properly. The straggling people had now congregated in the doorway, further cutting out the light. A huge man, fat falling around his body, lumbered up from the table. He slung his sub-machine gun across his stomach, the only place it seemed it might sit, and then uncomfortably, and motioned the British colonel to follow him. With apparent reluctance he pointed at the grimy wine bottles but the colonel shook his head and the fat man seemed relieved. '*Avanti*,' he said and staggered for the door.

There was a cart waiting outside now, a cart pulled by two donkeys. 'You must go with this thing,' said Nico apologetically. 'Sometimes the Tedeski watch from their planes and if they see a jeep they will see where it is going and we don't want them to know, do we?'

Straight-faced the colonel climbed onto the cart beside the driver, a boy no more than ten who looked unwaveringly ahead. Kate and Hopkins were directed towards the back and they climbed into the cart. There was smelly straw on the floor and a dog, who might have been more dead than asleep, in one corner unbothered by flies flitting around his mouth.

The fat leader shouted at the boy and the boy shouted at the donkeys. He flicked his whip and they moved off languidly, the leader walking alongside with Nico in deep discussion. The conversation turned into an argument which was still in progress when, fifteen minutes later, the donkeys climbed onto a firm stretch of bricklaid road and moved into the high shade of a wall. They were clear of any houses now but something was going on within the wall: there was a rattle of chains and a wrench of an iron door. 'This is the cemetery for the village,' Nico called up to them. 'It is the safest place.'

Kate whispered to Hopkins: 'I don't like cemeteries.'

Hopkins replied: 'I'm not all that keen myself.'

As if they knew this was as far as they were going the two

donkeys stopped and both shat on the path. Nico swore at them and then at the boy but neither took any notice. 'They do business outside the homes of the dead,' he grumbled.

He slung his gun on the other shoulder and courteously tried to help Kate to the ground. She did not need his hand and she jumped most of the way. Hopkins followed looking unhappily at the iron gate. Colonel Irvine stood beside them. 'Splendid place to hide,' he said mildly.

There were some men inside the gate examining them through the bars as they scraped it fully open. One who pushed his head into the opening as if to get a better view was as cross-eyed as Nico. 'My cousin called Tonio,' said Nico.

The party went into the cemetery. It was like a little town, tombs like miniature houses with figured roofs and windows, each with a decorated door. There were angels in the small plots of land in front of each tomb and neatly kept pathways. Against the far wall was a large vault and the door was invitingly opened. 'My family,' explained Nico. 'For three months I have been living with my grandmother.'

The colonel and Hopkins both glanced at Kate but she followed Nico between the people and into the dry-smelling vault. The village people pressed curiously but cautiously after them. Some of the women began to point out coffins that were lying on slabs against the walls. Nico turned and pushed them out as they muttered protests. He said something stern to them and they finally backed away. 'This is my family,' he said again to Kate.

She was looking at the coffins around the wall. Hopkins followed her looks. The colonel said: 'Very cosy.'

One coffin had slipped from its slab and was lying awry, its lid slid away. Through the aperture stared a skeletal face wearing a toothy grin. 'My Uncle Sandro,' introduced Nico. 'He was the barber in the village. Always smiling, just like now.' He took a moment to return the dead smile. 'I worked in his shop.

Sweeping up the hairs, you know. But I could not be a foot-baller, like I told you, and I could not be a barber. You cannot have a cross-eyed barber.'

There was a disturbance from the doorway and two men, hung with firearms and with fierce expressions, came into the vault. One took off his hat. 'They have come,' said Nico moving away. He touched the colonel's arm and said: 'Please, officer, sir. These men have come to speak to you.'

Hopkins moved forward with the officer but Nico said: 'Stay here for just now.' He eyed a warning at Kate. They stood and watched. The discussion was not protracted, a map was produced, and there were more exchanges.

Eventually Colonel Irvine turned back towards Kate and Hopkins. 'I have to go on by myself,' he shrugged. 'They are all right, these people, trustworthy I hope, and they've got enough weapons to look after me.'

'We should come, sir,' said Hopkins strongly. 'My orders are to escort you.'

Kate said: 'And mine are to drive you.'

Irvine patted each of them like a father. 'Don't worry. They'll look after me. I've got to contact a partisan group behind what is at this moment German territory, if anyone can find out where that is. But this lot are on our side and they hate the Jerry. You two wait for me to come back. I should only be a few days.' He smiled firmly at them. 'That's your orders.'

The colonel turned and they exchanged salutes, watched with new approval by the Italians who then began exchanging salutes between themselves. Hopkins looked anxious and Kate held his arm. 'I still don't like him going,' said Hopkins. 'I'm supposed to be his bodyguard.'

'It's orders,' said Kate. 'And they came from him.'

Nico was watching them. Irvine, with three men festooned with guns and grenades, was sitting in the back of the jeep.

He turned and waved with reassuring casualness towards them. Nico walked to Kate and Hopkins. 'It's okay,' he said. 'Your officer will be safe with these men. The Teds will not get him.'

Kate said in a low voice: 'It's not the Tedeski I'm worried about. It's the present company.'

'Me as well,' said Hopkins. He turned to Nico: 'Do you know where they are heading?'

'Heading? Like in football?'

'Going,' said Hopkins. 'Where are they taking our officer?'

Nico shrugged. 'Some place, I don't know. After Assisi, some place.' He indicated vaguely. 'After . . . well, behind . . . that's right . . . behind the Teds . . . they don't tell me. Me, I am just a soldier. I am the one who has been hiding with my dead grandmother.'

Hopkins said: 'What do we do?'

'We're not going to live with anybody's dead grandmother,' said Kate seriously.

Nico laughed showing his spread teeth below his crossed eyes. 'No, no. Anyway we will all move from there soon. The Teds are gone from here and they'll come back and bomb the tombstones. We think they know now where we live.'

'And us?'

Nico said: 'I must take you to a place. A safe place. It is very nice. They even keep some animals there. From the circus.'

Very little surprised them now. When Nico turned they obediently followed him back to the cart. There was only one donkey now and the boy who drove it was bending forward, asleep almost between the donkey's ears. It was noon and very hot. Nico shouted at the boy who awoke at once and shouted at the donkey. 'We will ride like this,' said Nico.

They climbed into the cart and the boy flicked the donkey's backside with his stick. The donkey snorted and moved forward. 'How far is it?' asked Kate.

'It is up and down, like most of this country. About twenty

to forty minutes, according to the donkey. Then a walk for a kilometre down to the place.'

'What is there?' asked Hopkins firmly. He was still suspicious of Nico. 'What is this place?'

Nico half-turned. 'Don't shoot me yet, Mister soldier,' he said eyeing Hopkins. 'It is a house. Everything will be good.'

'It had better be,' said Hopkins to Kate.

'The colonel didn't seem to be worried,' she said. 'So we'll have to wait and see what is going to happen. Perhaps we can feed the circus animals.'

Nico understood. 'They have been taken there because of all the noise and the fighting in places. Sometime they have been in Assisi – at the saint's festival. San Francisco of the animals. But at this house it is quiet and they are not frightened by the guns. They have been there for a few months. Even the Tedeski did not shoot them, only sometimes to eat. They used to go and feed them when they had something.'

The road had narrowed to a track scarcely wide enough to take the cart but the donkey knew where it was going. Kate closed her eyes when she saw the green drop on her side of the vehicle. Hopkins saw and touched her elbow and made her change places. On the other side the scrub and bushes rose like a wall, the caps of hills bent against the sky. There was a round white tower on one. They could hear a river grunting its way far below.

There were no habitations, no people, no domestic animals, and no birds sounded. 'I've never been in a place without birds,' said Kate.

'All gone,' said Nico half-turning again. 'Shoot and eat or just fly away. Don't blame them.'

They travelled for more than half an hour, the boy nodding in time with the donkey. They came to a farm but there were no people or animals. The roof of the farmhouse had been blown open like the lid of a tin. A dog which was lying fearfully in a pile of dung lifted itself and came pitifully towards them. From the cart they could not see that it was stumbling along with them.

Abruptly the track widened and the donkey stopped. The boy said something and Nico announced: 'We are here now. Now we must go on our legs.'

Hopkins left the cart and helped Kate down. She smiled at him as if he had done something out of context. The dog cowered behind the truck, trying to hide from them. Nico shouted to the boy and he turned the cart around in the widened space but not without difficulty, shouting and beating the donkey as it did its best. 'Cruel little bastard,' said Hopkins.

'Yeah,' said Nico uncaringly. 'No tip for him.'

The boy urged the donkey back the way they had come. The dog remained pathetically by the roadside. 'Looks like we've got a dog,' said Kate.

Nico asked: 'You want me to shoot him? I could shoot him now.'

'No, don't,' said Hopkins hurriedly. 'We'll take him.'

Nico looked bemused and shrugged. 'English.'

'Welsh,' corrected Hopkins.

They had walked a few yards through the scrubby trees into a high clearing and suddenly, wonderfully, the valley opened out before them, far down, flat and green with a river curling and the house sitting lovely and white in the midday sun.

'La Serena,' said Nico.

As they descended the ragged path the valley appeared to change shape, opening and elongating before them. It seemed green and cool in the heat of the day, the river rippled around its curves, the trees stood like gathered shadows. And at the centre the white calmness of the spreading house seemed to call to them.

An old man with two donkeys abruptly appeared around a bend in the path, his head bent like those of the animals. As they approached Nico muttered something to him and the man grunted: 'What the fuck.'

The way was narrow and they moved aside to allow him to pass. He did so without raising his eyes and the donkeys did likewise. Nico said: 'His name is Albinetto. He only says in English: "What the fuck." That is all he learned from the Americans.'

As if to confirm it Albinetto muttered from behind them as he and the animals moved up the track: 'What the fuck.'

They reached the flat of the valley and took a worn path towards the house. Now they could see it had a wide veranda skirting its exterior on three sides. The dog that had followed them seemed to recognise it and for the first time limped ahead. Another dog came from the wooden shadows and moved towards it amiably.

'How long will we stay here?' asked Kate still studying the nearing house. Some of the roof had fallen at one end and the covering of the veranda was missing in some places letting in bars of sunlight. They could see furniture now, almost merged with the interior. A woman in a clean flowered apron came out. She waved what seemed to be a large spoon, like a greeting.

'Signora Eleonora of La Serena,' said Nico. 'She has always been here.'

'How long are we staying?' repeated Kate.

This time Nico answered: 'As long as you must stay. They will tell us. They will come for you.'

Kate said to Hopkins: 'It's amazing. It's so peaceful. You wouldn't know there was any war.'

'I think it might be a nice place to be,' suggested Hopkins.

'For as long as possible.' She smiled at him. 'Maybe we could desert and stay here for ever.'

There was a deep afternoon smell about the place, warm and loaded with wood scents.

They were sitting at a rough, round table on the veranda,

drinking almost clear white wine. Hopkins could hardly believe where he was. 'Last week I'm getting shot at and I'm scared out of my trucks and now I'm sitting here like this.'

Signora Eleonora came from the dim interior and said something in Italian to Nico who interpreted cautiously: 'There is some difficulty. There are two bedrooms but one is very noisy because of the doves. They are in the roof and they make big love in the early morning and sometimes in the night. There is another room below, but there is a pig there!'

He turned and questioned the Signora. 'She says the Germans never found this pig. When they came to the house they hid the pig and, because he knew the Germans would take him, he make no noise. He is a brainy pig.'

Kate smiled at the lady. 'We will stay in the one room,' she said. The Signora smiled faintly but sincerely and said something more to Nico. Nico said she was glad because she did not want to upset the doves.

Hopkins said: 'What about these circus animals you told us about? Who looks after them, feeds them and that?'

'There are not so many now,' said Nico. He repeated the answer to the Signora and she shrugged and told him.

Nico said: 'The Tedeski ate the giraffe.'

They stared.

'They came and shot the giraffe which was not good because they cannot shoot straight and the head was . . . you know . . . swinging. But when they did they cooked it in small pieces.'

Again he questioned the Signora. 'It fed about fifty men. They had to eat it quick because it would be rotten. They gave some to the Signora and she said it tasted okay for a giraffe. The camel was next but they had to get out quick and so it is still here. You must see them. They like people to come and see.'

He finished his wine and stood. 'I must go.'

Hopkins regarded him anxiously. 'You're leaving us?'

'My auntie lives near. I will be back. You will be okay here looking after each other in the room. If the Germans are coming I will hear. In some days from now your officer maybe will come back. I don't know. They don't tell me nothing.'

He made to walk away but turned back. 'They have a special eating here in Umbria,' he said. 'Tonight it is for you. It is pig's foot.' He hung out his hand to illustrate. 'It is the special thing of the region. Very good. When the pig lies down you will notice he puts his foot underneath him and then falls down. The other three of his feet get strong . . . you know muscles . . . but this one foot, the same every time, it keeps sweet. It must be kept a long time – marinated it is called. Then it is very nice to eat. They have some.'

He shook hands with them a second time, bowed towards Signora Eleonora, and then walked from the place. This time he left.

Kate and Hopkins lay dozing and naked, almost entwined, in the old and ornate bed. Signora Eleonora had showed it to them with pride. It had belonged to her grandmother who was known as the most beautiful woman in Umbria seventy years before the war.

What was left of the afternoon sun slipped between the slanted shutters of the window and lay quietly across their skins. It was a cool, wooden room. When they stirred they could hear the pig groaning in the room below.

They sweated gently against each other. She was so much softer without her uniform. Hopkins put the palms of his hands across her backside and began to gently smack her. 'You've got broad hands, Hopkins,' she said still sleepily. 'One of them could just about cover my bum.'

'Fishing,' he said. 'You get broad hands on the boats.'

'Will you go back to it?'

'Not if I can help it,' he answered. 'I can't see you taking to that sort of life.'

190

'Is this a proposal?' she asked. 'Odd way of putting it. Talking about fish.'

'I don't want you to go away,' he said. 'I'd like us to be together.'

She moved more closely to him. 'Let's get together now. Would you like that? We're both rested.'

There was no need for her to ask. They rolled together, her breasts lying on his chest, the nipples against his ribs. His hands were still behind her and, with care, he eased her above him and kissed her face. She pulled herself clear for a moment, then opened her legs and eased him into her.

'I believe I killed a man once,' she mentioned when they were lying quietly again. The sun was almost gone, reduced to the weakness of a candle through the window blinds. He opened his eyes without hurry.

'I've never met anyone like you,' he said frankly. 'How did you kill him?'

She giggled and pushed her nose against his cooling cheek. 'Not like you think,' she replied. 'Not in this sort of situation. But I did kill him. I'm sure I did.'

'How?'

'I shoved him in the river, in the Thames, at Marlow,' she said. 'He was a Yank.'

Now he knew she was serious. He half-sat up and said: 'Christ.'

'I'm pretty sure he drowned. He was drunk and he was trying it on with me. A bit too heavy. I was pushing my bike along the towpath and he started to play up. He took his willie out so I gave him a push. He was off-balance and splosh, he went, into the water. He came up briefly but then he went down again and I never saw him again.'

'Have you told anybody else?'

'My mother, she knows. But you're the first otherwise. The funny thing is nobody has ever said anything. It was just before the D-Day invasion and lots of things were being kept under wraps, and he *was* a Yank. It was never mentioned in the local paper and the police didn't come around or anything.'

Hopkins eased himself up on his elbows. He was grinning. 'You're the limit, darling,' he said.

'I'm sorry now,' Kate said seriously. 'I've often thought about what happened. You won't tell on me, will you?'

He kissed her softly. 'Never.'

'I feel like a drink,' she said. 'What with making love in the afternoon. Let's have a shower together.'

Hopkins rolled from the bed. The sheets were embroidered at the edges. He went to a thin wooden door at the end of the room. 'There's not much room for two,' he observed.

'We'll squeeze in. Without any clothes I don't take up much room.' She slid from the sheets and padded across the floor to him. Inside the rough room was a big iron bath half-filled with water. Kate put her hand into it. 'Cold but clean,' she said. There was a large tin can with holes punched in it. 'You stand there and get somebody to pour the water over you with this.'

'An American jerry-can,' he said picking up the container. 'Who's going first?'

Carefully he lifted the can and just as carefully let the water cascade down her body. 'It's cold,' she whispered. 'But good. It feels very good.'

They came together again standing in the wooden room, her legs clutching him, his hands like the seat on a swing enclosing her backside. The room rattled as they moved and downstairs the pig grunted heavily, disturbed by the commotion.

'By God, Hopkins,' she said as they lay afterwards on the wide bed, their legs entwined, his face in her fair hair. 'I'm in love.'

Hopkins said: 'I am too. I'm not surprised.'

'Let's run away, as I said. Desert.'

'They'd find us. We're soldiers.'

She said thoughtfully: 'And lovers.'

He repeated: 'Soldiers and lovers.'

Chapter Seventeen

Signora Eleonora rang a tinny little bell, waking them in the early evening. They poured another jerry-can of water over themselves, dried on the threadbare towel and went downstairs. Nico was standing on the veranda in the late light. 'The Teds have been thrown out of Florence,' he announced as if he had done it himself. 'Soon the war will be over.'

Signora Eleonora poked her head from the room and asked him a question. He replied in Italian and she shook her head. 'The Signora says that soon the rains will come. We will have to wait for the end of the war until the rain stops. Nobody in the north of Italy will be able to move because of the mud.'

There were three glasses of opaque wine on the round table. Nico made sure the table was balanced and they sat down. 'Tonight,' he said, 'for you to eat there is *culatello*. It is a great honour. If you do not like it, please pretend you do.'

He said he had to run an errand for his auntie and he sauntered away in the dusk, his sub-machine gun slung carelessly.

The Signora came back to the veranda and crooked an old finger towards Kate, saying: '*Signorina.*'

Kate followed her into the room and returned in a few moments with a pleased expression and holding a beautiful long white linen dress against her.

'It belonged to the Signora when she was a young woman,' she said. 'She wants me to wear it when we are here. I am going to put it on.'

Hopkins waited. She was not long. She returned, framed in the door, wearing the slim dress. Taking two steps onto the veranda she turned around gracefully. The Signora followed her beaming. '*Bella*,' she murmured. She touched the embroidered sleeves tenderly.

'It feels so wonderful,' said Kate making another turn. 'And after that uniform. Thank you, Signora Eleonora,' she said. She kissed the Italian lady on the cheek.

'It does look lovely,' said Hopkins as Kate sat beside him. 'Like a wedding dress.'

'It's only on loan,' smiled Kate. 'While we are here.'

They sat with their wine glasses but now in silence, a silence brought on by their strange and temporary situation and the fact that they were still, in many ways, virtual strangers.

'The trouble with us,' said Kate eventually, 'is the same trouble as people who have romances like this always have.'

'What's that?'

'We don't know each other. We have no history. I mean, we *could* run out of conversation.'

Hopkins smiled. 'I can't see you running out of conversation, Kate. And I can just grunt if I can't think of anything to say.'

Slowly he put Small's knuckledusters on the table. 'I saw you had that,' said Kate. 'It doesn't look nice.'

'For punching people in the teeth,' said Hopkins. 'It was my pal Small's. He had it when I found him with the other killed blokes.' Pensively he picked them up. 'He had them since he was a kid, I expect. He came from a tough family in a tough part of London. His father used to loot bombed houses, so he told me. Sometimes before they were bombed.'

Kate touched one of the lead knuckles with her fingertip. 'Didn't do poor Small much good, did it?'

'He thought they might. Like a good-luck charm. He came out of prison to go in the army. He should have stayed inside.'

They drank reflectively. 'You didn't have much of a time as a kid, did you?'

Hopkins said: 'It wasn't that lucky. My old man was drowned in the Bristol Channel and my mother went a year after. I was about nine. They weren't much of a family and nobody wanted to take me. So I ended up in this home, orphanage. But I survived. Then, when I was fourteen, just about to leave school and, more to the point, old enough to go to work, my uncle got me out of the place and before long I was working on the fishing boats and bringing them home a wage.'

'And they were unkind to you.'

'They didn't care about me or me about them in the end. She got to be completely batty . . .' He screwed his finger against his forehead. 'And he didn't give a damnation about anything.'

From the room came a deep grunt. 'The pig,' grinned Kate. 'They've brought the pig to see us.'

Signora Eleonora was with Albinetto, the old man they had seen before. 'What the fuck,' he said. He pointed to the pig and then poked it on the snout and the animal at once collapsed its rear right leg and rolled into a lying posture. The man gabbled in Italian and the Signora joined in. Nico appeared on the step. 'Ah, it is *culatello*,' he said. 'He is telling you about it.'

Albinetto explained as if they understood him perfectly. Nico interrupted: 'This leg, trotter you call it, you will eat tonight, for more than one year it is saved . . . kept . . . as they say marinated,' said Nico. 'It is from another pig, of course, you understand. This pig you see still lives. It is not his time yet. They keep him for after the war. When it is ready it is tender as cream. It is the special thing of Umbria. Tonight, in the honour of you, they are serving you this trotter on your plate.' He regarded them warningly: 'You must like it.'

He became pensive. 'In Umbria,' he said, 'we say that each

time you sit at the table you eat twice. Once the food, then the talking about it.'

The next morning they went around the back of the house to the compound where the circus animals were kept. There were only a few left, so listless, so fatigued it seemed that they did not even attempt to escape although the wooden fence of the compound was flimsy. 'Perhaps they think it's safer where they are,' said Kate.

Two of the circus horses had escaped, Signora Eleonora told them in her sign language, and could sometimes be seen running wild in the hills. But the other animals were dispirited and sad. There was a camel, its eyes almost closed, which chewed on any single piece of straw it could find. Its coat was ragged, bare in places, and its hooves curled like eastern slippers. Once it had suffered agonies of toothache, the Signora succeeded in explaining, but the tooth had fallen out. There were three dusty dogs which lay in the shade with, they saw, the dog that had joined them when they journeyed to La Serena. They lay with lassitude and did not bother to scatter the flies around them. There were also three goats that seemed the most active although they stared through the weak fence as if it were impenetrable.

Signora Eleonora explained that the circus had contained many more animals, had once toured the towns of middle Italy and had taken part in the St Francis Carnival of Animals at Assisi. When the fighting had been going on the owners had trooped them from place to place, always moving just ahead of the war, although all the monkeys had been killed by a solitary unlucky hit from a bomb.

In the compound was a wrecked vehicle, a van, rusting in the sun, with faded painted scenes on its sides. The engine had been taken out and so had the seats at the front. Kate and Hopkins walked around it. On the far side they found the complete skeleton of the giraffe which the Germans had shot and cooked and eaten.

It was laid out on the dusty ground like an exhibit, every bone in place from the dog-nosed skull, down the long neck, to the narrow, gentle shoulders, and the slender legs.

'My God,' said Kate as they slowly walked the length of it. 'Have you ever seen anything so terrible as this?'

'They must have boiled the bones after they'd eaten it and laid them out like this,' said Hopkins. 'It's a bloody shame, isn't it?'

'Everything is,' Kate said. She began to cry. It was the first time he had seen her cry.

The river curled three times as if performing a dance in front of the peaceful house. Hopkins found some tangled fishing tackle in the hall and spent a patient hour unravelling it. 'Never done this sort of fishing,' he told Kate as they walked on the brown path to the river bank. 'One at a time, like. Always by the thousand, by the netful.'

Kate sat beside him on the bank in the shade of the last of the cypresses. He let the line loop aimlessly into the unhurried current and watched the float make a modest dance. She lay close against him, her eyes almost closed.

'We could stay here for ever,' she said quietly. 'Damn the war and the army.'

'Desert,' he said. 'Go AWOL.'

'AWOL doesn't sound very romantic,' she said turning her face into his shoulder. They had abandoned their uniforms. He was dressed in a rough shirt and sagging trousers the Signora had given him. Kate kept the white linen dress for the evening, and had found a girl's smock, blue with red hems, and she wore it easily. She had bare feet. Hopkins still wore his army boots.

'We could though, couldn't we?' she pursued half-seriously. 'Just simply hide. No one would find us in a country like this.

We could come out when all was quiet, when this wretched war was finished.'

'It's gone on so bloody long that most people have forgotten what it's for. I have, for one.'

'This afternoon,' she agreed. 'It seems a long way away. Everything does.'

They saw Nico coming from the house. He came towards them along the bank of the river. 'Something's up,' said Hopkins. 'He's had a wash.'

But Nico said: 'No news. Your officer has not come.' He studied the pair. 'Maybe they have lost you.'

Kate said: 'That's what we were hoping.'

The Italian shook his head. His eyes, for a moment, seemed to come into alignment. 'They will come,' he said. 'Nobody forgets. The fighting is going further away, the Germans are falling back, right back into the arms of the Russians and the Americans. In the shit they will be.'

'Then everybody can go home and begin again,' said Kate.

'Maybe. But some will be not alive, lady. Some men from here. The Teds bombed the cemetery where we were at two days gone.' He curved his hand like a plane. 'Boom, boom, boom.' We had four men killed and all the dead of the village were thrown up. It was a bad sight. My granny was there.'

He studied the far bank of the river. 'It was this place, just here, that my friends caught twenty Teds. Some fishing, like you are, soldier. Some swimming.'

Hopkins asked: 'And your friends? What did they do?'

'Wiped 'em out,' said Nico emphatically. 'Every one. Killed them. Bang, bang, bang. Machine guns. They had no chance. This river was like blood.'

'And what happened after that?'

Nico sighed. 'The Germans sent a big lot of soldiers, storm troopers eh? They took all the men in the village . . .' He pointed. 'Three kilometres that way. All the men and shot them against the church. There are no men there now. Only women and *bambini*.'

They remained in La Serena four more sunlit days. The Signora shyly brought a scratched old visitors' book for them to sign. Around them the countryside, even the trees on the hills, seemed scarcely to stir. Far off they could see an isolated white tower in the green mountains, against the heavy blue sky. A deep, peaceful happiness was with them.

Chapter Eighteen

Now the seasons had begun to change; one morning there was mist among the trees and although the sun was still strong, rain moved in the mountains. The Signora said it was the coming of the autumn. She made up-and-down sweeping movements with her hands and swashing sounds. Then she plodded her feet as though moving through mud.

'Do you think they really could have forgotten all about us?' asked Kate lying against him in the early light. 'I mean, really. It happens easily in a war, doesn't it? The old colonel goes off and nobody ever knows what's happened to him and we're just left here, overlooked.' She moved her breasts up his ribs. 'It could happen.'

Hopkins, half-awake, aware of the luxury of her skin, said: 'Could be. But I don't think so. You can have only so much luck.'

'All right then,' she said attempting to sound decisive. 'Then we'll do what we said – we'll desert. We'll just disappear and they'll never find us, them and their bloody war.'

He eased himself into a sitting position against the pillows. As if responding to the movement she wriggled and with grace slid from the bed to sit astride the chamber pot on the floor. 'I'll try to be quiet,' she promised.

He sighed. 'I don't mind if you're noisy.' He regarded her pleasurably as she crouched. 'But I'm sorry to say their war will have to come first.'

Kate rose from the pot without looking towards him. She

climbed back into the bed. Hopkins kissed her gently and she slid down his body. Their lovemaking was easy now, unhurried, sometimes even without passion. 'It will be like this one day,' he said. 'When we've got plenty of time.'

'God, I hope so,' she whispered. 'If nothing goes wrong before then.'

At ten thirty in the morning they saw Nico loping towards the house, his sub-machine gun bounding across his chest. 'Now, we go!' he called. They were in the shade of the terrace. Hopkins felt his heart drop. Kate looked at him. 'Too late to run now,' she said.

Nico was excited. 'They came back. Your boss, the officer, is okay. We will meet them.' He pointed vaguely out of the valley. 'We must be going now.'

He had parked the jeep under a rough roof at the side of the house. He went towards it, his step animated as if he were glad to have a task. Kate rose slowly and embraced Hopkins. He held her gently and kissed her hair. 'Whatever happens now,' she said, 'it has been so wonderful here.'

'Yes,' he said solemnly. 'And whatever happens to us after this, we'll always find each other.'

'And love each other,' she answered. 'Promise?'

'Promise,' he said.

They heard the jeep's engine cough and start and they turned in to the house. The Signora was standing in the shadows, knowing they were going. She looked sad also. 'Everything is paid,' she said. 'Nothing to pay now.'

Albinetto emerged from the back of the house. He was wearing a strange velvet cloak. Looking at the sky he gave a small shiver. He shook hands with them. 'What the fuck,' he said.

They went to their room and lay for a few seconds together on the light sheets of the bed, silent and deeply thoughtful. Kate was crying and without a word she went to the door first.

He heard her shoes going down the wooden stairs. His Sten gun was in pieces and he took a few moments to click it together. He looked briefly around the room where they had been so happy and with a grunt made for the stairs also.

The Signora was standing away from the sunlight, as she always did, and they shook hands with old-fashioned formality. Kate had washed the white dress and now handed it back. 'Thank you. It was lovely,' she said. Kate and then Hopkins gently kissed her on the cheek. She smiled with real pleasure and murmured: '*Bellissima.*'

Hopkins went back inside the house to pick up the Sten gun which he had been cleaning. When he reached the veranda Kate was two hundred yards ahead, behind Nico and walking in the sharp sun towards the jeep. Hopkins called: 'I'm coming, Kate.' Then the dogs began to bark and the old camel in the compound put its head above the broken stockade and humphed loudly.

It was a moment before he realised why. A spread shadow abruptly flitted over the brown grass in the distance, at the far end of the valley. He saw the plane itself a second later and shouted. Nico and Kate had seen it too and the Italian was trying to pull her aside, away from the jeep.

With a huge roar the German aircraft came up the valley, its machine guns sparking, bright in the sun. Then it dropped a precise line of little bombs, each one exploding as if sprouting from the ground. Hopkins halted in horror as one bomb exploded in front of the jeep and the next hit it squarely. There was a shattering detonation and a bulb of flame. Impotently he raised his Sten gun. Another second and the plane was spread over him and horrified he saw the next bomb bouncing unerringly his way. There was a great explosion, which he only half-heard, and an orange, burning sheet of fire which flew around him. He threw up his hands against his face and then knew nothing. Nothing.

Chapter Nineteen

It was snowing. Opposite his bed was a tall bare window, ceiling to floor, and it framed the thickly falling snowflakes. Hopkins moved carefully. He realised he was fixed in various parts of his body. Both arms were encased in plaster of Paris and his face felt stiff and unwashed. He had a thick beard. But he found he could move his eyes enough to discover that he was in a long, large room, with white figures moving silently around. It was either a hospital ward or he was dead and in heaven.

He had been half-conscious before, and he remembered the shadows of moving figures and being in some sort of vehicle rolling roughly through a cold country, but he had drifted away again, gratefully into the unknown. And for a long time.

Now he realised this was something different. He was awake. Where he was he had no idea. A man in a white smock smeared with bloodstains appeared at the bottom of his bed, smiling unsurely, putting his head forward a little, like a chicken, to make sure Hopkins was seeing him. He seemed pleased when Hopkins came out with some words: 'Where is this place?'

The bloodstained man said: 'Vienna.'

He seemed anxious to withhold any further information and he hurried away and returned quickly with another man in a cleaner smock. 'At least you have come back,' said the man. His accent was heavy but he was apparently pleased with his English. 'My name is Varisilov. Do you know your name?'

'Hopkins,' said Hopkins. 'I think.'

Varisilov clapped his hands lightly like someone who has won an unexpected prize. 'That is very good. It was Hopkins or it was Small.' He regarded the British man questioningly. 'But it is not Small? You had some things like lead fingers, with the name Small.'

'No, Small was my pal. He was killed. I don't remember anything after that.'

'It was some time gone,' said Varisilov. He sat on the edge of the bed. The man with the bloody smock went away as if he had done enough. 'Months.' He smiled again. 'I speak good English, yes?'

'Yes, very good. Where is this place?'

'It is Vienna. The Russians have taken Vienna. The war will be over soon, in a few weeks. This is a Russian hospital. You are the only Englishman here.'

'I am Welsh,' said Hopkins.

'Ah, Welsh is different. I understand. You have bad wounds. Every part. We thought you were dead.'

'So did I. I don't remember anything about it. Small being killed was the last thing.'

The Russian produced Small's knuckledusters from the pocket of his smock. 'These were his,' he said. 'Do you remember that? They are for boxing, I think.' He fitted the knuckledusters over the fingers of his right hand and threw an imaginary punch. Then he handed them to Hopkins. 'You see, his name is on them. Each one has a letter – S–M–A–L–L. Like so.'

Hopkins took the knuckledusters. 'I remember that much. He was dead. He was still wearing these. He wanted to fight the Germans with these.'

Varisilov smiled grimly. 'It would not be good against a Tiger tank.' A nurse, a square-jawed woman, came and handed the Russian a clipboard of papers. He sniffed as he read. 'You were carried to Milano by some of these crazy Italian partisans. You were not much alive, mister. You were brought here to Vienna and you have been here, in this hospital, for three months nearly. A lot of people die here, mister, but you came out lucky. What do you remember now?'

'Things before we landed on the beach at wherever it was. I was driving the landing craft because everyone on the bridge was killed. Then I found Small and he was dead. And there were the others, Delmi, Rabbit and the rest. Delmi, I knew him years, even at school. After that nothing. How did you know I was called Hopkins?'

'You had identification discs – the dog-tags as the Yanks say – but it seems that nobody was sure they were yours. They were not around your neck. A lot of men have been dying.'

'Will I be here for much longer?'

'Now you have woken it is good. But you still have injuries and they will have to be fixed. It will take some more time. So be glad you are alive.' He rose from the bedside and tapped his head. 'And try to remember some more.'

Even when they allowed him to sit he could not see the full extent of the long ward. From his bed it stretched bleak and high to what seemed a great distance, the tall windows, clogged with snow, continuing down the wall in front of him. The walls were cold stone.

There were four ranks of beds, two down the walls and two back-to-back in the middle of the room. At a rough count, because he could not see all of them, he thought there were about a hundred. From above glared temporary lights that had been fixed, their wires looping around the spaced rafters.

At the very centre of the huge room, in an area clear of beds, was an iron stove that burned almost red hot. There were some benches, curiously ornate as though they had been taken from some park, arranged at a distance around it. Here patients wearing nightshirts and filthy pyjamas and other bits of clothing, sat and mostly stared into the heat coming from the stove. On the floor before them was an upright radio set, its wires trailing over the floor, which played interminable American jazz and dance music. Nobody listened to the music and there was little talking. The men only stared in silence at the stove.

At night there were groans and nightmare screams. Patients would get from their beds and walk about like distracted ghosts. The nursing staff, mostly blank-faced and slow, did their basic duties but their condition seemed not far removed from that of the patients'. Hopkins wanted to get out.

Apart from the incessant dance music there were few distractions other than the early-morning collection of urine from the many bedpans. The resigned men who did this task ran wagers on who had provided most urine in one swoop. They bet whatever money they had and the contents of the bedpans were poured out and solicitously measured. It seemed to give them an interest.

Hopkins discovered that there was an American at the far end of the ward, a young, small black man who always had a group of other patients standing at the foot of his bed. 'They just come to look – see,' he said to Hopkins who had reached him by using the beds like stepping stones, sitting at the foot of each one and moving to the next. 'They ain't never seen a man with black skin before. They're just hicks, Russian hicks and that sort of hick, and they come from asshole places where they've never seen a guy like me. And they don't have movie houses so they never see them on the movies either. The bastards just come and stare. It's like I'm in Barnum and Bailey.'

He eased his left leg from the ragged blankets. The foot was missing. 'Shot clean off,' he said with a sort of pride. 'And I was a fuckin' cook.' Despite his youth all his hair had fallen out so that his teeth shone with excessive brilliance from his small head. His eyes shone too. 'I kid these guys, these Ruski hicks, that all black people have a foot missing. And they believe me. They really do. I tell them the white folks cut off the feet to stop the slaves running away. There's one guy who kinda translates. Where do you come from? You a Limey?'

The young man said his name was Coney. Hopkins could not shake hands although Coney offered his. 'Sort of,' said Hopkins. 'I'm from Wales.'

'Wales? Where's Wales?'

'Next to England, like attached to it.'

'Like France.'

'Something like France.'

'Got you. But I don't know things. I don't even know where this fuckin' place is. I was in Italy. I know where Italy is.'

'It's called Vienna. It's Austria.'

Coney said: 'Wherever it is, I want out of here, these guys staring at me. And I don't like this fuckin' snow stuff. Do you have snow in your country?'

'Quite a bit in Wales. We have to dig ourselves out of our houses some winters.'

'We don't have snow, not where I come from. Rain maybe. And mud. Plenty of mud. And rain, but no snow.'

Hopkins returned next morning. He had a crutch now but he still moved from bed to bed. 'What's new?' asked Coney.

'My bedpan won the piss contest,' said Hopkins. 'Other than that not much.'

Coney said: 'One guy, down the end there, died last night. They carried him out.'

'I didn't hear them. They usually make a lot of row, don't they?'

'Maybe it's to make sure we see them taking him away,' said Coney. He brightened. 'I got news. I hear they may be shipping me out. Handing me back over to the Americans. I can't wait for that.'

Hopkins said: 'Christ, I wish they'd let me go as well.'

'There's the guy,' said Coney pointing. 'The one who looks like a hog. Ask him.'

The Russian who had spoken to Hopkins when he first regained consciousness, the one without the bloodstains on his smock, was walking through the far aisle between the beds. Coney whistled shrilly and the man turned around but with no annoyance. He walked to them. 'He wants to quit,' said Coney pointing at Hopkins. 'Like me.'

'Yes, I have been looking for you,' said the Russian. 'This place is so big you cannot find people. I forgot where your bed was. You are going too.' He took a grubby piece of paper from his trouser pocket, searching for it under his smock. 'Tomorrow. Handed to the Yanks. We need the beds.'

The snow gave an eerie illumination to the streets. The blackout had been lifted but the war had left few lights to shine. Damaged buildings were hunched against the sky; there were ragged clouds, a few stars and a piece of moon.

'Now you go to the Yanks,' said the driver of the small truck. 'Lots of money and fucking with girls.' He jovially handed around a bottle of vodka, which both Hopkins and Coney drank. There was a pale young Russian officer who turned it down. 'Nice, nice,' said the driver. 'Fucking with girls.'

It was not far. They pulled into a square, the buildings at its edges melted into the dimness. The snow glowered. There was a group of soldiers to one side, standing about a jeep. 'Yanks,' said the Russian driver. 'Good-time boys.'

They shook hands formally and the two guards in the truck climbed down as if to ensure that the transfer took place as planned. Then the Russian junior officer who had been crouched at the back of the vehicle and refused the vodka bottle, climbed down and pointed to the grouped shadows of the Americans. A tramcar came along one side of the square, some drunks noisily aboard, and its clanging startled them. The

Russian soldiers fell to their knees and brought their rifles into position. The officer snarled something at them and they stood again in embarrassment. 'Tramcar,' said the officer scathingly. 'Not Panzer tank.'

He indicated that Hopkins and Coney should stagger beside him across the snow towards the Americans. Coney, like Hopkins, had been given a crutch and he eagerly swung himself along on this until the officer called him back for going too fast. He and Hopkins were wearing padded Russian jackets and cheap fur caps. Hopkins still had his British army trousers and Small's knuckledusters. He had shown them to Coney before they set out from the hospital and the slight American had tried wearing them. 'Too big,' he said.

It was only a hundred yards across the tight snow. One of the Americans detached himself from the group standing against the jeep. He and the Russian saluted each other a little lamely and there was an exchange of papers. The Russian officer pointed to Hopkins and Coney, as if there was some doubt about who was being handed over, saluted again and with the two soldiers marched away, back towards their own vehicle.

All the Americans watched the Russians go, as if marking them down for future reference, then the officer said: 'Okay, Hopkins.'

'Yes, sir, that's me,' said Hopkins.

'British. How are the British getting on in the war then?'

Hopkins eyed him but said: 'I don't know, sir, I've been out of it for a while.'

The officer then turned his attention to Coney. 'And you're a deserter,' he said.

Coney tried to look shocked. 'No, not me, sir. Maybe some other guy. Same name. Look, I got no foot, I can't desert. I can't even run.'

Unimpressed, the officer checked the papers on his clipboard. 'It says here you're AWOL, Coney. Maybe you had two feet when you snuck off.'

Another tramcar ran into the square, rattling and clanging, with another clutch of drunks on board. In a moment Coney made a dash for it, hopping over the snow on his one leg and his crutch. Hopkins tried to shout to him. He was heading for the tram which had stopped no more than a hundred yards away.

'No, Coney, no!' bellowed Hopkins almost tipping over with the effort. Then he saw the American officer's hand go to his white canvas pistol holster. He flicked up the cover. Hopkins tried to get in front of him. 'He'll come back! I'll get him back!'

But Coney was ten yards from the tram, bounding like a rabbit, when there was a succinct shot, followed by another. It came from the Russian group who had just reached their truck. Two of the soldiers had their rifles to their shoulders. They were clearly outlined.

Coney pitched forward into the snow. The American officer pushed his pistol back into the holster with almost a gesture of disappointment. 'They shot him!' howled Hopkins. 'The bastards, they shot him.'

The Russians were casually getting into their vehicle. The Americans were turning their backs and heading for theirs. Hopkins made to run towards Coney but the officer held him. 'Coney . . . Coney . . .' Hopkins sobbed.

'You're going nowhere,' said the American easily. 'Not him either. He's dead.'

Hopkins could not believe what had happened. 'But . . . Coney . . . why . . . ? Why did they shoot him?' He sat down and began to cry. Roughly the American hauled him up.

'They try to shoot somebody every night,' shrugged the officer. 'Tonight it was him. Get in the jeep.'

They took him to an American hospital, a series of huts and tents, at the edge of the city. They gave him a shot in the arm to calm him and he awoke at daylight in a tent by himself. He realised with horror what had happened. Coney. He could not believe it. 'This war,' he mumbled to himself. 'This fucking war.'

'Sure is,' said a round-headed American appearing at the bottom of his bed. 'It's a real fucker. You want some coffee?'

Hopkins nodded without saying anything. The man poured thick coffee into a tin mug and, without asking, added two heaped spoonfuls of sugar. Hopkins thanked him heavily and said: 'They shot my mate. He was a Yank.'

'Sorry to hear it,' said the man without conviction. 'People die regular. You got to go for assessment at ten o'clock. You can get some chow before then.'

'Where is this place?' asked Hopkins.

'Hell, I don't know. It's US Army Base Medical Facility Number something. I can't remember the number exactly. I only got here myself three days ago. They keep giving me jobs to do.'

'It can't be far from the city. Vienna.'

'Not too far, I guess. You can see the buildings. What's left of them. But the war will be finished soon. The Nazis are on the run just about everywhere. We can all go home.' He pointed to a canvas washbasin in the corner of the tent. 'You'd better get scrubbed up before you see the assessment officer. They like you to be clean. Got any shaving kit?' He studied Hopkins's ragged face and answered his own question. 'Maybe not. I'll get you some.'

He went out and Hopkins sat on the single chair and drank the coffee sadly but gratefully. He could still see Coney falling, lying in the snow. He wondered if they had collected him yet. They would not leave him lying there. They would clear him up.

The American soldier came back with a jug of hot water, a bar of soap and a razor. 'I'm doing this,' he admitted, 'so I don't have to wash wounds. I don't like washing wounds.'

'I don't blame you,' said Hopkins. He muttered to himself: 'Christ, what a bloody thing.'

'Shooting your buddy. Sure is, to you. But nobody else cares. They've gone past giving a fuck for anything. When you're ready the chow is just in the next tent. It ain't bad. Make you feel better.'

He went from the tent but soon came back carrying a pile of neat khaki clothing. 'Uncle Sam had this made to measure for you,' he said cheerfully. 'But maybe it won't fit anywhere. It's new stuff though. Don't spill your eggs on it. This assessing officer don't like eggs. He's got hang-ups.'

The assessing officer seemed the size of a boy. He had a shining face, small hands and rimless spectacles, and he sat behind his desk like a pupil at school. He told Hopkins to take off his clothes. It was difficult because of the plaster of Paris on both arms and the crutch but the officer filled in the time by studying a single sheet of paper in front of him. 'Hopkins,' he said as if finding something of interest.

'Yes, sir,' said Hopkins. He was down to the US Army drawers. He had lost weight and they sagged. 'Keep those on if you can,' said the officer. 'You're a mess anyhow.'

He was belligerent. He stood up behind the desk, all five feet of him, and said: 'I'm Captain Henry. That's my family name, Henry. I've got to assess you.'

'So I understand, sir.'

'There's not much information about you on this sheet. I take it you are British?'

'Yes, sir. British.'

'Some asshole has put "French" with a question mark.' He crossed it out vigorously. 'Army number and rank? You got dog-tags?'

Hopkins told him. He was wearing his identity discs.

The little man looked at the paper again. 'Amnesia,' he said as he wrote it. 'For how long can't you remember?'

'A lot of the time since I left England, sir. I remember being on a troopship and some things after but not much. I remember the training camp in England and my butties there.'

'You recall your butties,' repeated Henry as though glad but unsure what butties were.

'Yes, that bit. And I remember one of them was killed in Italy.' He leaned over and felt in the pocket of his trousers lying across the chair. He took out Small's knuckledusters. 'These belonged to him.'

Henry took them from him and returned them at once. 'Cute,' he said.

Consulting the paper again, he asked: 'What is your recent recall? When did you start remembering again?'

'When I woke up in that Russian hospital,' Hopkins told him. 'I'd been out for weeks they said. Months even.'

'Did you miss Christmas?'

'It looks like it.'

'You're lucky. I hate goddamn Christmas.' Henry gave his small head a good-sized nod: 'It happens. Battle shock. Do you remember being wounded? According to these notes you arrived in Milan with some Italian partisans.'

'That's correct, I believe,' muttered Hopkins. 'What's going to happen to me now, sir?'

Henry took out a clean, neat handkerchief and blew his nose. 'This climate,' he complained. He looked up at Hopkins. 'Repatriation, that's the ideal,' he said. 'Send you home.' He looked concerned. 'You *do* know where you live, don't you?'

'Yes, sir. Wales.'

'That's good. Everything is in such a state, son. No records, no background. People, soldiers, hundreds, thousands, wandering around Europe, milling around, not knowing where they're going, where they've come from, even who they are. Records are nil. And the war's not even concluded yet. Wait until then. It will be the most eternal screw-up.'

He tapped his pencil vigorously as if to mark a decision.

'We'll get you to the British who'll send you home.'

Hopkins said: 'As long as it's not back to the war. I've seen enough of the war. There was a woman, a girl, involved, you know, sir. I keep thinking, wondering who she was.'

'Yes, there usually is,' said Henry philosophically. 'Mighty good thing too. Gives you something to work out in your mind. She may come back or she may not.' He made a confession: 'Sometimes I wish I could forget my women.'

'How long will it be before I can go ho . . . back?' asked Hopkins.

'You were going to say "home",' said Henry tapping his pencil against his temple, as if he had uncovered a clue. 'Then you changed it. Don't you want to go home . . . your own home?'

'Not very much,' answered Hopkins.

'There'll be plenty of guys like that,' said the officer. 'They won't want to go home. And their wives won't want them back either. It's one of the advantages of war. Separation.'

For the first time he seemed to notice Hopkins's body. 'You don't look in good shape,' he said. 'We'll get the surgical team to give you some attention. I'm not an orthopaedic man but who did this carpentry?'

Hopkins lifted his plastered arms and looked down at his wounded leg. 'I don't know,' he said.

'Your leg's not right,' Henry said. 'And if they don't reset your arms you'll be walking about like a chimpanzee.'

Chapter Twenty

They moved him from the tent into the main, two-storey building. Not long before it had been a school, the classrooms now wards, blackboards still hanging on the walls, desks piled outside in the snow. There were ten men in the ward where they put Hopkins. They lay on beds or low cots, grunting and turning balefully when he was brought in as if somebody was disturbing a private world.

'The surgeon man will be coming to see you,' said the round-faced orderly who had looked after him in the tent. 'He's got to fix your arms and legs. After that everything should be okay.'

There was still chalk writing on the blackboard at the back of the room although it was in German. A later addition, across the top of one board, was written: 'Fuck This Place.'

He lay in the bed they gave him, his limbs aching. A tough-faced woman nurse came along and went around making attempts to straighten the beds. The response from the men was groans. 'They don't seem too good,' Hopkins said to the nurse.

She studied him but decided he was joking. 'They complain,' she said. 'It's only wounds.'

An iron stove was at the front of the classroom and a big black man came in and poured coal from a scuttle making a pile on the floor. A cloud of dust rose and settled on the nearest beds. Hopkins wanted to get out of there and he told the man in the next bed. The response was a coarse laugh. 'Every mother-fucking guy wants to get out of here,' croaked the man. Hopkins could only see his forehead, the rest of him had retreated below the blankets. 'Dead or alive.'

Another orderly came to the door and bellowed: 'Att-en-tion!' Nobody moved.

A man in a white overall came through the door. He saw 'Fuck This Place' written on the blackboard and nodded as if in agreement. He went to Hopkins's bed first. 'You're the new man,' he said. He had a clipboard. His accent was not American. 'Let's see yourself.' He motioned to the orderly who pulled back Hopkins's blankets. His nose wrinkled. 'Get him some clean pyjamas,' he said, then reconsidered it. 'After surgery.'

Hopkins said carefully: 'What are you going to do . . . sir?'

'Do? I'm going to try and put this jigsaw right. Who screwed this up?'

'I don't know,' said Hopkins. 'I don't remember who or where. Even why really.'

'Good thing you got here now before it all knits together. In no time somebody would have to pull you around on a cart.' He continued to stare at the leg and the two arms. 'Never seen anything like it,' he said. He became decisive. 'We will need to start again. Break your arms and your leg to fix them right. It's not too late. You got here in time.'

'Thanks, sir,' said Hopkins. 'Thanks very much indeed.'

After they had reset his arms and a week later had repaired his leg, he remained in the ward for another month. It stopped snowing for a while outside the windows. Someone came and erased 'Fuck This Place' from the blackboard and the coal pile around the boiler was swept up and a container put in place for the black man to fill.

Little else happened. A man who said he was a physiother-apist, although Hopkins did not know what he did, approached the bed and took a single look at him. 'I'll be right back,' he said. But he never was. Hopkins could not use a crutch because of his reset arms and he needed one now that they had reset his leg. He stayed in the bed. They carried the man in the next bed out early one morning and he was never seen again. No one took his place.

He had harboured a hope that under the anaesthetic, while they were resetting his limbs, might come some memory of the time he had mislaid. 'I think there was a girl, a woman,' he said to the doctor who came to check on him after the operation.

'Sure,' said the doctor. 'There nearly always is. *Cherchez la femme*, as they say in France.'

Hopkins muttered: 'Fuck me.'

Food was brought in three times daily by a series of mainly unspeaking orderlies who spooned into his mouth whatever had been cooked. It all tasted the same. Sometimes they brought coffee as well and, once, schnapps because it was the orderly's birthday.

One morning a neat American woman in uniform appeared. She was straight-haired, straight-backed and straight-faced. 'Is there anything I can do for you?' she asked. She thought it strange that he could not think of anything and he thought it strange also.

'I come from New England,' she said. She carried a small canvas stool with her and she set it up by the side of his bed. It was as though she was under orders to fill up some time. 'A place called Woods Hole. It's by the sea. It's a really nice place.'

'I come from by the sea,' said Hopkins. He realised he was entering a conversation. 'In South Wales.' He hesitated. 'That's on one side of England.'

'I know where it is,' she said. 'My name is Gloria.' She picked up the chart from the bottom of his bed. 'You are Hopkins. That's all it says here. Don't you have another name?'

'Davy, David that is, but I'd almost forgotten it. I haven't used it. Just Hopkins.'

'Well, we'll change that. I'm supposed to help to make this place a little more human, so we can start by calling you David. What seems to be keeping you here?'

'I've got a broken leg which they've reset because it was no good the first time. And two broken arms.'

'That's some accident. Or whatever it was. How did it happen?'

'I don't know. That's the other trouble with me. I can't remember.'

'There's a lot of that complaint in here. I try but I get nowhere.' She became thoughtful and then said: 'There's a recreation place right at the end of this corridor. You can play dominoes and cards and that sort of activity. But you can also have a drink, if you're permitted by the medics.' She paused and summed up his injuries. 'And there's dancing.'

It was a bleak room, big and scantily lit although above the small dance floor a mocking silver ball revolved. There was another over the small bar. The music came from a nickelodeon shining brazenly in a corner. 'You don't need to put any nickels in,' Gloria said. 'It's on all the time. I guess the war chest pays for it.'

Hopkins told her he did not have any money of any kind but she shrugged and moved to the bar. 'You wouldn't be able to carry any drinks anyhow,' she said. 'I like this schnapps stuff. Okay?'

'Okay,' replied Hopkins. He watched her sparse figure go towards the bar.

A cheerful Oriental behind the bar exchanged some banter with her and put the glasses on a small tray. 'Doubles,' he laughed. 'One on Uncle Sam. I'll bring them over to your table. They're heavy.'

He was four times the size of Gloria who followed him across the room shyly. The jukebox was playing non-stop Glenn Miller, one after the other. 'In The Mood', 'American Patrol', 'Moonlight Serenade' and all the others. As the barman went back he did a few steps to the music but he was the only one. The dance floor under its spinning ball was vacant. Hopkins could see there were several tables occupied at the dim far end of the room and a group of men laughed madly over glasses.

'They're the loonies,' said Gloria. 'They're only allowed soft drinks and it does that to them. At nine o'clock they have to go back to their ward. There's a whole bunch of them at the end of the hospital. The war's driven them crazy.'

Hopkins said: 'It's enough to drive anybody crazy. Look at me. There's weeks, months, I can't remember at all. I keep thinking it will come back but it don't. It's probably gone away for ever.'

They began to drink the schnapps. She said: 'I quit Woods Hole, got myself this cute uniform, and got here because of me. I wanted out. I wanted adventure. And here I am.'

'I was a fisherman,' he said.

'Catching fish?' she asked vaguely. 'Like real fish, big ones. Not with a worm-on-a-pin kind of thing?'

'At sea, Bristol Channel, off South Wales. It didn't suit me. So I got out and into the army. And I've landed up in this place.'

She had finished her drink swiftly and, to his surprise, rose and went again towards the bar. This time she returned with a bottle of schnapps on the tray. 'No point in doing things by halves,' she said. She saw Hopkins's concern. 'I don't need to pay. I write it off to professional expenses.'

'I'm a professional expense?'

'Not at all. But I'll lie.'

She poured out two more glasses. Hopkins began to feel better than he could last remember.

'Woods Hole, Massachusetts, wasn't great. Not for me. I wasn't the type. And even when I was eighteen I could just see that most of the men were dumb. I only had one boyfriend and he was older than my father so he wasn't really a boyfriend. He was called Wally Whelk. Like the band conductor Lawrence Welk. That wasn't his real name, but everybody called him that. He smelled of whelks too. I could never face a whelk again.'

'Don't know a lot about whelks,' said Hopkins. Because of his limited arm movements he had to bend low to his glass. She casually helped him, lifting it to his lips. 'Nothing as small as whelks.'

'They smell,' she said. 'Wally couldn't get rid of it. I had to leave.' She sighed and poured two more glasses from the bottle. 'And see where I've ended.' She leaned towards him confidingly. 'This place is full of sick and wounded and dying or crazy men. There's no one you can socialise with.'

'Staff,' suggested Hopkins. He tried to keep his voice in order. 'The medical staff.'

'No point.'

'Why no point?'

'They're black or they're homos. Haven't you seen some of these guys holding hands?'

'Haven't noticed. I see what you mean. But there's others.'

'Oh sure, there's some dreaming of the cute blonde wife in Wyoming. There's the patients, like I said, either injured or crazy.'

She leaned again confidingly, picking up the bottle on the way. She filled their glasses. 'Two nights ago one guy climbed into the bed of another. This guy fell out the other side of the bed because he was scared, broke his kneecap. Big scene. The kid had a lung wound, a broken kneecap and a sore jacksie.'

For the first time in months Hopkins began to laugh. The schnapps was helping. 'Anyhow,' sniffed Gloria. 'They don't want me. I came to the war where for Chrissake there are plenty of goddamn men, and I'm still high and dry.' She regarded him hopefully. 'Would you like to dance ... ? "Moonlight Serenade" has come around again.'

Hopkins regarded her thin, hopeful face. 'I won't be able to hold you,' he said raising his hands as far as he could. 'And there's the leg.'

Gloria smiled mistily. 'No matter. I'll hold you up.'

He was three inches taller and holding him up was difficult. They reached the dance floor, knocking over two chairs as they did so. The barman gladly picked them up. 'No customers, no pay for him,' said Gloria. Under the slowly spinning silver ball they stood as closely as they could. She put her hands under his elbows and leaned against his stomach. He revolved on his one workable leg. The barman turned the music lower and the light as well. The romance swept over them. 'Oh, David or Davy,' she whispered raising her head to blink up at him. 'I love you, screwed up though you are.'

Hopkins answered: 'Screwed up is the word. I've got screws everywhere.'

They both began to laugh. She felt like a stick against him. 'My room is just down the lobby,' she said. 'Let's go dance there. I have a phonograph.'

There was not much space to dance in her room. It had been a school store place and two blackboards were propped in one corner and a clutch of flags in another. 'I have my very own Nazi flag,' Gloria said. She went to the pile and took one banner out. 'See?'

Unfurled it was red, black and white with a swastika at its centre. She began a little pantomime marching alongside her bed with one finger under her nose like a Hitler moustache and the flag held out before her. Hopkins hazily watched her, his pain held at bay by the schnapps working around inside him.

She stopped her goose-step. 'Not now,' she said twirling the flag and lobbing it back into the corner. 'We came to dance.'

He sat heavily on the side of her single bed, his feeble arms before him in their slings. The bed had a flowered counterpane which she told him she had brought from her own room in Woods Hole. There was another bottle of schnapps on a table and some glasses. She poured two and held one out to him. 'You can get to like this stuff,' she said.

'It's very likeable,' said Hopkins carefully choosing the words.

'And we are going to dance,' she repeated. From the floor she lifted a portable gramophone, plugged it into a socket and switched it on. 'Let's have Glenn Miller again, shall we?' she said spinning a record already on the turntable. 'I like Glenn Miller.'

'He's all they play,' said Hopkins.

She stood him in the middle of the small space between the bed and the door. 'Moonlight Serenade' began to drift into the room and she leaned against him. As before he revolved on one leg. Her eyes drifted to the opaque and she became lost in the music. He thought she was dropping off.

'Enough,' she said sharply apparently speaking to herself. She remained before him. 'I think I'll need to undress you. Is that okay?'

Hopkins said: 'I can't manage it myself.'

He stood, holding onto the wardrobe while she unbuttoned his trousers. She pulled his braces away in a businesslike way but then became softer as she pulled the trousers down. 'There,' she said, her voice becoming hoarse. 'Now we're getting someplace.'

The place was his groin. She rubbed him affectionately and he found himself responding. He stroked the back of her neck and her straight hair. 'Now these,' she said. 'We don't want these getting in the way. I wish the army would make prettier drawers.'

Pushing her away gently he sat on the side of the bed. The

counterpane felt cool against his backside. 'I'll get rid of these,' he said in a practical way trying to undo his boots. She helped him energetically, then she tugged his socks clear.

'Footwear only looks sexy on a woman,' she said. She lifted her skirt and displayed her skinny legs, her dark stockings making them like feathers. She dropped the skirt hem and slid the garment away from her thighs in one movement. In seconds, it seemed, she was naked. Her thinness seemed to accentuate her nakedness. 'Lay back, baby,' she murmured vaguely. 'Moonlight Serenade' had become wedged in a groove and was emitting a repetitive moan. Gloria stretched a leg as if it were in elongating sections and gave the gramophone a kick. It tipped onto the floor with a crash. 'I'll come on top,' she said.

She inserted herself between his stiff, wounded, plastered arms and drew herself up his legs. He began to groan gently. She stopped and said: 'You sound like that goddamn gramophone.' Then she lowered her head as if entering on an adventure and advanced up his body firmly inserting herself onto his penis as she progressed.

Hopkins lay back only half-conscious of what was going on. He kept wondering when he'd last done this. Who was it with? Who was she? He tried to hold Gloria with his injured arms and even her slight weight made his leg ache. He attempted to shift her sideways to take the pressure from the limb but the movement brought him to his climax and his climax provoked hers. She began to scream in a strange subdued way.

'God, God, God.' She wriggled even further into him.

'What's the matter?' asked Hopkins.

'Nothing. Oh, God, I have to tell you . . .'

He realised she had forgotten his name. 'Hopkins,' he told her. '. . . Hopkins.'

'You're crazy, not to mention crippled,' she told him looking up his body to his chin. 'But that was so exciting. I've been waiting for that for a long time.'

'I'm glad,' he said sincerely. 'I've had a decent time too.'

She wriggled against him. 'Just lie like this. Only for a while. I have to be away early in the morning. They're posting me. Away from here.' She paused and kissed his chest. 'We will never see each other again.'

They lay like that for ten minutes. He had gone to sleep and started snoring, but she stirred and after prodding him awake helped him along the corridor. They stumbled together, holding each other up until they reached the door of his ward. 'Go now,' she whispered pushing him softly, then she went away for ever.

He reached his bed, groaning with all that had happened to him. The men in the other beds began groaning also, joining in like a dire chorus. Carefully he got into the bed and slept. When he awoke he heard it was raining outside and standing at the foot of the bed was an orderly.

'Okay, you're the Limey. And are you the lucky one! You're out of here today. They're going to ship you out of here. Back to Limeyland.'

Chapter Twenty-one

The country the Americans called Limeyland came into view, a smudge on the horizon of an April day. The pre-war ferry, clanking across the English Channel, set her scarred nose for Dover. Men who could move stumbled to the deck to see. Hopkins went with them. He had been sitting on a threadbare seat near a window but he got up and went on his crutch to the deck.

Men began to cheer. 'Good old Blighty!' somebody shouted. 'A pint of old and mild!' shouted another. Wounded, out of the war, some of them derelict, they were going home. Hopkins felt nothing. He was going back to things he could scarcely remember. He thought of his vague uncle and aunt in Wales and wondered if he would want to see them, or if they would want to see him.

It began to rain on the deck and the men returned to the ragged shelter of what was still grandly called the lounge. Two craggy nurses came around with a trolley and served Oxo. 'Home soon then,' said one to Hopkins. She lifted the Oxo to his mouth.

He answered: 'Yes, not long.' Where would he go? Was this sense, this shadow, a real person he had known? Would he ever find her?

It had been what seemed a never-ending halting journey by train across Europe. Although it was now spring the freshness, the greenery, was only grey in the landscape he could see through the slowly travelling window. The war had laid low the towns through which they travelled on the long route from Vienna to Calais, black buildings, blocked roads, woods severed down to their roots, farms flattened. Sometimes a field or a river would shine and Hopkins took in the brief view as he sat upright in his bunk. It was a pre-war sleeper train; it crept unsurely over the rails. There were two hundred wounded men aboard. They lay under red blankets, some of them scarcely moving throughout the journey; some sat up and got together with others to play cards, some could walk about.

There was a red-faced man from Ireland who had a battered concertina. He played old songs and, raggedly at first, the bedraggled soldiers joined in:

> 'When this blinking war is over,
> Oh, how happy I will be.
> When I get my civvy clothes on,
> No more soldiering for me.'

And the train had gone on through the night along miles of track, over river bridges, through tunnels and towns, the soldiers' voices sounding through the dark and broken countryside. They were the victors but the songs were not songs of triumph. It seemed there were no winners.

When the food was brought around in army mess tins by steamed-up men from the Army Catering Corps, they talked roughly over the stew. Hopkins, by lowering his mouth, found he was able to use the fingers of his right hand to hold a spoon and feed himself. Nobody else offered.

'I'll tell you what it'll be like,' said a soldier. 'Just like it was before. The rich and the rest of us, the country run by the Jews.'

The man who was bringing the food said: 'They used these trains, so I heard, to take Jews to the concentration camps. Killed 'em off. Millions.'

'I don't mean *them* Jews, I mean the ones we've got in England. They've made a bleeding fortune from this ruddy war. They always do, don't they?'

Another man said: 'All I want is to go into my 'ouse and see my mum and get my job back.'

'Some 'opes,' said a fourth. 'It'll be just like it was before. They only want us when there's a war. We're only any good for fucking fighting. So until the next one we'll just 'ave to take what we're given.'

'Another war,' said the first man. 'Against the soddin' Russians. That'll be some war that will.'

Now they saw the white cliffs take shape and cheered them from the deck. April sun was lying over them. The sea became pale.

Dover harbour lay amid the rubble of the ancient town. There were half-sunken ships and the ferry had to be edged between them. Many of the inhabitants, shelled and bombed from France, had lived in caves.

On the jetty were ambulances and mobile canteens warm with tea and pies, with eager women behind the urns. Hopkins had a cup of tea with a group waiting for the train.

The motherly woman who served him raised the cup to his lips for him. She said: 'You'll soon be better, love. It's nearly all over now.'

He thanked her but he had difficulty in framing any other words. There were pats on the back from a group of curious spectators and applause as an ambulance took them the short distance to the station where the train for London was waiting.

He felt as if he was in a dream, a dream where he was going to a place but did not know where. Every faltering step he took was going nowhere. A railwayman was helping the wounded soldiers onto the train. He helped Hopkins, then handed his crutch up after him. Soon there were snorts of steam from the engine and people on the platform waved as the train moved off through the first fields of England.

Hopkins watched them and the villages, church spires standing against the springtime sky. Roads and ploughed fields. Inland it was as though nothing had been any different. The other men in the compartment had fallen silent too, looking with subdued eagerness at the passing scenery. 'I'm never going away again,' growled one man with his neck in a cast. 'Never. I don't bloody care who orders me. They can stuff their orders.'

He felt apart from the other men. They at least knew where they were going. Even the blind soldiers waved from the train windows when they heard their companions being cheered. But Hopkins, although he raised a broken arm, put it down again and looked out at a landscape that could have been anywhere.

At Victoria people had come to see them arrive. People often gathered to see the hospital trains come in and to clap the wounded men as they were led or carried to the line of waiting ambulances. Hopkins used his crutch as well as he could. The spectators waved to him and he tried to wave back. It was difficult with his arms as they were and in the end he resorted to a series of nods.

There were three other men in the ambulance and they were eagerly trying to look through the slits in the darkened windows. 'We're getting towards it now,' said one who claimed to know the way. 'I know where this is, I reckon. Not that you'd know it after Jerry's done 'is best, the bastard.'

Another soldier said: 'Here's the river. I can smell the Thames.'

All except Hopkins crowded to see. 'Still as mucky,' said one man.

'It's still the Thames.'

They were going to Millbank, the main military hospital, on the embankment at Westminster. The ambulances turned into the forecourt. A staff sergeant in the Medical Corps banged on the doors and those on each one of the six vehicles were opened to reveal the apprehensive faces. 'Right, lads, don't 'ang about just 'cause you're a bit wounded. Form up in two ranks. Those what can. Those what can't, sit down somewhere, but nice and tidy. Straight lines. You're still in the British army.'

Hopkins stood in the second rank and, leaning on his crutch, tried to come to attention. 'Bollocks to that,' said the soldier next to him. He also had both arms in plaster. 'And I ain't saluting anybody.'

He glanced at Hopkins's injuries and added conversationally: 'Can't even scratch my arse, I can't. So I ain't saluting.'

'Parade, parade, right turn,' ordered the sergeant-major but he did not shout now. They shuffled around and he called: 'Squad, squad, quick march.' It was more a suggestion than an order. 'Well, march anyway.'

The hospital was a cavernous and cool building. Hopkins was taken by a young and cheery nurse to a ward where twenty other men were lying. Some of them, as if at a prearranged signal, began to sing:

> *'Holy Moses I am dying,*
> *In my little wooden bed . . .'*

He attempted a grin. The nurse in her young voice told them to stop and some of them did.

'Doctor will come and see you as soon as he can. It gets busy when there's another intake. I'll help you undress.'

Hoots and catcalls came from the other beds. She said: 'Ignore them. I do.'

She helped him out of his clothes and brought a pair of pyjamas, thick and comforting. He put them on and she helped him into the high bed. Every bed had red blankets. There was more badinage and the girl blushed. Hopkins said nothing. He wearily lay back on the stiff, clean sheets and stared upwards.

There were liquid patterns on the ceiling and he realised they were reflections from the Thames. Somewhere he could hear traffic. He lay back and closed his eyes. He wondered what would become of him.

It was evening before the military doctor came to the ward. The other men fell quiet and a radio which had been playing indiscriminately suddenly stopped.

He was a round-faced man, middle-aged, with bright eyes behind glasses. He peered at two sheets of paper. 'You don't seem too bad, lad,' he said genially. 'Fractures on the mend. You should be up and out of here in a few weeks. Once you can get around.' He turned to the second page. 'And amnesia. What can't you remember?' He gave a chuckle. 'Daft sort of question, eh? But what's missing, I mean?'

'I can't remember much from when I arrived in Italy,' said Hopkins. 'After the troopship. Then there was a landing on a beach and a lot of shit and shooting. I found my butty dead in a tent where they put all the bodies. But after that it's blank, sir. Nothing.' He held up both plastered arms. 'I got blown up, I suppose.'

'Ended up in Milan. Brought in by some Italian partisans.' The doctor's eyes came up from the documents and he sniffed. 'It's a shame the Eyeties couldn't have started the war on the proper side, isn't it? They're not a reliable race.'

He surveyed the casts on Hopkins's arms and on his leg. 'Nothing much to do there,' he said. 'Once you feel a bit better we'll get some nice lady to help you to walk. Do you have a wife or a girl?'

'I believe I have someone,' replied Hopkins, 'but I don't know who she is or where she is.'

'They may have told you, I am what they call a psychiatrist. It's a new-fangled thing.'

230

Hopkins said: 'Yes, sir.' He was sitting awkwardly, directly in front of a man with a white coat and pink skin who was peering keenly at him through spectacles.

'I suppose the best explanation is that I am a psychologist who does something about it. That's what I always say to you injured lads. Been going for years, of course. Freud and Jung and such people. But the Americans have got hold of it now and it's going to become a big thing, as they say. There's certainly plenty of scope for it, don't you think?'

Hopkins said: 'Yes, sir.'

As though on impulse the man suddenly sprang to his feet and said: 'Henry Bean.'

Taken by surprise Hopkins stood unsteadily and extended his right-hand fingers.

The officer took off his glasses and stared towards Hopkins as if he thought something new might be revealed.

'And I am an army captain, to make matters worse. Hah! Hah!'

Hopkins tried to laugh with him. The man said: 'It may seem mad, a psychiatrist in a war. The whole world's mad.' He leaned forward again. 'Well, let's try and get to the bottom of what's wrong with you.'

'I can't remember,' said Hopkins simply.

'You can't remember what? What's wrong with you?'

'No, sir. There's weeks, months it could be, which are just blank. I missed Christmas.'

Bean began to rustle the papers on his desk. He picked up two pinned together. 'Ah, yes. Hopkins, isn't it? Corporal Hopkins.'

'Private, sir. Private Hopkins.'

'It says here you were promoted in the field. In action. You must have done something.'

Hopkins felt oddly lifted. 'Corporal,' he repeated. 'Well, I should be due for some back pay.'

'I'll say. Jolly fine too. They seem to have got some of your records together by now. It's a devil of a job trying to keep things in order you know. Battles, bangs, men moving about. Dying, wounded. It becomes quite impossible to keep things tidy.' He looked at the small sheaf of papers. 'But here you are now, more or less.'

'Yes, sir.'

'At least you know *where* you are. How long was your memory failure?'

'I don't know for sure, sir. I've tried to work it out. I remember getting to Italy but after that some things are all right and others have completely gone. There was an amphibious landing.'

'Not Anzio?' He checked the papers again.

'No, sir. It was after that one. But it was a landing of some kind. I was on the wheel of the landing craft. The crew were wiped out and I used to be a fisherman so I know about boats. But I remember being on the wheel and then ashore, after going to a tent and seeing one of my mates lying dead. He had some knuckledusters in his pocket. He always carried them. I thought I'd look after them for him and I've got them with me now.'

He took the knuckledusters from his pocket and laid them on the desk. 'His name was Small and it's spelled out on them – on each knuckle, see? S–M–A–L–L.'

Henry Bean stared at them. 'Whatever next,' he said.

He picked up the knuckledusters without enthusiasm and quickly returned them to Hopkins. 'It was probably on the landing craft that you were promoted to corporal. That doesn't happen to many soldiers, promotion at sea.'

'No, sir. I suppose not.'

'Anyway, make sure you claim the back pay.' He pushed the glasses towards the end of his nose, making himself look older and perhaps wiser. 'I don't know what we can do to bring back the missing weeks, or months, corporal. I don't see any point in sending you to classes where you have to build bricks or put shapes into holes. You appear to be all right otherwise, apart from your arms and legs, that is. I think we'll just keep you here until you are physically able to move about and then send you for a few walks with an escort. It will give you time to think.' He visibly brightened. 'Something may occur to you, you never know.'

They fitted him with a deep blue suit, white shirt and red tie – the uniform of wounded solders. 'You look as if you're lucky,' said the medical corps sergeant looking at a clipboard list.

'It's about time,' said Hopkins. 'What is it? They've found my memory?'

'Now, now, corporal,' said the sergeant. Hospital sergeants were often gentle men. 'Your memory is lying around somewhere. It could turn up any day.'

'Yes. Thanks, sarge. We'll have to keep looking for it.'

'Right. In the meantime you're going out for a walk today. You've got your blue suit.' He studied the clipboard. 'And, you could be in luck. There's a lady going with you. She's one of these volunteers. Quite posh some of them and this could be one. The Hon. – it says here – the Hon. Felicity Brough. You don't know her, I suppose?'

'No, sarge. I'd remember that.'

'Yes, you would I'm sure, lad. I don't know what she's like. She's new to the list. But she sounds posh.'

The sergeant moved away. The Hon. Felicity Brough. Hopkins shook his head. What next?

Two o'clock, it said, on the list. There were still three hours. He sat back on the red blanket and looked beyond the ward and out of the window, full of flat blue sky. It was a light spring day, mostly clear. The London traffic sounded below. He tried, as he had done every day many times before, to recall what had happened. He remembered Naples clearly and even some part of Rome, with Delmi. Abruptly he sat up in bed. Delmi! Delmi might know. If Delmi was still alive.

The sergeant was walking almost politely down the ward. Hopkins called him and he came to the bedside. 'Sarge, I just thought. I had a butty called Delmi in Italy. He might know what happened.'

'Delmi what? It's got to be Delmi something.'

'Bugger it, I forget. But somebody could trace him. I'll remember his full name. He lived near me in Wales. I went to school with him.'

The sergeant said: 'Well, think hard about it, Hopkins. File it away. We can't start a major search, can we? There's still a war going on. Tell the padre about it when he comes around. He's found blokes before. Mind, they've often been up with the angels by then.'

Chapter Twenty-two

The Hon. Felicity Brough was young, blonde and bright. 'I don't know what to call you,' confessed Hopkins.

'Felicity, I hope,' she smiled. They were in the echoing foyer of the hospital.

'Not Hon. or anything?' She giggled engagingly. Her face was round and clean, her hair pulled back, her form slight.

'Don't you dare,' she said. 'And what do I call you? Not corporal, I hope.'

'I've got a first name, Davy, but for some reason everybody calls me Hopkins. Maybe I look like a Hopkins.'

'Do you like it?'

'It's what I've got.'

She leaned near to him and whispered: 'I told them I was twenty-one and they believed me. They didn't even ask for my identity card.'

Touching his elbow in a proprietorial way she guided him with care towards the door and the sunlight. Blue-suited patients were around the foyer and there were smirks and low remarks as they walked out.

The afternoon sun fell across them like a gentle hand. 'They're just jealous that I'm going for a walk with someone like you,' smiled Hopkins. His own smile surprised him.

'Am I any different?' she asked. 'There are plenty of lady volunteers, so I was told. I don't know since I'm new. You don't mind, do you, Hopkins?'

He smiled again, this time at her. 'Far from it. I've been feeling pretty low.'

She squeezed his arm. 'Well, if you're happy that's fine. Let's walk along the Embankment. The river looks just as murky even with the sun on it. Have you been out much, away from the hospital?'

'This is the first time. I haven't been here long. They brought me back from Italy. They've only just taken the plaster off one arm.'

She hesitated then said: 'Were you nearly killed?'

'I can't tell you because I don't know,' he replied. A tug and two black barges were going downriver, pushing into the brown water. 'I can't remember anything about it. All I know is I ended up with these knocks. Two broken arms and a broken leg. Whoever tried to mend them first didn't do it right and it had to be done all over again. It's been months.'

A touch of afternoon sun caught London like a moment of encouragement, but nearer, the Palace of Westminster stood solidly almost as dark as the river. 'Do you think it will all be over soon, the war?' she asked as though he might have advance information.

'According to the papers it should be. The Germans are falling to bits,' he said. 'But I don't know. They don't tell me.'

'I've been feeling quite useless. Nobody wants me to do anything. I'm seventeen. I could do something. I'm so glad I thought of volunteering for this. Would you like some tea?'

'I thought you'd be just taking me for a walk.'

'Like a dog on a lead! No, thank you. Let's sit and have a chat. We'll get a taxi.'

'Oh, no. We can't. I haven't got any money on me. I've got plenty of back pay owing but they only let us have a few bob in hospital.'

She grinned but said nothing. A black cab came by, one of the pre-war Hackney carriages that had the look of a century before. She hailed it. Hopkins climbed in first with difficulty and she gave him a gentle push to help. She sat beside him. She was wearing a light coat and a dark green dress with a white collar. 'The Savoy, please,' she said to the driver.

Hopkins sat on edge and silent beside her in the taxi. The Savoy? How would they get into the Savoy? How much did the Savoy charge? He only had three shillings and fivepence. He glanced nervously through the travelling windows. He had never been in a taxi before.

'How long will it be before they repair London?' asked Felicity. 'I wonder.'

Hopkins took in the skeletal buildings, half-walls, basements overgrown with weeds and new flowers. 'Looks a bit more than a repair job,' he said. 'But it's work. That's what the men coming back want. Work.'

He was aware of the slender legs under the dress, the good coat, pre-war, lying open.

'I've been spoiled,' she said. 'I didn't know anything about other people's troubles, their lives. Mind, I was only twelve when it started.'

He had no idea where the Savoy was located. They kept to the Thames Embankment and were soon there, turning up among the destroyed and damaged buildings of the Strand.

'The Strand,' said Hopkins looking at the street sign. 'Now I've heard of the Strand. There was a song they used to sing about it.'

Felicity began to sing lightly: '*Let's all go down the Strand!*'

'*Have a banana,*' he laughed.

'Bananas, I wonder when they'll come back?' she said. 'After all the terrible things that have happened, it seems ridiculous that all people can think about is having a banana. I remember bananas, horrible things, all bent and yellow.'

She said 'Here we are,' as the taxi turned into the short

approach road to the Savoy. Hopkins began to fumble towards his pocket. Although they had taken the plaster off he still found it difficult. She put her slender fingers on his wrist. 'Don't,' she said. 'I get an allowance.'

Hopkins said: 'I'll give it back to you. When I get my pay.'

The pair walked into the marble foyer of the hotel. A man in a tailcoat appeared and held the door so that the limping Hopkins did not have to use the revolving door. He touched his top hat to Felicity. 'Miss Brough,' he said. 'How nice to see you again.'

There were other men in tailcoats and tall hats standing at intervals, seemingly staring into unknown distances. They minutely nodded and smiled. Behind the long reception desk two other men and two ladies added theirs.

'They all seem to know you,' whispered Hopkins.

'My father has an account here,' she said. 'I charge everything to him. It's his contribution to the war effort. He's at the War Office and over military age so he doesn't seem to do that much. Sometimes he's home by four o'clock.'

Hopkins walked awkwardly and just as awkwardly gazed about him as they descended the wide carpeted steps. It was a huge and luxurious room with windows along the end wall, through which the genteel sun added its decoration. A perfectly poised waiter approached. There were twenty or more people in the room and they stopped their conversations to see the wounded soldier enter in his blue suit. A woman in a red hat started to applaud and others joined her. 'Jolly good,' called a high-class man's voice and another said: 'Good show.'

Hopkins thought they might be engaged in some game, some entertainment, perhaps like housey-housey, and did not look towards them. 'It's you they're clapping,' pointed out Felicity. She lifted her hand in a half-wave towards the people.

'Well, as long as nobody wants me to dance.'

One waiter handed them over to another who shepherded

them to a rounded table with padded and curved seats against the wall. It was covered by the whitest and smoothest tablecloth he had ever seen. On it were set shining silver implements for tea. 'Afternoon tea, if you please,' said Felicity to the waiter. She accepted a menu nevertheless and said: 'You have fruit cake?'

'Fruit cake is on, miss.'

'You can never be sure these days.'

'Will it be your usual, miss? Earl Grey?'

'English afternoon tea,' Felicity returned firmly. 'Cakes and sandwiches.'

Hopkins's eyes were drawn to the menu the waiter placed back on the table. 'Christ,' he whispered. 'Tea is seven and sixpence. For one. That's fifteen bob.'

'My father's bank can stand it,' she smiled. 'We might even have an extra lump of cake. If they're not rationing it.'

Hopkins looked around him: the subdued light, the shadowy movements of waiters, the understated conversations of the room. A man appeared and began playing a violin.

'I can't believe all this,' said Hopkins.

They sat for more than an hour. She wanted to know about him and he told her as much as he knew, or could recall. 'It's only a few months in Italy I can't remember,' he said. 'God knows what happened then.' He looked into her young, clean face, her fresh eyes. 'I bet you're still at school,' he said.

'Commercial college,' she said biting a segment of cake. 'I refused to go to some crummy girls' school while there was a war going on. I wanted to join something, do something, but they kept saying I was too young for anything. I could have gone into a factory next year but it's nearly over.'

Two men and two women, dressed in country tweeds, paused by the table on their way into the room. They stood staring at Hopkins in his bright blue suit, white shirt and red tie. Then one said: 'Jolly good,' and the others agreed before moving off.

'Patronising bastards,' said Felicity quietly. 'They've done bugger all, I bet.'

'Some people have managed it, I expect,' he said. 'They've gone through the lot, the whole war, without anything happening to them. Either they've been lucky or they've kept their heads down.'

'Not got involved,' she agreed. She held the fruit cake between two fingers. He watched her then did the same. 'My mother's like that,' she said. 'The moment war was declared she packed her bags and cleared off to some ghastly hidden hotel in Cornwall. Right away from it all. She's not been back since. I expect she will once the final all-clear goes.'

'Where do you live?' asked Hopkins. The waiter approached but Felicity waved him easily away and poured them another cup of tea.

'Kensington,' she said. 'Bombs everywhere, up the street and down it. But they all missed, by an inch sometimes.'

'You live with your father?'

'And two old retainers. God, they can scarcely scrape along the carpets now, but they've been with us for ever. Half the house is under wraps anyway. He comes back from the War Office and sometimes we have a meal together. And I've been deep into Pitman Shorthand and touch typing. I've learned to type to music. They play a gramophone and you type in time. It's quite fun. Will you be going back to Wales?'

Hopkins thought about it. 'I don't know what I'll be doing. There's only my auntie and uncle there and we're not close. They don't even know where I am. I wouldn't go back to the boats anyway.'

'The boats?'

'The fishing. That's what I did. It's too wet and cold. Heavy too. And all the fish look the same.'

She giggled over her tea. 'Would you come to London?'

'What would I do?'

'There's boating on the Thames. They'll be in full swing again next summer.'

He laughed now. He found her company comforting. 'I can see me doing that. "Any more for the *Skylark*?" I don't know, really. It will all work out, I hope. Before I think about the future I've got to try and remember what happened in the past.'

She came to the hospital again at the end of the week. 'Last time they insisted I took somebody else out,' she said. 'You're not allowed to take the same chap out all the time.'

'I sat by the window to see if I could spot you.'

'What else have you been doing?'

'Having my arms back.' The plaster on each arm had been removed and he held them in front of him proudly. They were thin and pale and had the scars of blisters. 'Oh, they look fine!' exclaimed Felicity. She took each hand and held them out.

'Bit of this physiotherapy to build them up, that's all they need,' said Hopkins. 'And my leg is on the mend as well.' He paused. 'All I need is my memory now.'

'It will come back. I'm sure,' she said. They walked through the hospital foyer.

'The hospital has been given tickets for the Albert Hall this afternoon,' she told him. 'It's the Welsh Choral Society and they're doing *Messiah*. Would you like to go?'

'I might join in,' he said.

She called a taxi as soon as they were out of sight of the hospital. 'They don't like you whizzing around like this,' she said as she climbed in after him. 'They want to keep it all a bit ordinary. Like going on buses. But you can still hardly walk.'

Hopkins said: 'It's getting easier. The specialist said he's hopeful I'll be discharged before the end of the month.'

Felicity said quietly: 'I hope not.'

It was the last month of the war. The April sun was lying across the scarred London parks. There were fire engines and tanks parked under the trees, the lakes were drained and the lawns trodden, but the air was clear and optimistic. 'So this is it,' said Hopkins as they walked up the steps towards the Albert Hall, its roof like a big cushion. 'In Wales, they think this is the wonder of wonders, you know. The choir people always talk about it and when they've been here they talk about it even more.'

'Have you heard *Messiah*?'

'Bits. Some of it. Before the war there was a lot of good singing in the Welsh valleys. I suppose they'll start it up again soon.'

'Do you sing?'

'I can't remember. But I doubt it somehow.'

'You haven't had much to sing about,' she said.

As they went into the rounded foyer she took the tickets from her handbag. 'Well, for a start,' she sniffed, 'we are not going in the gods.' Disdainfully she held out the tickets. 'Mean blighters. Fancy sending balcony seats to wounded soldiers. You'd never get up the stairs. It's miles.'

She patted his arm to stay where he was and made off with her youthful stride and determination. In a few minutes she was back, waving new tickets. 'Ten rows from the front,' she said triumphantly. 'And I should think so.'

The auditorium was filling gradually, then rapidly; the orchestra appeared, and the hundred singers. There was a scattering of coughing. The conductor and the four soloists were applauded. Dimness fell over the great round room. They settled down together, close, and listened to the famous music as it grew around them. Hopkins had not felt so happily peaceful for a long time.

It was still bright with sunshine when they walked out. 'Wonderful,' said Felicity.

'Never known anything like that,' he said.

'Now, for some tea. I want you to come to my house. I do a good tea. As good as the Savoy any day.'

In his bright blue suit people were always patting him on the back or saying: 'Well done,' as if he had won a competition. He found he was shifting his shoulder away from the well-intentioned pats and grunting at the praise. This time as they were about to get into the taxi a man, too old for the war, pressed a pound note into his hand and said: 'Have this on me.'

'Keep it,' suggested Felicity firmly as he angrily wound down the window to throw the money back. 'He was only treating us to a taxi.'

It was not far. A few crescents punctuated with bomb-sites and they stopped outside a tall house in a Georgian row. 'Number thirty-four, love,' said the driver. He was regarding them curiously in his mirror. 'War'll soon be over,' he said as Hopkins passed him the pound note. 'Get on wiv things then. Mind you, I ain't been doing much. Just driving this cab.'

It came to three and sixpence and Hopkins, after a moment's hesitation, gave the pleased man five shillings. The change was all in half-crowns. He put them in his blue suit. The man honked the taxi's bulbous horn and drove off down the curve of the crescent. Hopkins surveyed the houses. 'This is posh,' he said.

'Can't help it,' she replied quite brusquely. She seemed nervous and he wondered who was in the house. They walked up the six steps to the front door and she had trouble finding the key. When she located it in her handbag she dropped it and he tried to reach and pick it up. 'No.' She restrained him with her small hand. 'You'll hurt yourself.' She picked it up and with a tight face turned it and opened the large door.

'They've got the day off,' she mentioned stepping into the hall. 'Peggy and George who help out. Her mother's been taken bad, she said.'

Hopkins took two steps into the hall and stood, rooted, looking about him. There was a fine, curved staircase rising to a balustraded landing. On the walls were large, dim but important-looking portraits. The furniture was heavy, a thick table and a gilt mirror above it, and some old solid ornaments. 'It's like a bloody museum,' said Felicity. 'She says nothing must be moved an inch until she comes back. I don't care and Daddy doesn't notice. He lives in his study and I live upstairs. Sometimes we cross and exchange a few words.'

Hopkins followed her cautiously up the wide staircase. 'I've only seen places like this in the pictures,' he said.

She had reached the landing and she held out her hand as if he might need help. 'That's about all they're good for,' she said. 'As soon as I can I'm going to get a flat.'

There was a small sitting room off the first-floor landing. A pair of flowered armchairs and a two-seater sofa with a low table between them. 'Utility,' said Felicity showing him the wartime label on one of the chairs. 'Not exactly Regency but they're all right. They'll do until Mummy comes from her Cornish funk-hole and starts changing the place.'

Only the sofa seemed capable of accommodating him. 'What does your father think about your mother being away?' he asked. 'He must miss her.'

She was standing close to his knees. She was wearing a blue skirt and a blouse in a lighter shade of the same colour. 'Miss her?' she giggled. 'For the first two years I don't think he noticed she'd gone. And he's only mentioned her a couple of times since. Certainly not since before the flying bombs finished. I'll make the tea.'

She turned but changed her mind and walked back towards him. 'Stand up, please, Hopkins. Stand up close to me.'

He stood with his normal difficulty. He could feel himself shaking. Her hands went to his forearms. 'Poor things,' she said. 'They feel thin compared to the rest of you.'

'I'll soon feed them up,' he said huskily, helplessly. He could not believe that she was not playing a game. Perhaps she was just sorry for him. But it was not that. And it was no game.

She lifted the arms until they were around her slight waist. He could feel her through the delicate material of the blouse. Still uncertainly he looked into her calmly determined face. Again she took his wrists and placed his hands on the sides of her breasts. 'You're seventeen,' he muttered.

'This is no time for playing birthdays,' she said. She was already unbuttoning the blouse and, as if demonstrating that she had come well prepared she tugged it away and exposed her white, small breasts. Then she put his hands against them. Clumsily he touched her. She took his index fingers and placed one on each rose nipple. 'You're seventeen . . .' he said again.

The big front door below opened with a bang. 'And this is my father,' she said, her face in a sudden sulk. 'And I'm seventeen.' She snorted: 'Sod it!'

Chapter Twenty-three

The train, with wartime tardiness, travelled west displaying the breadth of England, at that distance, apparently undamaged by the past six years. The trees and the meadows, with dotted cows and sheep, were bright green, the sky large and blue with random clouds and circling birds, church steeples and towers outlined against it.

They had given him a fresh uniform and a rail warrant. When they asked him where he wanted to travel, where was his home, he hesitated but then told them. 'You'll get a good welcome in Wales,' said the army clerk who scribbled the warrant. 'They'll have all the choir out.'

Hopkins doubted it and limped away. He was able to pick up his big pack now but he needed some help to get it on his back. On the train at Paddington he wrestled with it before a motherly woman helped to lift it clear. 'You don't seem strong enough to fight,' she complained.

The train burrowed below the Severn tunnel and the mild Welsh hills rose at its approach. They were grey and deep green and dotted with farms and sheep. But the towns seemed to crouch below the western sky. He changed at Cardiff and the same woman helped him on with his pack again as if she was dressing a son. She had not said a word the whole journey and other occupants of the compartment had been silent also. Now she adjusted the awkward khaki webbing and said: 'You need your mother.' She folded her knitting and helped him from the train.

He had a cup of greyish tea at the station while he waited for the West Wales train. The buffet was crowded and pungent as an air-raid shelter. The country was like somewhere facing defeat rather than victory. On the platform were some American airmen, laughing as they usually were, but without meaning.

On the connecting train he sat next to the window. Nobody offered to help him with his pack this time and he left it on his back, uncomfortably leaning forward like a tortoise. But the contours outside the grubby window became increasingly familiar and he began to wish that someone would be there to greet him.

No one was, although he had sent a telegram to his uncle saying that he was coming home. Leaving the train he searched the platform for a recognisable face, somebody from school perhaps, but there was no one. It was like an unknown place.

As he went out the little man collecting the tickets at the barrier, leaning on it as if he had been there too long, gave him a glance and muttered: 'Back again then,' as if he came there every week.

'Aye,' he replied. 'Back.'

Outside the station he pulled his pack higher on his shoulders and looked one way and then the other. Nothing had changed as far as he could tell. He did not have to sniff the air to smell the fish. They were still bringing them in. Not that he would be. No more trawlers for him. They would not have him anyway; not in his state. There was nothing for it but to walk up the hill. He plodded carefully, the stony-faced houses watching him go. He slowed even more as he passed Gwen's house. The door had been painted blue and the window frames yellow. They must have run out of paint. There was no sign of her, no face at the dull window. The curtains looked as if they had not been moved since he last saw them.

He passed and glanced back but there was nothing to see, only a boy on a bike putting the evening paper through the letter-boxes.

His step slowed even more as he neared his uncle's house. He thought he was getting tired or more hesitant. What if he walked right past, caught the bus at the top of the hill, went to Swansea and eventually back to London? He might end up living in Kensington! He shook his head wryly and sniffed above his slight smile. He opened the gate with its everyday creak and walked to the front door. A woman came from the next house, Mrs Ivor Davies, the widow, who had always been there but was rarely seen except framed by her curtains. 'This came,' she said uncaringly. 'But there was no answer.' She handed him a telegram which, when he opened it, turned out to be the one he had sent. He thanked her. 'The door's open,' she said. 'Like always.'

Hopkins turned the dull brass doorknob and the door scraped open. Even from the short passage he could see his uncle sitting in the same position in the same chair. The old man hardly looked up but said: 'You're back then.'

'I sent this telegram,' said Hopkins holding it out. 'Mrs next door just gave it to me.'

As if it explained everything his uncle said: 'Why would I be getting a telegram?'

Hopkins struggled from his pack and set it on the floor. 'Where's Auntie?' he asked.

'Oh, her. She's upstairs . . . wait, no she's not. She's dead.'

'Dead. Auntie? Oh . . .'

His uncle half-turned his head. 'And I tell you who else is dead. It's just been on the wireless. Hitler.'

On the day the war in Europe finished the sun fell brightly on the Bristol Channel, the town band played by the shore, there were parties for children in the streets, and his Uncle Unwin died in his chair.

In that dim room and that dark old chair he had not had a great deal to do with the war, but it was as though he had only been waiting to see it out of the way before he went. Even in the days since Hopkins's return he had said very little, not even enquiring as to where his nephew had acquired such a bad limp. It was almost evening before Hopkins noticed he was dead.

He was carried out from the chair. Beneath him Hopkins found a copy of the *Western Mail* from 4 September 1939, the second day of the war, and a neatly folded comic, *Radio Fun*, which Hopkins remembered going missing during his early days as a boy in the house. He recalled it well because he had always had to pay for the comic himself.

In the end, though, he was sorry to see the old man go. The chair looked so empty. He did not have a solicitor but Unwin had posted a note to the undertaker some months before, saying directly: '*The boy gets the house. There's nothing else and nobody else.*'

Hopkins found a pile of tins outside the back door. The old man had eaten directly from them and must have stashed them for years because tinned food had been on coupons. For the first time he went into his uncle's bedroom. It smelled as if it had not been used for a long time although the bed was unmade. In his aunt's bedroom, across the passage, the bed was unmade also and there was a chamberpot half full. He sighed and shut the door. A man came around a week later and told him the house was probably worth a good deal, anything up to three hundred pounds.

He was now truly alone. He had collected a demobilisation suit from a depot near Haverfordwest. They issued it with two shirts, a tie and a pair of shoes. He also received his back pay of seventy-eight pounds, ten shillings. 'You're set for life with that,' said Willie the post who stood inquisitively on the doorstep while he opened the envelope.

But the missing slice of his life remained as remote, as untouchable as ever. Without it, without her – whoever she was – he was still lost.

Two days after the victory celebrations he was walking up Talbot Street past Gwen's house and, on a sudden temptation, he turned to her door and knocked. She smiled when she saw him and he smiled back. 'I was wondering when you'd come by,' she said. 'I heard you were back.'

Guardedly she kissed him on the cheek and invited him in. 'They said you'd been crippled,' she observed. 'Walk up the passage for me.'

'You sound like you're still ordering me about. Like you did at the school,' he said.

'Nobody ever ordered you about, Davy,' she said. He took a few steps to the door of the room. 'Not that bad,' she assessed. 'I wouldn't call you a cripple. There's people around here walk worse than that and they've hardly been out of their street.'

'They say it'll get better.'

'Where did you come by it?'

'Italy,' he said. 'Somewhere. I don't remember. I was wounded in the brain as well.'

'Come on through, I'll make you a cup,' she said as if closing that part of the discussion. 'Allan is dead, you know. My hubby, if you remember.'

'I'm sorry. I remember him coming back from abroad. My Uncle Unwin's gone too.'

'I heard. On VE Day. That was a shame. Spoilt it a bit, I expect. Allan did it himself. Couldn't cope. Cut his throat under that bit of a tree in the back garden.' She pointed vaguely through the window. 'It's going to have some apples on it this year. First time.'

'Funny things happen,' he said. They were still standing apart. She moved towards him and kissed him quietly on the cheek. 'You were always a lovely boy,' she said. 'I don't like to see you limping. I've got somebody else now. It will be a surprise. He's out in the lav at the back. We've got one inside, of course, but we kept the old one outdoors as well. You never know. Here he comes now.'

The scullery door sounded and Hopkins turned towards the

closed door of the living room. It was opened unhurriedly and standing there, small and cherubic, was the comrade he had last seen running up the beach in Italy.

'Christ!' he cried. 'Delmi!'

'It's one or the other,' said Gwen.

The June sun had dropped towards Haverfordwest. Hopkins had been back more than a month, living in the cleaned-up house, cold without the couple who had lived in it so quarrel-somely long. He made himself food and slept in his own room. The rest of the place remained undisturbed including his uncle's chair. He was restless and sad. He did not know where to go next.

Delmi had promised to be at the Institute that evening. He had been medically discharged from the army: flat feet. 'I can get out for a bit, an hour,' he promised. 'She's out herself so she won't notice.' Hopkins had no one to order his life. 'She gets upset if I'm out and she don't know where I am,' said Delmi when he had settled at one of the scarred wooden tables. The Institute had major plans for new wallpaper after the war. 'Why don't you stand up to her?' asked Hopkins. 'Be a man.'

'She's bigger than me,' said Delmi. 'And if she throws me out it's my last chance of getting a married life. Who else would have me? At my size?'

'There's that to it,' agreed Hopkins. The beer had seemed less watery since the end of the hostilities. There were a few people at the gloomy tables and Mrs Powell was occupying the business side of the bar. The landlady had come through the war unscathed.

'What you going to do?' asked Delmi. 'You got to do some-thing, man. You can't just 'ang around. Even if you've got a couple of quid in your pocket.'

'I know. There'll be plenty like me soon. Coming back and feeling lost. Wandering aimlessly. You get through it all with your life, more or less, and then you don't know what to do with the bloody thing. Do you want a Scotch? I'm fed up with this beer.'

Delmi said: 'That's what going foreign does for you. Gives you tastes. Yes, boy, I'll have one. Make it a double if you like.'

Hopkins rose. 'You don't want to stagger back,' he warned.

'All right. Just a single. But get me two glasses.'

When they were seated again Delmi said: 'You don't have to go back fishing, on the boats?'

'Couldn't anyway,' said Hopkins. 'There's no strength in my arms. Nor my legs for that matter. I'd be overboard in a tick. I'll have to do something else.'

'There's a couple of jobs at the shipping office,' suggested Delmi. 'Sitting down, quiet. Some women working there. Might suit you.'

Hopkins said: 'Del, listen a minute. You know how I can't remember a bloody thing for those few weeks?'

'You told me. Half a dozen times. Don't tell me you've had a brainwave? You've thought of something?'

'No, that's the trouble. Bugger all. But you told me I went out with a girl in Rome.'

'Well, yes. But it was only one night. They shifted us from there.'

'And you can't remember anything about her?'

'No, I told you. I don't think I even saw her. And there was a girl what you took a shine to on the troopship. I was thinking about it and I fancied you'd met her before some time. You and poor old Small both tried to get mixed up with them. But they were reserved for officers.'

He was showing signs of anxiety. 'She'll be back soon,' he said. 'I'd better be indoors first.'

There was a commotion at the door and five of the fishing men came in, young and thick and with pound notes. They went to the bar where Mrs Powell tried to calm them. 'You go to one of those nasty pubs and then you come in here to a decent Institute to cause me trouble,' she complained. They all had whiskies and then turned their backs to the bar and surveyed the room. 'Hopkins,' shouted one called Morris. 'Why don't you come out with the boats?'

He strode across. His approach was not friendly. Another youth called Howells followed him and the others watched. 'Don't want to,' said Hopkins. He remained in his seat.

'Come back from the army, have we? Been foreign. So the fishing's not good enough.'

'I don't want it,' said Hopkins. His eyes were steady on the other man. 'It's just wet labouring.'

'Wet? You calling me wet?' Morris came close. The group at the bar became attentive. Delmi looked anxiously around. 'I ought to be going,' he said to Hopkins.

'Go on, Delmi, go,' said Hopkins. 'I'm not taking anything from a bloke smelling like a kipper.'

Morris clenched his fist and hit him while he still sat in the chair. It tipped back and Hopkins was saved by Delmi's arm. 'Now pack it up,' said Delmi. 'He's got no strength. Don't you know he's been wounded?'

Morris said: 'He'll be more wounded if he says I smell of fish. I wash every night, I do.'

Howells put his body across Delmi. The small man tried to look around his bulk. Hopkins, grunting with the effort, got to his feet. Morris came at him again and Hopkins stemmed him with the nearest weapon. His head. He butted Morris in the face, aiming for the nose. There was a squelch of blood and Morris stumbled away. Everybody in the bar began fighting. The fishermen put down their glasses at the same time as a group of farm boys who had been sitting watching got from their seats and joined in. Nobody much cared who was fighting who. Mrs Powell slammed down the shutters of the bar and began shouting for the police. The police station was only across the street, and as it was a quiet night some officers quickly arrived.

Hopkins and Delmi spent the night in a baleful cell.

'What happened to that tortoise?' asked Hopkins. 'The one you found in Italy.'

'Ran away,' said Delmi. 'Buggered off once the shooting started.'

'He could run?'

'Like the wind, boy, like the wind.'

They had breakfast of tea and hard pieces of toast, and were taken up the steps to the magistrates' court by a portly and puffing officer.

Crestfallen they arrived at the entrance to the courtroom as the others, the five fisher boys, came out. At a distance they viewed each other's injuries. Morris said to Hopkins: 'Ten-quid fine,' and Howells following behind said: 'Me as well. A week's bloody wages.'

Inside the courtroom the pair were shepherded into the ornately wooden dock, a coat of arms poised above the chairman's head as if it might fall on him at any moment.

'Back from the army I see,' said the chairman looking at some papers before him. His name was Williams, a confectioner known in the town as Sticky Williams.

Hopkins and Delmi agreed they were back from the army. 'He's been wounded,' said Delmi pointing gamely at Hopkins. 'In the legs and arms and in Italy.' He stood only to Hopkins's shoulder in the dock. 'He's a hero.' He added sombrely: 'We're pleading guilty by the way.'

Hopkins muttered: 'Guilty.'

'Ah,' said Mr Williams. 'I do not doubt it for a moment. But you young fellows must not bring the war back with you. The fighting must stop when you get home. We can't have our peaceful town made into a battlefield.'

254

Hopkins and Delmi nodded in agreement.

'Do you agree to be bound over to keep the peace in the sum of ten pounds? You may walk from here this morning but if there are any more fisticuffs then the ten pounds will be forfeited on top of any punishment imposed at that time.' His face took on a fatherly air. 'Lads, lads,' he pleaded. 'Think first. That was a bad night in the Institute. Poor Mrs Powell put her foot through one of the floorboards.'

They were told they could go and they trooped from the dock, through the lobby and out into the damp street. 'Bound over, no fine,' said Hopkins with a touch of triumph to Morris who was loitering outside.

'Mustn't do it again,' said Delmi. Morris scowled.

He regarded Hopkins apologetically. 'Wasn't our fault anyway, was it?'

'Not our fault,' agreed Hopkins. He wondered where he was going now, where he would go from there.

'I'll have to get back to her,' said Delmi apprehensively. 'All night. She'll have noticed.'

Walking down the hill towards the town, Hopkins saw an older man he recognised coming up the slope towards him. He was the brother of Emrys Prothero, the trawler skipper. 'I'd like a word,' he said to Hopkins. 'Let's go and have a cup of tea.'

'Your Uncle Unwin was a good man,' said Mr Prothero who had been the union convenor at the fish dock. 'Before he went mad.'

'He was mad you think?' asked Hopkins. 'I just thought he had no go.'

'Inert, he was, yes,' said Mr Prothero. 'But that was part of his madness, see. He went mad just after your auntie died. They always did things more or less together.'

They both drank the tea noisily. 'He wouldn't have liked to see you in trouble like you've been,' said the union man.

'Wasn't my doing. I was the one they went for.'

'But you're in a position to be attacked, boy. What are you doing with yourself? I've seen you wandering about the town. You hardly know how to put one foot in front of the other.'

'It looks like that,' agreed Hopkins. 'I feel lost. But I'm not going back on the fishing. I'm not strong enough to start with and I don't want to go anyway. I hardly know this place, really, I hardly know anybody.'

'Your uncle did a lot for the fishermen, for the union,' said Mr Prothero. 'And I don't forget it. Your auntie sang at the concerts, not so much appreciated, mind, but there you are. I think you're letting them down. You were before the magistrates today and it won't be the last time.'

Hopkins nodded miserably. 'I can see that. I'll just have to get my head down, Mr Prothero, find a job. Find a girl, get married and all that.'

'There's no need to go to extremes, son.' He leaned forward over his heavy cup. 'Listen, there's a ship sailing out of Cardiff tomorrow. Afternoon tide. Bound for God-knows-where. General cargo. I can get you a berth on her. You've still got your union card?'

Hopkins looked up in genuine surprise. 'Yes, but what will I do? I've never been deep-sea. And I'm nowhere near as fit as I used to be. I can't bloody lift anything.'

'Watch your language. This is a Christian café. I can get you a berth on deck.'

Hopkins looked at him with continuing astonishment. 'But I won't be able to work on deck. Christ ... Sorry ...' He glanced around. There was a terse woman in white wiping down the counter. 'Sorry I swore. But what can I do? I can hardly lift my arms let alone anything else.'

Mr Prothero studied him. 'You can paint, can't you? Painting, you don't have to lift anything but a brush. And chip rust. She's thick with it.'

Chapter Twenty-four

In those days men would hang in peril over the sides of ships and paint the hulls while they were at sea, sometimes in uneven weather. On occasions they were lowered with a paint pot and a brush and never seen again.

The SS *Santa Clara* had only just cleared the sulky Bristol Channel when Hopkins found himself suspended on a cradle, chipping years of rust from the side of the vessel and then painting over it.

In the summer weather it was not so arduous; the sun beamed as the ship grunted slowly south, and Hopkins knew that unless an officer leaned riskily over the rail he could not be seen. He took his time, chipping and painting, and watching the porpoises faithfully following astern waiting for the time when the vessel's rubbish was jettisoned into its wake. There had been plenty of time to think, to puzzle. Who was she? Where was she now? Now there was more.

It was a scraggy cargo vessel, formerly Italian. No one had bothered changing her name on the bow, five thousand turgid tons carrying a cargo of war surplus material, it was rumoured to Italy. Italy again. He was going back. Perhaps he would remember something there.

There was a crew of fifteen of several nationalities, although some of them never spoke, the flotsam of war; two were missing an eye and at least two arms were absent. Hopkins could never surely detect which man owned only one arm, because they moved among each other in the dim lower decks so silently that they were not much more than shadows. There was little talk, no laughter and not a note of song. It was not a happy ship.

Two deck officers, as unkempt as the vessel, sometimes appeared and shouted random orders. Hopkins never saw the captain until the final day. The captain drank alone and a lot.

After his painting and chipping was over for the day Hopkins would descend to the mess deck and fill himself with clogged food and a liquid he could not identify; he went to the heads, then climbed into his bunk and waited for sleep. After a few days he attempted short conversations with the men in the bunks on either side of his but one had no tongue in his mouth and the other was a Yugoslav. The days and nights drifted on. He was glad for the darkness of his bunk or to be over the side with pot, paintbrush and chipping hammer, watching the movement of a sea of deepening blue.

The ship turned to port at the Strait of Gibraltar and the officer of the watch recognised, with some self-congratulation, the famous rock. All shore leave was cancelled in Gibraltar itself but two men jumped ship and were never seen again. It was only when one of the more alert harbour staff surveyed from the dockside the bow which the pair had been painting that it was discovered they had changed the name, on both sides of the ship, from *Santa Clara* to *Santa Claus*.

Although conversation was not rife on board there were half-rumours that the voyage would not proceed any further than Naples and these proved to be true. The Maltese steward who fed the captain, sometimes literally spooning the food into his sagging mouth, had the information. He believed the skipper would drink himself to death before he got ashore.

Captain McBrane managed to stay alive but he fell from his bunk as they arrived and had to be carried in a chair to the hatch cover where he summoned the whole ship's company for a special announcement. Around them spread the Bay of

Naples. The skipper, food stains decorating his uniform coat like medals, sat like a dissolute king on a creaky throne, facing the blank expressions of the crew he commanded. It was the first time most of them had seen him, although one man had sailed with him before.

McBrane had a six-inch-thick Scots accent. 'Boys,' he announced throatily, pointing towards them as if unsure who they were. 'Boys, lads, men. We've been sailing this bucket o' shit for long enough now. Meself, I'm doubting if she could sail another mile. But that's none o' my business. Nor yours now. Boys, the ship and cargo have been sold for scrap, all together, and we are goin' ashore here in Napoli.

'Each o' you useless swines will be paid off by the agent here and presented with a railway warrant to get you back to good old Britain, although it might take you a wee time. Weeks, I expect, maybe never.

'You'll be paid off and given subsistence . . .' He appeared pleased with conquering the word and said it again. '. . . Subsistence allowance so that you can eat a little and sleep somewhere on the way. You'll drink that away, I expect, before Rome.

'God bless us all. The agent with his money bags will come aboard in an hour and once you've signed you can fuck off ashore. Goodbye.'

The captain in his chair was carried away by the same two stokers who had borne him there and the men dispersed, those who had understood telling those who had not, what was happening. Most were pleased.

Hopkins went to the rail and looked out onto Naples with its volcano beyond. It was over a year since he had landed there. Now he was back. Perhaps here he might find her.

What had once been a covered market close to the port had been converted into a domed dormitory for servicemen passing through Naples. It still smelled pleasantly of grapes and melons. Hopkins was directed there as it accommodated merchant seamen. It was afternoon when he carried his single bag there, the place stifling beneath the lofty curved glass roof. It was not until night-time that the space began to cool down.

There was a mass parade of beds, line after line, with gushing latrines and showers at one end. Lost-looking men sat on beds staring at the walls or lay stretched out gazing at the roof. Hopkins was pointed in the direction of a bed in a distant corner by an ancient and silent woman who had a desk at the door. He paid her his handful of lire.

He did not waste long in there. He went into the street, stretches of it still flattened by the battles of the year before. There was a café almost opposite and some of the servicemen from the lodging were sitting drinking beer. He found an empty table at the shadowed back and had ordered a beer when two British military policemen stamped up the street. They turned purposefully into the café and two men nearest the exit slid out.

'Papers, papers,' droned one of the redcaps like a news vendor. 'Identity papers.' They took a surly look at the documents offered and spent longer over Hopkins's discharge book. On a thought Hopkins said: 'Is there a place in Naples, a sort of transit camp for troops? I was here last year and I was there but I'm not sure where it was.'

One of the military policemen, his chin so burnished it caught the rays of the setting sun, sniffed: 'There's a bloody great big one ten miles away.'

Like part of a double act his colleague put in: 'And there's a place that's small, just up this street and around the corner, left. It's where the pox-doctor's post is.'

'That sounds like it,' said Hopkins.

'You got the pox?'

'No, I don't think so.'

260

'You'll soon know. Naples pox is incurable. Dynamite won't shift it.'

The pair nodded at each other and went into the street again. An odd feeling was taking hold of Hopkins. He had paid for the beer but he left it on the table. The soldier at the next table watched him go, picked it up and drank it.

Hopkins hurried along the pavement. It was fully evening now with the sun dimpling the cobbles. At the next junction he turned left and saw the place. It was the right place. He recognised it.

Purposefully slowing his step he crossed the road. All around was becoming busy with evening crowds. He weaved among them and stood at the gate of the camp. There was a guard-post manned only by an Italian policeman smoking the last life out of a brown cigarette.

Hopkins ignored him. All at once he felt the excitement welling inside him. He remembered being there. Crossing the street. Carefully he crossed again, so slowly that a tramcar clanged its bell at him. Now he was on the far pavement. He looked left and right and chose to walk right. Then he heard the parrot, the screech: '*Santa Caterina! Santa Caterina!*'

He stopped dead in his step. There it was again: '*Santa Caterina! Santa Caterina!*' He almost rushed towards the sound. The café was set back from the road. It fitted loosely into his memory. '*Santa Caterina!*' bawled the parrot again.

He went into the front of the café, to the tables on the pavement with a little fence around them. Sitting down he let the feeling of the place seep into him. He knew it. He knew it. He was close to her. Across the street was the church the old lady had pointed out. Santa Caterina. Suddenly he knew *her face*, he knew *her name*. She had been sitting opposite laughing at the parrot and saying: '*My name is Katherine . . . Kate.*' Kate, that was it. Christ! Kate!

He rammed his face into his hands and tried to force himself to remember more. A loose-looking waiter tapped him on the shoulder. '*Signore?*'

Hopkins stared at him. 'Ah, yes.'

'A beer, *signore?* Or wine?'

'Yes, beer. That will do. I was listening to the parrot. He says "*Santa Caterina*".'

'*Si, si. Santa Caterina*. It is the church over there. He also learns much from the soldiers. He can say "bollocks".'

'Bollocks,' said the parrot.

For four days he remained in Naples, seeking anything that might arouse his memory. Now he knew her name was Kate and she wore an army shirt. It was just a snapshot. Her sitting in the café laughing at the parrot and its squawk of '*Santa Caterina! Santa Caterina!*' But nothing else: nowhere did he find another semblance of a clue. He was chasing a shade.

Each evening at seven he went to the restaurant with the parrot which continued to call '*Santa Caterina, Santa Caterina.*' It said nothing more. The waiter appeared each evening with the menu and a beer. 'Where is the lady?' asked Hopkins. He meant the older woman who had served them, the woman who had told them about the church, Santa Caterina. He could not see her, remember her, but he knew she was there at the edge of the picture.

'Gone now. Gone away,' said the waiter. He waved his arm and ended the movement with an upward pointing finger. 'Signora is upstairs with God in 'eaven.'

Each morning Hopkins set out walking, aimlessly at first and hopelessly, but then thought with more care and the thought led him to each of the British military establishments in the centre of the city. He was still travelling blind. At each gate he was stopped but with no great authority for the war was over, and each time all he could lamely ask was if there had been a woman soldier there called Kate, perhaps Kate Smith. He was sure her name was not Smith but the army needed to have surnames. The enquiry provoked unbelieving stares though, and once the military police were called. He told them he was looking for a lost friend.

Despondently, at the end of the third day, with the sun drifting down behind the patched buildings, he arrived at the gate of a small military camp in the process of being dismantled. He stood in his civilian clothes and looked carefully at the printed board above the guardhouse. It said: *Military Movements Office.*

An angular woman soldier appeared and asked him what he was staring at. He asked after Kate Smith, who might have been at that posting a year or so before. The woman regarded him curiously and then laughed. He walked away.

As he did so a girl, on the short side for a sergeant, came to the guardhouse and said something to the angular woman who had been speaking to Hopkins. 'Not long now,' he heard her say. 'Glad to see the back of this dump.'

'Me as well,' said the taller woman. 'I'll go anywhere, as long as it's home.'

The small sergeant was called Dotty. Kate's small friend. It would only have taken a moment for her to have a careful look at Hopkins and she might have realised who he was. But by this time he was walking disconsolately away.

It was a regulation that after four nights in the wide-roofed hostel its lodgers had to move on. Hopkins had finished anyway. Worn and dispirited he packed his rough brown suitcase and tightened the strap. Then he walked out and towards the main railway station. All he had was her face, her voice, her laugh, and her Christian name. Nothing else. How many army girls were called Kate?

He got on the train for Rome but there was nothing there for him. All he faintly recalled was the American soldier shouting about 'prostit-toots'. He wandered loosely knowing too well that the trail had gone cold. She was still almost as far away as ever.

Two mornings later he showed the rail warrant given to him on the ship and caught the train for Florence, the next stage of his return to England, his sense of failure hanging around him. After an hour he was hunched in a corner of the ragged carriage, staring without hope at the passing countryside. But it was becoming more green, more hilly.

With a small but growing awareness he looked at it, the sudden hills, the bright sunlight on the high trees and inclined meadows. Then moving across the carriage windows, slowly now as if to afford him a long look, there appeared a white tower on a green hilltop, standing out against the Italian bright blue sky. Now he stared. He stood from the seat, his movements almost dreamlike. There was a young Italian girl in one corner of the carriage and she regarded him with curiosity. Clumsily he took his single case down from the rack. 'I've got to get out,' he said to the girl.

She understood his meaning. 'Next station, Treni,' she said. 'Now soon.'

Treni was still a town reduced almost to ground level. The wartime steelworks, the main target, was the only part relatively untouched by the intensive bombing of the Allies; the houses were destroyed. It was only now crawling back into life. People came in from the countryside, the hill villages, and were trying to reassemble the town. They had made some habitations among the ruins and there were shabby little stalls selling things – fruit, vegetables, damaged household goods – in the tracks between the rubble that had once been streets.

Outside the station Hopkins found a new and optimistic map under the banner '*Informazioni Turistiche.*' He put his single case on the ground and studied it. He worked his finger from Treni up through the marked ways into the mountains. The name

264

Spoleto seemed to mean something, he could hear a voice saying it, an old woman's voice: 'Spoleto. Spoleto.'

There was a crouched man almost next to the map with a tray of nuts wrapped in twists of rough newspaper. Hopkins bought two packets and the vendor was grateful. 'Spoleto,' said Hopkins. 'How do I get to Spoleto?'

The man looked at him as if he was surprised he did not know, then pointed behind onto the cleared area in front of the station. An ancient bus was vibrating there, the only bright thing about it the word '*Spoleto*' newly painted on its destination board. Hopkins climbed aboard.

The seats were threadbare, some worn through to the metal framework. The driver, as rough as his bus, got aboard and stumped towards Hopkins, his sole passenger, and held out his hand for the fare. Hopkins gave him some coins and he seemed to find them sufficient. He produced a grubby ticket which appeared to have been issued many times before and indicated that his passenger should sit at the rear of the bus where the seats were in better condition. Hopkins went there.

A woman, thin and bent as a stick, staggered aboard and continued to stagger as far as halfway up the aisle. No one seemed to be able to walk. She took no notice of Hopkins, although she might not have seen him. Sitting down with a sigh she began to sing a miserable, low song which she continued without pause until she left the bus in a mountain hamlet where a lively white stream tipped between the houses. She went painfully in through the door of the stone cottage next to the cascade.

Hopkins was taking everything in, looking for anything that might give him even a glimpse of recognition. As the road wound, sometimes back on itself, and the green land rose steeply to trees against the sky, he felt there was something, something only as familiar as a shadow, but something. But now his fear was losing the memory of her face. He had seen it in Naples,

the laughing word: '*Caterina. My name is Katharine . . . Kate,*' as
the parrot performed above her shoulder, the khaki collar of
her uniformed shirt against her slender neck. He must not lose
the face now, he must not let the memory escape. He closed
his eyes as if to cage it. Kate . . . Kate . . .

Some other passengers boarded the bus as it journeyed: a
man with a dog and a dead duck, two grumpy-faced women
who sat by each other but did not exchange a word. None of
them seemed to pay any fares. The man had a ticket, which
the driver passed with a nod.

It took an hour to reach Spoleto, the bus climbing and
twisting up the mountainway and down again, until they crawled
up a final hill and, edging through stone streets so tight Hopkins
moved away from the window, stopped with a grateful heave
in the square of a small and beautiful town. Spoleto.

It was late afternoon now and the sun had fallen behind the
hills. There was a café on one side of the cobbled square, a
poor-looking place but the only one. He took a rusty chair and
sat at an uneven table with a beer. A man with a mule and a
cart came across the square, the mule pausing to empty its
bowels at the very centre, and a few people straggled by, on
foot or on bicycles.

'No people,' said Hopkins to the waiter. He was another old
man and seemed grateful for the custom and the conversation.

'No more Italy,' shrugged the man. 'Italy broken. No more
Italy.'

The buildings around the square were low and sad and one
at a corner had collapsed. On a wall opposite, however, was a
long plaque that stood out newly against its surroundings.
Hopkins asked: 'What's that?'

'The resistance,' the waiter shrugged. 'In the German war.
Those men dead.' He stared at the plaque also. 'You like some
pasta? We have pasta plenty.'

266

Hopkins had not eaten all day. He had a bowl of spaghetti with a trace of meat sauce. 'Once, before the German war,' said the waiter, 'we had *culatello*, the pig's foot. People came here from many parts to eat the pig's foot.'

'They did, did they,' muttered Hopkins. He knew he had heard it before.

They had a room above the café and he stayed there for the night. Through the evening there was scarcely a sound in the square – only figures moving about – and no lights shone through the night. He went down and had another beer and some of the same pasta before going back to the room.

He lay on the decent bed in the downtrodden place. The waiter said that it had belonged to a German officer. He tried to think it out again. What did he do here before? How did he remember the white towers on the green hills? Had he eaten pig's trotters? Where, oh where, was his Kate? He could hear people breathing in the other rooms.

Splinters of sun pointing narrowly through the shutters woke him. It was seven o'clock, there were sounds below and the smell of coffee rose through the floorboards. He got up, washed his face in a basin of cold water standing on a small table, wiped it on a towel the size of a handkerchief, and went down the unsteady stairs.

There was fresh bread and more coffee. He paid for his stay but told the waiter that he might be back that night. The waiter said he hoped so, but shrugged as if he did not really care.

At that time of the morning there were more people about; old and trudging most of them, moving through the sharp shadows and the early sunshine, paying no attention to either. He walked across the cobbles and read the names of the resistance fighters on the memorial plaque. One of the men he had known but he did not remember. It meant nothing to him.

Opposite, near the café, was an iron railing with a gate

clamped shut by a huge and rusty padlock. He looked between the bars into the sunken area and saw it was a small amphi-theatre, or the ruins of one, square grey stones and the roots of ancient columns. As he watched a hesitant old man approached, carrying a small wooden chair, and tried to open the padlock with a key. He could not make it turn and comi-cally sat on the chair and began to curse. Hopkins said to him: 'Let me have a go.' The man's hands looked frail. He nodded gratefully and handed over the key.

The lock was thick with rust but in the end Hopkins turned it. The frail man rose from the chair with delight. '*Signore, signore,*' he enthused. '*Bravo. Bravo.*'

He pushed the iron gate and it opened with a groan. Going inside the overgrown enclosure he looked about as though wondering if anything had been stolen. Apparently nothing had. Placing the chair on a weed-clogged piece of path in front of a shuttered wooden hut he invited Hopkins beyond the gate. 'I am the guide,' he explained. 'I can speak English unless I have forgot.'

Hopkins surveyed the amphitheatre spread below. 'Today,' said the man with a sort of private pride, 'is the first day open for business. You are the first visitor here since I closed the gate in the war. Now I will show you the Roman work in this place. But first I must charge you for admission.'

Holding out a handful of change Hopkins let the man select the coins. Having been paid the man said: 'First person to buy. My name is Signor Vincenzo.'

'I'm Hopkins,' said Hopkins.

The man rose and produced another, much smaller, key, with which he tried to open the shutter bar on the wooden hut behind him. Again Hopkins took the key and did it for him.

'Ah, Hopkins, you are clever,' said Signor Vincenzo. 'I would like to give you your money back but I have to make accounts to the authorities.' He pulled away the shutter creakily and looked into the little kiosk. He sniffed the dust but said: 'It is the same. Four years since I locked up. Even the Tedeski did not try to steal.'

Hopkins was not surprised. There were a few oddments on the shelves, some browned-over guidebooks, three pencils in a box, some china animals, and a bunch of curled postcards. 'You would like a postcard?' asked the guide picking them up as if they were valuable. 'The first since the German war. And for you.'

He handed over the old pictures. Those at the centre of the pile were not too faded. Hopkins passed them through his hands. 'I give you for price before the war,' said Signor Vincenzo. 'Because you are first.'

There were sepia photographs of mountains, several of what he saw was the main square of Spoleto. And then one that made him stop. He had almost passed it from hand to hand. Fiercely he tugged it back into view. He put his face closer and he felt his eyes expand. Hurriedly he carried it out into the sunlight.

It was a beautiful house set in the flat of a valley. It was faded and brown. But he knew it, he knew where it was. And beneath the dusty picture were the words: 'La Serena.' That's where it had happened!

Chapter Twenty-five

Hopkins, wobbling on the donkey, watched the valley as it broadened in front of his eyes. Ahead, the old man, Albinetto, grunted with the movement of his beast and sometimes shouted at it before progressing at the same pace. The sun was clear of the mountains by now, full over the house and making the river shine.

He could hardly take his eyes from La Serena. Everything was coming back, flooding back, now, with every step the donkey took down the slope. He could see Kate again, her face before him, her eyes and her laughing. He almost choked with the realisation. But where was she now?

He stared at the house as if he expected her to walk from the door into the sunlight. She was wearing a white dress. But too much time had gone, a whole year, a war.

It was only coming back gradually, a piece at a time. Then he saw something at the side of the dirt path below – the skeleton of a vehicle; an army vehicle, the jeep. When they reached the flat land he called out to Albinetto and slipped from the flank of the donkey. He stumbled over the hard rough ground towards the vehicle.

They had never taken it away, only stripped it of everything that could be stripped, from wheels to roof. The framework was deeply charred. With growing horror he was beginning to see it again. He stopped by the wreck, putting his hand on the bonnet which rattled at his touch. It was both a support and a touch of sadness. That was what had happened.

Now he looked towards the place where he had been that deadly morning forty paces behind. The bare ground was still scarred, a scoop from the blackened earth. It had not yet faded, or been grown over. Now he knew again, saw again, what had happened in those few terrible moments. He saw Kate and the Italian, Nico, approaching the jeep, then heard the plane, high and harmless at first, but suddenly roaring and swooping. Putting up his hand to cover his face he relived the vivid moment, the little toy-like bombs bouncing towards the jeep and past it towards him. With a choking horror he saw the explosions around the jeep and, in his imagination, thought that Kate's body was thrown into the air. A darkness closed around him as it had done then. He leaned against the side of the jeep, then, after a few moments, climbed slowly into the metal of what had been the driving seat, the place where she had once sat, and leaning forward against the warm metal in front, cried softly, deeply. Now he knew it. She was dead.

The sun was high now and he could feel it burning on his head. He lifted his face and looked about without hope, bending and peering into the recesses of the wrecked jeep. There were open gaps, sun-bleached weeds grew and the last winter's rust was coating much of the metal. With an infinite weariness he climbed from the skeleton of the vehicle and patted it as if in apology.

Next to it was a ditch which continued alongside the path, steep and stony. He looked there, again without hope, imagining that something, anything, a piece of material perhaps, was wedged among the growth. But there was nothing. Only weeds.

He turned and walked along the track towards the house, pausing at the place where he thought he might have been when the bombs tumbled, the last place before the long blackness fell upon him. At the side of the ditch there was a clear hollow in the earth, a bowl of hard dirt and stones. He must have been blown into the ditch. The ditch had saved his life. He gave the hollow a disconsolate kick, then scraped the earth back into place and trod it carefully down.

Before him the house stood as he remembered it during those few days when they were there: the haphazard roof, the deep shadows within, the cool veranda. Somebody came out of the shadows, a young man holding a broom. He smiled uncertainly. 'The Signora,' said Hopkins standing below the wooden step. 'Is she here?'

'Spoleto.' The youth pointed with the broom.

'Is she coming back?'

He understood. 'She come after today.'

He went into the room where they had been together. Someone had crudely repaired a hole in the roof but otherwise it seemed the same. He stood inside the door and sadly took it in. Even the chamber pot was in the same place. There was the bucket of water in the place used for washing. The bed was covered with the same quilt. Now he remembered everything. But for what? She would not be back. He had found her too late. He lay on the quilt and stared at the ceiling, every moment coming back. Now he could remember her name in full – Kate Medhurst. He felt deeply desolate and closed his eyes.

He lay down and slept for three hours and awoke with the last shreds of daylight fingering through the shutters. Once again he lay thinking about her. Then, slowly and miserably, he got from the bed and washed his face in the water from the bucket. He stared at the chamber pot, then turned from the room and went downstairs.

Without asking the young man had laid a table for him on the terrace. He knew it would be pork, he remembered that, and it was. But not the special trotter.

As he ate the darkness folded over the valley. He could see

the sheen of the river glimmering through it. He drank a beer, then got down from the table and walked through the warm evening to the water bank.

There was still light enough for him to distinguish where they had been together that bright afternoon, Kate's face in the sun. He could hear her voice. Now the memory was complete, all in place, everything but her. He sat until it was dark, the only sound the movement of the river. He put his head in his hands. It had been a long journey to find nothing.

His sleep was crammed with dreams: Kate with him in the Russian hospital, his uncle and aunt shouting for him to go back to the boats. He woke early and wearily went down to the room where the young man now introduced himself as Peppe. 'Today Signora come,' he said.

Signora Eleonora arrived on the first bus at mid-morning. Old Albinetto took one of his donkeys up the path and brought her down on its back. She seemed to know that Hopkins was there for she made a great fuss when she saw him. She remembered him and the '*bella signorina*'.

When they were in the shadows of the house she sat him down and made him coffee. Then, at a thought, she went up the loud stairs and returned carrying the white linen dress she had given to Kate to wear. Hopkins stared at it and stood and touched the hem. She then said something he could not understand; she spoke rapidly and then raised a finger, went into the room and opened the heavy desk with a key. He knew now what she was about to show him.

She brought the bulky visitors' book, its leather dark and scarred. He nodded that he remembered it. She opened the pages and painfully he saw their signatures – David Hopkins and Kate Medhurst – written on that morning that now seemed so long ago.

With his fingers he touched her name, then smiled his quiet

thanks at the old lady. But she was insistent; she wanted to show him further.

There were a few other meaningless signatures on the lines of the pages but then she turned to the last page. She pointed triumphantly. *There was her name again* – Kate Medhurst, Marlow, England! The date was 15 June 1945, just a few months before.

She was not dead! She had been back! Christ!

Riding an erratic bicycle the man came along the dust track, past the wrecked jeep, and turned into the forefront of the house. Signora Eleonora was eager and wrung her hands vigorously. She pointed Hopkins out to the new arrival and the new arrival to Hopkins.

The man dismounted and left the bicycle on the ground. He was young and smiling. 'My brother's friend,' he said.

Hopkins realised. He was remembering fully now. 'Nico.'

'Sure . . . I am Alberto his brother.' They shook hands. 'I have been in England. I was a prisoner-of-war. At Worksop.' He smiled. 'It was better than the war.'

He sat at the table and the Signora brought coffee for him and refilled Hopkins's cup. 'You know about Kate, Kate Medhurst?' said Hopkins. 'She is still alive. I have just found out.'

'She was here,' said Alberto. 'Only a few months ago. She came back to see.' He looked searchingly at Hopkins. 'She was sure you had been killed. She told me she had tried to find out, from the army and other places, but half the people in the world are still missing. After the war nobody knows anything. Did you look for her?'

Hopkins said slowly: 'I lost my mind, my memory. Only for that time, those few days and after.'

'They thought you were dead, also,' said Alberto. 'I have heard the story, complete. The Americans came and took the lady, Kate, away. She was only just alive. My brother Nico was dead. And then some partisans, some of the Italians from the hills, came and took you away. I came back here from England. I liked Worksop. It was nice.'

Slowly Hopkins said: 'I can't tell you how I feel. She is alive. A few days ago I could not remember her at all. Who she was, her name, anything. There was someone there, like a shadow in my mind, but I could not find who it was. Then, in Naples, only at the beginning of this week, I saw her face again. There was a parrot . . .' He tailed off. 'You wouldn't want to hear all that. But I began to piece it together. Now, what you have told me, makes it all fit.'

Alberto smiled. 'And what, *signore*, will you do now?'

Hopkins rose and pushed his coffee cup aside. 'I am going to find her,' he said.

He sat looking at the telephone for ten minutes, then another ten. Then he got up and left the shabby London hotel room with his leather case. He would go himself. He would get a train.

At Maidenhead station there was a bus waiting obligingly labelled 'Marlow' and he got aboard. 'I want River Lane,' he said to the conductor.

'We stop right at the end.'

He sat looking out of the window but seeing nothing. He felt rigid in his stomach. Say she turned away from him.

'Come far?' asked the conductor, glancing at his worn suitcase on the next seat. It was not a busy morning.

'Miles,' said Hopkins.

'I'll tell you when we get there.'

It took half an hour. It was just as he had pictured it would be, just as she had described it when they were finding out about each other at La Serena. When the conductor called out: 'River Lane,' he remained stiff in the seat. 'River Lane,' the man called again. 'Where you wanted.'

He picked up the case. It seemed to have doubled in weight.

It bumped against his leg as he got from the bus. When the bus pulled away he remained in the road, immobile, not knowing what to do. He felt like running after the bus. It stopped as if in answer to his thoughts and the conductor leaned out. 'There,' he called. 'River Lane. Right in front of you.' As if only to oblige the man Hopkins began to walk. Halfway down was a cottage with a cascade of roses overhanging the lane. He walked, set-faced, slowly, woodenly.

Then Kate came out through the gate.

She had a brown-paper carrier bag and a dog was trying to get out with her. She said something to it and tried to shut the gate. At that moment she saw Hopkins.

'Oh, Christ,' she whispered. 'Hopkins.'

'Kate,' he called. They were thirty yards apart. 'Kate, it's me, Hopkins.'

She was wearing a summery dress and her hair shone. The shock on her face suddenly evaporated and she dropped the carrier bag and began to run towards him. The dog, pleased to have escaped, followed her.

He moved, stumbled a few steps forward, and she reached him. They stood apart, as though frightened to touch, and then folded into each other's arms, both weeping, both trying to say things.

'Oh, darling Hopkins. I thought you were dead.' As if she had suddenly remembered she put her lips to his and they kissed lovingly, fiercely, in the lane. The bag had overturned and tomatoes were rolling. 'Your bag's tipped over,' he mumbled. Rugga, the dog, began to moan ecstatically.

'Oh, that. It's for the harvest festival.' They pulled away a few inches from each other. 'I lost my mind,' he said. 'I couldn't remember.'

'Oh, darling, you've found me now. And I've found you. Come . . . come into the house. We can tell what we have to tell later.'

Her mother had come to the gate. She began to pick up the spilled tomatoes. They were just breaking off their embrace, but still holding on to each other. Kate kissed him fiercely again. 'Someone you know?' enquired her mother.

'He's come back, Mother. Hopkins! He's back. He thought I was dead. I thought he was.'

'You'd better have a cup of tea,' said her mother. 'Does Hopkins take sugar?'

Kate held Hopkins's hand towards her mother and the older woman took it and shook it gravely, studying his face as she did so. 'You'll have some catching up to do,' she said.

They almost staggered into the house. He had left his suitcase in the lane and he turned and went to retrieve it. 'Don't go!' pleaded Kate. 'Don't go again!'

He brought the case into the house. 'I'll put the kettle on,' said Mary Medhurst.

'Mother, I must make a telephone call,' said Kate. She could scarcely keep her words straight.

'To William?'

Hopkins watched them.

'Yes. I've got to tell him the wedding is off. Again.'

Chapter Twenty-six

Kate and Hopkins married the following winter and lived the rest of their lives in the Thames Valley. When Kate's father died in 1952 they moved with their two children into the cottage with her mother.

One day, about four years after this, a stranger appeared at the door. Hopkins was working as an estate manager and was not at home. 'My name is John C. Seely.' He was an American. 'Are you Miss Medhurst?'

'I was. I'm now Mrs Hopkins.' She regarded him quizzically and asked him to come into the living room. Her mother appeared from the kitchen.

Kate said: 'We have a visitor. Mr Seely.'

He was a weighty, affable man. 'I come from Medhurst, North Carolina,' he said. 'That's how I remembered your name.'

'Yes?'

'Years ago, when I was here in the war, you pushed me in the River Thames.'

Slowly Kate put her hands to her mouth. Her mother gave a little squeak and sat down. The American took the chair Kate shakily offered. She could not take her eyes away from him. 'We were on the riverside,' he said. 'And I was being forward with you. I was drunk, I have to confess to my shame. And, when I became too forward, you . . .'

'Pushed you in the Thames.'

They all stared at each other. Then the American said: 'But

I floated away and got out and here I am. It didn't do me any harm. I didn't even tell anybody.'

Kate's mother began to laugh, then John C. Seely, then Kate. Rugga, the dog, started to moan deliriously.